The Pleasure of Your Company

Carolyn Steele Agosta

Text copyright 2011 by Carolyn Steele Agosta

Published by
Carolyn Steele Agosta
North Carolina
Visit my website at http://www.carolynagosta.com

First Paperback edition: April 2011
First Kindle edition: March 2011

Agosta, Carolyn Steele, 1952—
The Pleasure of Your Company / by Carolyn Steele Agosta, 1st ed.

Summary: Valerie, Miranda and Helen, three Baby Boomer sisters, discover some long lost secrets as they deal with their late father's estate. While they're grappling with the fallout from these secrets, they're also caught up in the financial hard times of the 2008-09 recession. Their extended family runs from 79-year-old Aunt Reenie, a former actress, to Helen's 18-year-old triplets, known collectively as The Trips, and each family member has their own idea of what should be done with the estate. Throw into the mix a runaway RV, antique cameras and an underwater ballet sequence, and you have the ingredients for a darkly comic family relationship novel.

ISBN: 978-0-9829561-1-3
Fiction

This book is dedicated to my extended family
who have always offered me their love, support,
and tons of inspiration.

The pleasure of your company is requested

at the home of Phillip & Helen Mitchell

2 pm, Thursday, November 27th,

to Celebrate Thanksgiving

and Discuss Dad's Estate

Be There or Be Square.

Chapter One

Monday, November 24, 2008
"Economy Shrinks at Fastest Pace in Seven Years," (Reuters)

VALERIE CATES HERON WAS A VIRTUOUS WOMAN. She was. Everyone said so. A cellist with the New York City Ballet Orchestra, she played Tchaikovsky and Ellington equally well. She exercised daily—yoga, swimming, walks in Central Park—and ate oatmeal for breakfast. At age 56, she could still fit into her college jeans. She couldn't quite zip them up but, hey, no one's perfect. Every Christmas, the Salvation Army received a generous donation. Every summer she volunteered her time to give free cello lessons to underprivileged teens. Valerie's long copper-red hair was always in beautiful condition, she never got lost or arrived late, and no one had ever heard her drop an F-bomb. Not even when she received the Thanksgiving invitation from her sister, Helen.

"Guck," she said when she read it. "Guckety-guck. Guckarooni. Shit."

Emotional blackmail was a powerful force. It could make people do almost anything to prevent being judged by the very person inflicting the blackmail. Valerie had been home to North Carolina for the funeral, only two weeks ago. What was the point of going now? What was there to settle that couldn't be handled by email? She probably wouldn't even be able to get a flight at this late date. Nevertheless, Valerie knew she'd have to go or risk being branded as a heartless sister. She'd have to be there or be square.

Even Seth, her own son, exerted pressure. "It'll be our first Thanksgiving without Grandpa Lee," he said. "It's going to be tough on Aunt Helen. If there's any way you can make it, you should try."

Seth, 26, was a graduate student at UNC-Charlotte and he seemed to be the keeper of the family conscience. It was easy for him to say 'come home'; he already lived near Helen. "The rest of you will be there to hold her hand," Val said. "Whatever's in the will is fine with me. It's not like Dad had a lot. You can divvy things up any way you want." Seth didn't say anything, just waited her out and she thought, damn, Guilt City. "Oh, okay. Okay. I'll do it. You stinker."

He laughed and rang off, leaving Valerie to stew all day about the possible ramifications of Dad's will. She could say she didn't care, but that wasn't exactly true. Although Dad's estate wouldn't be huge, it might be enough to set the family members against each other. She'd seen it before. When Dad's father died, siblings came swarming out of the woodwork. No matter that they hadn't bothered to visit Granddad Hector in years; they all wanted a slice of the pie. It had even come to blows. Who needed that kind of drama?

Unfortunately, she was able to book flights out Wednesday night and back Friday morning. It figured. The one time she would have liked them to be full up, the airlines let her down. She packed a bag, loaded up on the latest fashion magazines, and generally composed herself to leave in two days' time. Meanwhile, she had the fall gala to consider.

The winter season was just beginning. The fall gala performance was the kick-off, and then the annual Nutcracker Ballet would commence on Friday and run for nine performances a week until after New Year's Day. On this Monday morning before Thanksgiving, Val made the six-block walk to Lincoln Center for rehearsals. Thoughts of the coming day and coming season filled her with anticipation, a welcome emotion after the difficult autumn just behind. Construction work at the New York State Theater had presented daily challenges. The weather had been unusually cold and damp. The elections were over, thank heaven, but the daily financial news filled everyone with a sense of gloom and her 401(k) had become the Incredible Shrinking Account. However, maybe the worst was behind them.

Valerie trudged down Columbus Avenue, pushing her cello in front of her. Two years ago, when the crummy little wheels on her cello case had to be replaced for the third time, she commissioned a friend to design some kind of push-buggy, on the order of a jogging stroller. It worked great, but always made her feel like someone's Nanny—or worse, a bag lady pushing a shopping cart. She stopped for a coffee-to-go from Starbucks and breathed in the wonderful aromas as she passed bakeries and cafés along the way.

She looked forward to rehearsal, working on a variety of pieces by a variety of composers for the gala. The ballet had not had a performance since their European tour ended in September. Although the orchestra did some recording in October and she spent a few weeks composing and recording music for an independent film, these were not the same as appearing with the full orchestra and ballet. There was something about the experience, all those musicians and dancers working so hard to create an unforgettable performance, that filled her up like nothing else did.

She arrived a little late at the rehearsal room, thanks to getting lost on a poorly marked construction detour. Several other people were late, too, but this did not explain the palpable tension in the room as Valerie walked in and took off her coat. A low buzz of voices filled the space, and Fred Zimmerman, the principal cellist, stood in conversation with Kurt Canon, the concertmaster. Fred had his eyes trained on the floor, and his arms folded across his chest, and he kept nodding as Mr. Canon murmured to him, in urgent undertones.

"What's up?" Val asked Zane Levitt, the cellist who sat to her immediate left. "Bad news?"

Zane glanced up from polishing his cello and shook his head. "I don't know. There are rumors some of our major benefactors are pulling out."

"Not David Koch?"

"No, I don't think so. You know a lot of our patrons are Wall Streeters. There's talk that a bunch of them have cancelled their pledges, plus the National Endowment for the Arts has announced they're drawing back."

"What does that mean?" Valerie opened her cello case and pulled Baby out, keeping an eye on Mr. Canon. He definitely had a frown on his face and kept jabbing at the air with one forefinger, as though arguing a case. "*This* season is safe, isn't it? We have a contract."

"Sure. A contract that allows for adjustments to the size of the orchestra if funding falls short. Early retirements, rotating mandatory days of leave. They can't actually *fire* us, but…"

Val sat abruptly in her chair and pulled Baby into place. Drawing a bow across the strings, hearing her instrument's sweet, mellow tones, she took a deep breath. All will be well, she told herself. Everything will be resolved. An old John Lennon tune came to mind. *Across the Universe*. How did it go? '*Nothing's gonna change my world. Nothing's gonna change my world*'.

Going home for Thanksgiving was beginning to look like an even worse idea than at first. If anything should happen to delay her return flight, making her late for rehearsal on Friday, she'd be in a position for a reprimand. Not a good thing if layoffs were being considered. Oh, don't think about that, she told herself. We have a contract.

Mr. Canon patted Fred on the shoulder and walked up to the conductor's stand. He tapped it with his baton, signaling the beginning of rehearsal. As the orchestra went through the motions of tuning up, Valerie concentrated on listening hard and centering herself on the familiar feel of the bow in her hand, the weight of the cello against her legs and shoulder.

Whatever Helen had up her sleeve, it better be worth all the trouble, she thought. Guck. Guckapalooza. Families were a pain in the behind.

Tuesday, November 25, 2008
"Accused Drunk Ends Up Running Over Himself", (AP)

Miranda Cates was *not* a virtuous woman. She wasn't. Everyone said so. She had run away from home at fifteen, been found in San Francisco and dragged back, and ran away again at seventeen. At age 53, she rarely exercised, smoked a joint a day, and got drunk every Saturday night. Every spring equinox, she got up at dawn to celebrate the return of the Maiden Goddess with her Wiccan friends, every New Year's Eve, she threw a party which became legendary by the next day. Miranda's long auburn hair was defiantly streaked with white, her tattoos were numerous and diverse, and everyone knew she felt no hesitation whatsoever about speaking her mind. Not even when

7

her sister's invitation arrived. *Especially* when her sister's invitation arrived.

"Damn it to hell," she said. "Damn it to hell by way of Cleveland. Helen can take this invitation, stick it in a southern fried biscuit, and roller-skate it up her ass. I am not dancing to her tune." Sure, Miranda wanted to know what was in Dad's will, but why do some drippy family hoo-ha over it? "Just spit out the news," she muttered, starting the coffeemaker. "Tell me flat out if Dad cut me from the will. I wouldn't be all that surprised."

"Mrow." Nikki Six, Miranda's cat, indicated her sympathy by noodling around Miranda's ankles. "Mrow-fffit." Which was cat for 'I hate it for you, honey. Now get me my breakfast.'

Miranda chopped half an onion into small pieces. "It's not like I ever had favored-child status. And I know I didn't make it to the hospital to visit Dad enough." She put a healthy pat of butter into the frying pan, cracked two eggs into a bowl, and began to beat them. "What could I do about it? I have to work, you know. The store can't run itself." She tore up a slice of cheddar cheese and worked it into the eggs. The butter began to sizzle and she poured the egg mixture into the pan. "And besides, Dad and I would have just driven each other crazy anyway. We always did."

"Mrrrrowow!" Nikki commented, standing pointedly next to her food dish. "Phhhfffftskie." Which was cat for 'Paranoid, much?'

8

At this point, Miranda noticed the chopped onion still sitting on the chopping block. "Crap! That was supposed to go in first. Jeez, I can't remember anything anymore." With a sigh, she added the onion bits to the half-cooked eggs. Their taste would be too sharp now, without caramelizing first, but what the hell.

Her memory was for shit lately, she thought. It was leaking away like men's brains out their ears whenever they saw naked tits. Damned menopause. If she wasn't having hot flashes, then she was having crying jags. Or murderous bursts of anger. Or she'd sneeze and then have to go change her underwear. It was a real bitch and her brains were turning to mush.

Cooking finished, Miranda took her plate and mug to the table by the window, where she could look down onto King Street. Too early for much activity, just a few people going into the diner across the street. Well, rats. She might as well go to the damned Thanksgiving dinner and find out what was what. Dad had a lot of antiques that she wouldn't mind getting her hands on, and who knew? Maybe the old fox had managed to sock away some investments here and there. She'd have to drive down the mountain Thursday morning and head back late that night or extremely early on Friday. The trip from Boone to Painter's Creek took about an hour and a half, if traffic wasn't heavy. Or maybe she could leave late Wednesday and sleep over at Aunt Reenie's. The couch was kinda narrow, but better that than a night at Helen's. Miranda packed a bong, located her stash of hash, and generally composed herself for a bout of family love and togetherness. Yippee.

Later, she headed down the outside stairs to go to work. The weather had turned nasty. It was extremely cold and windy, and snowflakes fell more and more heavily as the day progressed. Traffic in the store was sporadic. At one moment, there would be students looking for art supplies, visitors shopping for unusual small sculptures or paintings to take back home as mementos, and the occasional artist hoping to persuade Miranda to display their works. Then the next moment, the place would fall silent, and there would only be wet tracks on the wood floor to show anyone had been there. Two years ago, she had returned unannounced to North Carolina, rented a storefront on King Street in Boone, moved into the apartment above it, and opened her shop. The family might have wondered where she got the money, but Miranda didn't tell them and since no one asked, she figured they'd decided collectively they didn't want to know. She'd been a model of small-town business acumen ever since. Keeping a store wasn't exactly what she'd dreamt about when she was young, but it seemed as good a plan as anything else for the present and she took a perverse delight in succeeding despite everyone's expectations.

The bell above the door jangled and a customer walked in, stamping snow from his feet as he did so. Miranda felt a hot flash starting, warmth rising up her throat and flaming her cheeks. Damn, she hated those. Valerie, having already been through menopause, told her to think of them as power surges, but Miranda couldn't. They were just vicious reminders of her age, ruthless attacks on her libido, her energy level, and her vanity. The customer walked forward, the snow-bright light behind him putting his face in shadow. He was tall, curly-haired, wearing a heavy sheepskin coat. "Miranda Cates?" he asked, pausing just shy of the checkout counter. "I'm looking for Miranda Cates."

Ian? she thought. No, don't be ridiculous. Ian's dead. Her pulse ran down her arms in jagged lightning bolts, giving her fingertips a quick *Yee-ha.* "I'm Miranda," she said, stepping toward him. "How can I help you?"

The man glanced back, toward the shop window, and she could see his profile. No, not Ian. But handsome.

"Hi. I was wondering—could I place a poster in your window? My wife and I have a new CD and we're performing this weekend at Bolter's. Would you mind terribly?"

Damn. Just another shameless self-promoter. And a married one at that. Double dippity damn. Miranda sighed and reached out to examine the proposed advertisement. The hot flash receded, leaving beads of sweat in her hair. Just like a good romp in bed used to do. What I need, she decided, is a man. That would cure what ails me. A handsome, interesting, sexy man. If only she could meet one.

A long-buried memory slipped out of its hiding place and came to the forefront of her mind. Tim Heron, Valerie's ex-brother-in-law. He still lived near Helen, didn't he? Miranda drummed her fingers on the poster, not seeing it any longer, nor the man who awaited her reply. Maybe she would go home for Thanksgiving after all. A person should be able to turn to the family in time of need, right? And she had needs. Big time.

Wednesday, November 26, 2008
"Parasitic Flies Turn Ants into Zombies", (LiveScience.com)

Helen Cates Mitchell was a very organized woman. She was. Everyone said so. A wife and mother of eighteen-year-old triplets, she was also the mainstay of the Painter's Creek High School PTA and a Band Mom even after her kids graduated. She sang in the choir at Holy Cross Church, ran her own part-time business, *An Organized You*, and had been the mainstay of her father up until his death nineteen days ago. She still assisted his sister, Aunt Reenie, who was fairly able to do for herself but could no longer drive. At the age of 50, Helen could pass for 40. Her short brown hair was bouncy and shiny, she always had spare antacids and aspirin in her purse, and no one had ever heard her say 'no' to a needy request. Up until she sent out her Thanksgiving invitations.

"No," Helen said. "No to you, and no to you, and no to you."

The triplets groaned simultaneously. "But Mommm," Dee whined, "we're on break. We want to see our friends."

"A whole bunch of the Guard girls are getting together to see *Twilight* tomorrow night," Erica added.

"You told me you already saw it."

"So? I know girls who've seen it five times already."

"No," Helen said again. She stood at the kitchen sink, cleaning silver. "This is a special Thanksgiving, don't you see? I want y'all to hang around. Your aunts are coming all this way to visit and that's what we're going to do. And talk about Grandpa Lee's will."

Devon, his hair sticking up, and wearing yesterday's cargo pants and a Disturbed t-shirt, put a Hot Pocket into the microwave and pushed the button. "Why do we need to hang around for that? It doesn't have anything to do with us. Murph and I want to see *Transporter 3*."

Erica turned on him. "I thought you were going to *Twilight* with us."

"I'd rather poke out my eyes with a fork."

Dee aimed a smack at him, which he ducked. "You never do anything with us anymore," she complained. "Ever since we started college." She leaned against the counter, next to her mother. "He's such a jerk now. Him and his dorm buddies. All they do is play X-box and eat Taco Bell. They live like animals, Mom. They have wall art made from empty toilet paper rolls and duct tape. It's disgusting." Devon ignored her and plowed into his breakfast.

Helen grinned. Now this was more like it. The familiar bickering presence of the triplets. How she'd missed it. "Okay," she said, relenting. "If y'all will at least wait and go to the late showing. We should be done before nine o'clock."

"All right!" The girls ran off to take their showers and phone their friends, and Devon washed down his Hot Pocket with a Dr. Pepper.

"Nice breakfast," Helen murmured. He responded with a belch. "I want your bedroom cleaned up, your laundry done, and you need to put away all that junk you dumped in the garage. We'll be taking down the Christmas ornaments from the attic and I can't lower the steps until you move those things." Devon nodded. He was a man of few words.

Dreamily rinsing the silver in hot water, Helen reflected on the rest of the day's activities. She had a little list on the refrigerator, held in placed with a magnetized photo of the triplets, taken last summer. Helen lived by her lists. This one read, "1. Iron tablecloth. 2. Pick up centerpiece. 3. Pull out serving dishes. 4. Bake apple pies. 5. Devon – full-length pants! Shirt with BUTTONS! 6. Wine, candles. 7. Make cooking schedule for tomorrow.

Phil would help her with the pies. He loved apple pie and would do anything to ensure they got baked, including peeling and slicing all the apples. She just hoped the pie would cheer him up. Economic woes had affected his business, Mitchell Furniture Specialties, driving sales down and making Phil come home stressed and uncommunicative. She knew he felt a great sense of responsibility toward his employees, and even more to his father's memory. Phil's dad began the business back in the 1950's, and it haunted him to think the business might falter and die now, due to factors far beyond his control. There was precious little Helen could do to help; the pies were hardly enough, but they were better than nothing.

If only she could come up with a lot of money to invest in the business and tide it over until better times. That was one reason for the family powwow tomorrow. Another was the importance of continuing family traditions now that Dad was gone. Her family did not have a good history of drawing together in the bad times; more the opposite. Their motto seemed to be *When you're worried, or in doubt, Run in circles, scream and shout*. The family had fallen apart before, after a family member's death. If they fell apart again, she just didn't think she could stand it.

"I don't know why you bother," Phil said that evening, as they worked in the kitchen. "No matter what you want them to do, they'll just resist. Miranda will be in your face about it and Valerie will just slip away. It's like trying to push a string. She'll have excuses, other important things to do. You might as well accept it." He cut a final apple into slices and popped one slice in his mouth. After chewing and swallowing, he added, "You should have just clued them in on the will right after the funeral."

"I'd planned to. But, then..." Helen paused, remembering the dispirited gathering in her living room after the graveside ceremony was over. Valerie was already fretting about catching her plane back to New York, and Miranda had been overheard to say she'd come home for the funeral 'only to make sure the old fox is really dead.' Helen didn't *want* to murder her sisters

15

right there in front of the rest of the family, and besides, this was the Bible-belt South. People would talk.

So she just clammed up, and a good thing, too. After speaking with the estate lawyer, she'd come to the unhappy realization that death was a complicated business.

"I'm not expecting miracles," she said, finally. "And I'm not going to throw hysterics, either." Helen had thought it out very carefully and tried to anticipate every problem. "I just want to go over the will with them, explain the things that have to be done for the estate, and assign tasks. You know, get us all working together. I have a list."

"You have a list. Well, that will solve everything." He heaved a sigh and pushed himself away from the table. "You need anything else?" She shook her head. "I'm going to watch the news. The Dow fell again today."

Helen, wiping her hands on a towel, watched him go into the living room and switch on the TV. He dropped into his favorite leather recliner but not with the air of a man relaxing for the evening. Weariness and frustration could be read in every line. She turned back to the counter, her workspace spread with all the necessary tools and ingredients for a great apple pie and said a silent prayer that her sisters would come through, for once. Maybe by forcing them to take part in dealing with Dad's pile of stuff, they'd all spend a little quality time together and grow closer. She really did love her sisters, as maddening as they could be. She'd just have to appeal to their better natures. If that didn't work, she'd reason with them, and

16

if they still didn't capitulate, she'd turn on the guilt. Helen had been a mom for over eighteen years now, and she had several different weapons in her arsenal. One of them was sure to work.

Chapter Two

Thursday, November 27, 2008, Thanksgiving Day
"World's Oldest Person Dies at 115", (The Shelbyville News)

REENIE CATES BELDEN HERSCH BONFIGLIO was quite fond of all three of her nieces and grateful for them. She was grateful for Helen, who did chauffeur duty and visited so often. She was grateful for Valerie, whose glamorous Manhattan lifestyle gave Reenie bragging rights when she played cards with her friends. And she was grateful for Miranda, who was so generous with her marijuana.

They shared a good buzz on Wednesday night when Miranda drove in from Boone. They sat bundled up on Reenie's tiny balcony—because God help them both if Helen got a whiff of pot the next time she visited—and drank some wine while talking lazily about everything from the sad state of affairs in the auto industry to the recent finale of Dancing with the Stars. Later, after they finally went to bed around two in the morning, Reenie passed a restful night, culminating in a lovely dream just before she woke in which three different men clamored for her hand at a dance. One of them looked remarkably like Jake Gyllenhaal.

The next morning, she dressed in a favorite vintage Chanel suit, deep coral pink with white trim. It was a gorgeous ensemble and the color was one that always made her feel bold and cheerful. That is, it did until she put on her shoes, ugly orthopedic lace-ups. "Feet, you've failed me now," she said, grunting as she struggled to tie the bows. "And you used to be so pretty."

She did her hair and make-up, sprayed herself generously with her favorite perfume, Coco by Chanel, added earrings and bracelets. Miranda was still asleep, of course, the lazy thing. Reenie went into the living room and shook her niece's shoulder. "Get up, Miranda," she said. "Miranda, get up." Miranda groaned and pulled the blanket up higher. "Damn it, Miranda, get up!"

With no further response, Reenie grumbled her way to the kitchen. It was an important day; discussing Leland's will. Although she and Lee hadn't been very close when they were young—he was nine years older and out of the house before she was halfway through grade school—they were the last two siblings left out of eight, and they'd spent a lot of time together after she returned from California four years ago. The least Miranda could do was get her lazy behind out of bed and support her aunt in this time of need. Reenie nuked herself a frozen waffle, made coffee and turned on the TV. Oh, good. AMC had *Christmas in Connecticut* starring Barbara Stanwyck and Dennis Morgan.

About the time the movie ended, Miranda came yawning into the kitchen. "Why does Helen have to have dinner at the crack of dawn?"

"It's after one," Reenie pointed out. "Honestly, if you can't hold your wine better than this, you should be ashamed. In my day, I could have stayed up all night, dancing, and still arrive at work on time, looking fresh as the morning breeze. Girls today aren't what they used to be."

"Neither are the morning breezes," Miranda snarled. Finally, she got dressed and they headed for Helen's house. Miranda wore dark jeans, a silky woven vest in bronze and gold with trailing flutters of fabric, a black turtleneck top, and a pair of gold ballet flats. Her make-up was subdued—foundation, mascara, lip gloss—but her earrings were gold pagodas and her bracelets chunky handmade creations of copper wire, black cord and glass beads. The only tattoo visible was the trail of stars up the back of her right hand.

Reenie's apartment was ten miles from Helen's house, which was outside the city limits, near the lake. Helen and Phil bought the place ten years ago, when the triplets were in elementary school. It had plenty of space, a big yard, and an above-ground swimming pool. The house looked serene, with pansies blooming along the front walk and an autumn wreath on the door, but the minute they crossed the threshold, they were enveloped in the usual cacophony of Helen's home. The television blared in the living room, buzz of conversation came from the kitchen and, upstairs in the family room, the triplets horsed around with Seth, playing some kind of video game. The house smelled wonderful and the dining room table was festively set, with a tall glass vase of mixed lilies in yellow, orange and white, in the center.

Miranda and Reenie went through to the kitchen, waving at Phil who sat hunched forward, mesmerized by the football game in progress, and found Helen pulling a tray of cheese and fruit from the fridge and Valerie standing against the counter, holding a glass of wine.. Miranda went directly to the fridge, pulled out a bottle of wine, and poured herself a glass. Reenie sat at the kitchen table, so she could get off her feet and observe. Val looked elegant, as always, in navy silk with white frilled collar and cuffs, sheer navy stockings and very high-heeled pumps. And as always, she was keeping her precious hands far from any toil. Helen, on the other hand, looked a bit frazzled. Her hair curled into tiny corkscrews at the temples, and judging from the way she kept pushing back the sleeves of her cream-colored sweater and pulling at its neckline, she felt too warm in the kitchen. Nevertheless, she and her sister were deep in conversation.

After stopping to greet Miranda and Reenie, Valerie continued speaking. "I was telling Helen how surprised I was when we passed the steam plant. What a change!"

"It's been a huge project," Helen remarked, setting the platter of appetizers on the kitchen table and removing plastic wrap. She pulled out a little box filled with colored toothpicks and began stabbing the cheese cubes. "It's supposed to make the steam cleaner. More environmentally-friendly. But it sure looks strange with all those conveyors and chutes and enormous new steam stacks. Kind of a Frankenstein's monster."

"More like the misbegotten love child of a giant Robby the Robot and a Wild Mouse ride. But the steam is pretty." Reenie dug in her overloaded purse on the table, trying to find her eyeglasses. She never wore them in public, but family didn't count. "I remember when there was *nothing* there, not even the lake. Just the river and farmland and acres of trees."

Miranda, already refilling her wine glass, muttered, "Yeah. And you and Dad had to walk ten miles through the forest to get to school. Uphill both ways and barefoot." She took a large swig. "Why didn't you just play hooky?"

Reenie turned her face away. Miranda could be so rude. "It was three miles, not ten, and that was to the crossroads where we caught the school bus into town. The whole crossroads area is underwater, now. They had to tear down the church and move the cemetery when the dam was built."

"Well, anyway, the steam *is* pretty." Helen opened a box and spread crackers on another tray. The house smelled wonderfully of turkey and stuffing. "I love to watch the steam come billowing out. It's so white against the blue sky, all tumbling and turning on itself. Sometimes I even pull into the parking lot of that shopping center nearby simply to watch it."

Valerie laughed and patted her sister's shoulder. "Oh honey, you need to get a life."

The triplets and Seth crashed into the kitchen to welcome their guests and filch hors d'oeuvres. The noise level swelled exponentially and Reenie made the decision to put aside her irritation and enjoy the day. Miranda was Miranda, after all. Besides, it was nice having all three Cates sisters together for a change. They were so attractive, each in their own way. Valerie, tall and long-legged, her coppery hair gleaming in a smooth up-do. She'd always been the talented one, winning so many competitions with her cello. Miranda had been the troublemaker. Talented, too, with her painting, but erratic and undisciplined. She was bustier than Valerie, and not as tall, but good-looking with wavy auburn hair, streaked now with creamy white. To an outside observer, Helen might seem to have been short-changed. She didn't have any artistic abilities, her hair was plain brown, and her figure, although trim, wouldn't stand out in a crowd. She had a sweet, pretty face, but otherwise, everything about her screamed Standard Suburban Mom until she smiled, and then she became absolutely beautiful.

With a sense of shock, Reenie realized all three of the girls were in their fifties now. Their brother Gary, if he'd lived, would have been sixty. What the hell? How did time pass so quickly? Oh well, fifty was the new forty, right? She herself was nearing eighty and age hadn't slowed her down much, except for her damned feet.

Time did march on. It was strange, not having Leland there. And who knew? Maybe next year, she'd be the one who was gone. It was a very unsettling thought.

"For US Auto Execs, It's a Working Thanksgiving Weekend",
(AutoNews.com)

Dinner was outstanding. The turkey came out juicy and tender and there were side dishes galore—stuffing, Grandma's sweet potato casserole with pecan topping, regular mashed potatoes and gravy, split-top rolls, cranberry sauce, sautéed green beans and mushrooms—all accompanied by nonstop conversation.

"Remember the time Great Aunt Katherine's family came and we cooked three turkeys?"

"Remember the time the creamed corn fell off the table and the dog ate it?"

"Remember the time the toilet stopped working and we had to go to the neighbor's house to poop?"

"No poop talk, please."

By the time the meal was over and the dishes done, Helen's back hurt. Still, the dinner had been a success. Everyone enjoyed it and nobody argued. It boded well for what was to follow.

"If y'all will take a seat at the table," she began, urging her own brood toward the dining room, "we'll get this discussion out of the way and then we can enjoy ourselves."

She saw Miranda eye the handouts and heard her murmur to Reenie, "I think somebody's enjoying herself already."

Ignoring the comment, Helen took a seat at the head of the table and waited for everyone else to give her their attention. She sat with her hands folded and resting on top of the stack of papers until they all stopped chattering and looked at her. After taking a deep breath, she said, "Okay, here's the thing. Dad left his estate to the nine of us, to be divided equally. That includes Phil, even though he wasn't a blood relative to Dad. As executor, it's my job to find out what exactly is *in* his estate, to make sure all the bills get paid, and the terms of the will are carried out. I've made copies of the will for each of you. It's short and to the point."

Around the table, eight pairs of eyes watched her and Helen fidgeted with the stapled corners of the papers. "I've met with the lawyer who drew up the will, Mr. Edgerton. He seems nice. And he gave me a list of things that have to be done. There's a lot of paperwork. An estate account has to be opened, we have to go through all of Dad's papers to see if he had any outstanding debts, and a full inventory of his possessions has to be done and evaluated within ninety days of his date of death. With all of Dad's antiques and stuff, this will be quite a challenge. I already received a check for his life insurance money. It wasn't a large policy but I'll use it to pay for the funeral expenses and I hope what's left will be enough for whatever medical bills Medicare might not have covered. Dad didn't have much in his checking account. He lived from social security check to social security check and those have stopped. We still have to pay property taxes within the next month, and the power bill, of course. Basically, there's a lot of work ahead to finish the ninety-day inventory in time." She stopped and took a deep breath. Glancing at her sister, she said, "Trust me, Miranda, I'm *not* enjoying this. Altogether, there are tons of other things to do, and the lawyer told me it usually takes a year to settle an estate, and *that's* if there are no disagreements between the heirs. So I guess my first question is, are there going to be disagreements between the heirs?"

"Like what?" Devon asked.

"Well, mainly what to do with Dad's things. The most valuable item, of course, is the house and property. Should we sell the house? *Can* we sell the house, with the economy the way it is? If we can't sell it, then what? How are we going to pay for the expenses? Who knows anything about antiques? Should we have an auction? Who's willing to help out with some of the work involved and how much? I mean, these are all big questions, and there are probably other issues I don't even know about yet." She pulled a notepad from beneath the stack of papers and produced a pen. "I thought we could make a list of who's going to—"

"I don't want to sell the house." This came from Dee.

"Me neither. Dee and I always thought we'd be coming there with our children some day. Go swimming in the lake. Ride the jet-skis. Let our kids ride on the wagon wheel and hide

26

in the tunnel, like we did. Can't we keep it in the family?" Erica sounded near tears.

"*Your* family, you mean," Miranda snapped. "It's not as though Valerie or I would ever have a chance to spend time there, nor like we'd want to. And good grief, some of us could use the money. The biggest problem is, who'd buy that crazy old house?"

"The real estate market is tanked right now," Seth pointed out. His voice was quiet, but authoritative. "Even lake-front property has gone way down in value. This would be a terrible time to sell. And," he added, glancing at his cousins, "I have to admit, I hate to see it leave the family too. It's such a great house. Every corner of it is a reflection on Grandpa Lee and Granddad Hector. I know it's not modernized, and not the kind of thing that just anyone would like, but it has character. I guess I always pictured it being there in my future. So we need to discuss options, maybe, not just say yes or no to selling."

"Discussing options sounds like 'not selling' to me. Which also sounds like those who live here in Painter's Creek get all the benefits." Miranda's glare was like a pointed jab at each person at the table. "Again, I say, what possible use does the house have for Valerie or me? Or Reenie, for that matter? Or maybe you figure you can hold onto it until we conveniently forget all about our shares?"

"Hey!" Phil slapped his palm down on the table, rattling the dishes. "There's no need to get ugly about this. We're still having an open discussion. Some would like to sell, some would like to keep it, but one thing's for sure. As long as we do keep it, even during the time it might take to sell, somehow we have to pay for electricity and insurance and someone would have to do the upkeep. And how are we going to do that? I sure don't have any extra cash right now, not with three kids in college."

That shut everyone up for a moment. Then Valerie, who had been staring down at her fingertips drumming softly against the tabletop, said, "Do we have to make the decision about selling right away? What if we concentrate on the ninety-day inventory first? Maybe we could auction some of the antiques and use that money to keep the house going for a while, until we all are in agreement about what to do with it."

"Auctions are no good," Reenie said. "Most of the time, they don't bring ten cents on the dollar. And Lee's antiques aren't *fine* antiques, they're simply old farmhouse stuff. They're worth something, yes, but not a fortune. Selling them at auction would be like giving them away."

"Helen, why don't you start with listing the different jobs that need to be done and—"

"What about the boat? We're not going to sell that, are we?" Devon leaned forward to look at his father. "Isn't it half ours in the first place?"

Dee jumped in with her thoughts. "I don't want to sell *anything*. Not the house or the furniture or anything! Why can't we all just share it? And if you're so broke, Aunt Miranda," she continued recklessly, "why don't you go back to pushing drugs, like the old days? I've heard you made a lot of money back then." At her mother's astounded *Denise Meredith!,* she reddened and stared down at the table, but muttered, "Well, it's true. We all know it."

Miranda just smiled. "I didn't 'push drugs', my sweet little Dee-Dee. I grew cannabis and hemp in the Netherlands, where it was very nearly legal. And yes, I made a tidy sum. But seriously, what does that have to do with the subject? We're still talking about the rights of each person at this table to have and control their share of the estate. Hey, if someone wants to buy me out, that'd be fine with me. I'd rather have the cash anyway. Any takers?"

No one replied. The triplets looked hopefully from one parent to the other, but in vain. Helen tried again. "Look, the thing to remember is we're *family*. We owe it to each other to work things out as peacefully as possible. How about this? I'll make a list with each person's name and y'all tell me what chore you're willing to take on. And when you can do it, because we have to be done by early February and—"

"Do you really need to go to all that work? I think you can use the property tax evaluation as a starting point, and then add a certain percent of that for the contents of the house."

"But Phil, would that be honest? Maybe if it was just regular furniture—" Helen didn't want to get in trouble for cutting any corners.

"But if you overestimate the value of the estate, the inheritance taxes will—"

"Oh, the two of you, for heaven's sake," Reenie said. "Lee's estate isn't going to be large enough to worry about inheritance taxes! The real question is, what's the best way to sell things? Timing is so important and when I sold my place in California, let me tell you—"

"What about Grandpa's old cars?" Devon asked. "We're not going to sell them, are we? What about the jet-skis?"

"The barn needs a new roof," Seth said. "And there might be other repairs needed around the house."

"Isn't Tim a contractor?" Miranda turned to Val. "Is he still around? We could hire him to do the repairs. I mean, I know he's your *ex*-brother-in-law, but he's still friendly, right?"

"Hold up, everyone! We're all talking at once." Valerie clinked her spoon against her wine glass. "Helen's trying to make a list. Let's get that much done, at least." She turned to Helen. "I appreciate that there's a tremendous amount of work ahead of you, and I'd like to help, but I don't have a break in my schedule until March. I might be able to put you in contact with antique dealers in New York for the evaluations. And whatever I can do by email or phone or internet, I'll do." Helen wrote *Valerie* on her notepad and stopped, frowning slightly. Er, what, exactly, was she supposed to put down as Val's job? Val leaned forward and spoke more urgently. "Really, honey, we'll all pitch in. Maybe Miranda can go through Dad's camera collection."

"Oh, goody, I've been volunteered. How very pitching-in of you," Miranda murmured. She turned to Seth. "Do you have your Uncle Tim's phone number? Maybe I could call and see if he's interested in doing some work at the lake house."

Val ignored her and continued. "The Trips can help with the physical inventory. Right, kids?" Seth suggested that he could do a thorough check of the barn and outbuildings, and help with keeping up the grounds. "The point is," Valerie finished, glancing around the table, "we all benefit from the will and we all need to help out. And be grateful that Helen's a very organized person to head this up. Dad knew what he was doing when he asked her to be the executor."

"He didn't ask," Helen said, avoiding everyone's eyes and handing the copies of the will down both sides of the table. "He never asked. He always just assumed."

I have totally lost control of this meeting, she thought. Here's where I should make my impassioned plea to everyone, asking them to step outside of themselves for once and work for the common good. This is the point where I should press the theme of family unity and togetherness, now is when I should lean on their heartstrings. But do they have any? She remembered the final conversation she had with Dad before he died, that brief moment of clarity he achieved before fading away. "You've always let me lean on you," he said, and thinking of it now, tears came to her eyes. The heck with it, she decided. Her sisters would help if they wanted to help, and she wasn't going to spend any more effort trying to coerce, bribe, reason or guilt them into it. She got up from the table and walked away, leaving behind her notepad which still had just one word written on it. All of a sudden, she felt very, very old.

Still Thursday, November 27, 2008, Thanksgiving Evening
"Man Auctions His Life on E-Bay, is Disappointed in Sale Price", (The Perth Voice)

"That went swimmingly," Erica said as she and Dee retired to their bedroom. "Mom's upset."

"No kidding." Dee stared at herself in the mirror and scrunched her short, curly black hair to make it stand up a bit more. "Typical Aunt Val. Nothing can interfere with her precious career." She snorted. "It's not like she's a soloist anymore."

Erica bent over at the waist, brushing her long red hair upside-down so when she stood up, it would fall in lush waves over her shoulders. "And then she volunteered the rest of us." She eyed her sister and started to laugh. "I can't believe what you said to Aunt Miranda."

"Fat lot of good it did. She's such a bee-yotch." Dee went to the closet to see what there was to wear. All the same old things, unfortunately. She pulled out a black sweater and held it against herself, appraising the effect. "Aunt Val came up with the name of an antiques dealer. Big whup. One email and she's done. Her basic message was Mom's the executor, so too bad, dear, you're stuck with it. You know what's going to happen."

She decided on a different sweater. Just as black, but with a better neckline.

"Yeah. Mom will do it all herself, getting madder and madder, and then one day she'll just quietly go berserk."

The twins looked at themselves in the mirror. Dee and Erica were often called "The Twins", even though they were really, along with Devon, triplets and despite the fact that it was Dee and Devon who looked alike. Without saying a word, they decided to lose the miniskirts and put on jeans instead. Erica found herself a tank top and a sparkly sweater while Dee applied more eyeliner. Although they were going to the movies with a group of girls, no doubt they'd run into a few boys.

"The important thing, though," Dee said as they got their purses and jackets, "is that we don't want the house to be sold. So we need to find out who's on our side and who's not."

"Absolutely. This be war. Arrrrrrh!" Erica grabbed a ring of keys before Dee could. "Dibs on driving!"

The triplets had to share a car. That fact was the bane of their existence and the cause of much bickering. Devon constantly grumbled that nobody he knew had to share a car with two other people.

"Consider yourself lucky to have a car at all," his father always replied. "You could be walking. You could be working full-time at Walmart instead of going to college. Three kids in college at once! I'm just hemorrhaging cash. Here's an idea— maybe you could buy your own car." This would usually make Devon shut up. Most of the money from his part-time jobs went to support his habit—a garage band in which he played bass guitar. They always seemed to need new amps or rent money for the storage unit where they practiced.

The problem had gotten worse since the triplets started college. They were all dorm students at UNC-Charlotte, but Devon's dorm room was across campus from the girls' and somehow the car usually ended up in the girls' dorm parking lot. Although their mom had drawn up a schedule to give each of them an equal opportunity to drive, they had, of course, thrown it away as soon as they got to college. This evening, they avoided an argument only because Devon's roommate, Murph, had picked him up.

They all ended up at the same movie theater, standing in the same line. Painter's Creek only had one movie house, so all the people in town, from little kids to dating couples to old farts, ended up milling around in front of the theater, and that was where Dee saw Brian.

"Oh geez, look who's here," she whispered to Erica. "And where he is, Jessica must be. Do you see her? " She glanced around in every direction but Bryan's. She should hate him after the way he dumped her last spring, but somehow the sight of him—tall, slim, good-looking despite what some people said about his wide-spread ears—still turned her heart to mush.

"No, she's not here. She might have gone to her dad's house for Thanksgiving. He lives in Winston-Salem."

Bryan sauntered closer. "Hey, Dee," he said in a crooning tone. "Whassup?"

Dee shrugged. "Going to see *Twilight*." She glanced around, elaborately unconcerned. "You?"

"*Quantum of Solace*." He pronounced it so-lace. Past him, Dee could see Devon with his friends, glancing their way. Devon looked at Bryan and made a gagging expression. The more Dee tried to ignore him, the more Devon pretended to puke. "Hey, come here. I want to ask you something."

Bryan threw an arm around her shoulders and walked her away from Erica, outside the circle of light under the marquee and toward the parking lot. Dee stopped walking. "What do you want?" she asked, pulling loose and turning to face him.

Other people were walking past them, headed for the ticket booth. Bryan drew her over to the wall, near a row of glassed-in movie posters. She stared sideways at an ad for *Saw V* and felt Bryan looming over her, leaning his arm above her head, his face only inches away. "Hey," he said softly, "go out with me after the show."

"Why? Isn't Jessica handy?" Her voice didn't come out as nonchalantly as she wanted, more like a toad's croak. She cleared her throat. "I don't do booty calls."

"Don't be like that," he whispered, leaning even closer. "I see you and I go crazy. Can't we just spend a little time together?"

"Um, don't think so. You already have a girlfriend and I am not your default." Tough words. She wished she felt as tough, but instead she was afraid her knees were going to give way and she'd end up slithering down the wall like a strand of wet spaghetti.

"No, you're not," he agreed, not the least bit ruffled. "You're the one who got away. Come on, Dee. I want to kiss you so bad." His face came down and her breath caught in her chest.

"No! Not interested." She pushed him away and walked back toward her sister, rubbing her temple violently and aware every moment of his eyes on her. It was the hardest thing she'd ever done.

"Are you crazy?" Erica hissed in her ear as soon as Dee returned. "He's just going to break your heart again."

"How can he? There's nothing left but tiny shattered pieces. Not that I'm bitter!" She managed a wry smile before the Guard girls engulfed them.

There were seven of them, all of whom had been in the Color Guard for the high school marching band with the twins. Some were still in high school and their shrill giggling did not help Dee at all. She knew Bryan was a skunk. She *knew* his words were just words, but he still had a strong effect over her. Just like Edward over Bella in *Twilight*. Not that Bryan was a vampire. He didn't want Dee's blood, but he wouldn't mind taking her virginity. The big difference was Bryan didn't love her. And he never had.

"Ugh," she said when her thoughts reached that point. "I need popcorn."

After they got through the ticket line, and were waiting at the candy counter, Devon caught up with them. He didn't make a point of speaking to his sisters, but he exchanged glances with Dee and his expression was crystal clear. *Don't be a dumb ass.* Then he leaned his shoulder against hers for one instant, in a gesture of support.

Sometimes, as brothers go, Devon wasn't the worst.

Chapter Three

Tuesday, December 16, 2008
"Wall Street Advisor Charged with $50 Billion Fraud", (Herald Times)

AH, BLISS. VALERIE CLOSED HER EYES and reveled for a moment in the blessed silence. Finally out of the crowds and off her feet. A chance to gather her thoughts.

"Where to, lady?"

Oh. Val sat up straight and gave her address to the cab driver. As he pulled away from the curb, she glanced back up at the glittering display outside. Christmas shopping at Macy's. It was everything their commercials promised and more. More crowds, more noise, more confusion, more bargains and more miles of walking than anyone could want or take. Valerie wondered whether she just dreamt up the financial crisis; it sure didn't seem to be keeping anyone away from the stores. Maybe this was just their breakout moment, following months of bad news. Or maybe these were the last few people in New York who hadn't been fleeced by Bernie Madoff.

At any rate, she'd left her shopping until way too late. A week of bad weather made it easy to put off the chore. Today had been a case of do-or-die.

No doubt her family believed she waltzed into Macy's each year, credit card in hand, and waltzed out again twenty minutes later, mission accomplished. Little did they know it was a real endurance test, an Iron Man competition requiring exquisite planning, razor-sharp reflexes and the tactical use of elbows. Not to mention, an instinctive inner GPS. Macy's was huge, ten floors and an entire city block, and they changed their floor plan frequently. No matter how often one shopped there, the place remained a maze and Val had often gotten lost trying to get from one department to another, or trying to backtrack to pick up that beautiful sweater she'd seen only five minutes ago. There were great sales, that was the incentive, and the knowledge she'd be able to purchase gifts that would be near impossible to find in Charlotte, let alone Painter's Creek, at twenty to forty percent off. No need for anyone to realize how close to the bone Valerie lived.

Indeed, that thought was what kept her going, and now, watching the buildings on Broadway slide past, she felt a sense of triumph. Designer handbags for all the women in her life, including a fabulous patchwork leather hobo for Miranda that reminded Val of the shoulder bag her sister brought back from San Francisco when she ran away in 1969 as a fifteen-year-old. Val had been mighty pissed at Miranda back then for upsetting everyone so much, but a bit envious too. That bag symbolized freedom. And, considering that Miranda still dressed like a hippie, it should suit her perfectly.

For the men, electronics. A video game for Devon, a Bluetooth for Phil who seemed welded to his Blackberry, and a bewildering range of PC add-ons and software for Seth, who'd given her an incomprehensible wish list, admiringly filled by the sales guy at J&R in the Macy's cellar. She'd have preferred to give her son some clothes, handsome items that would set off his good looks, but she knew he wouldn't want them. Seth couldn't care less about clothes, and if he had a favorite item, would wear it to death. Not that he was sloppy; his shirts might be frayed but they were ironed. She just got tired of seeing him wear that same black leather vest all the time.

The worst part of the shopping trip was the long wait in Gift Wrap and Customer Service, but at least now she had the pleasure of knowing everything was finished and winging its way to Helen's home in North Carolina. God bless the post office. As the cab rounded Columbus Circle, her cell phone came to life with a ringtone of Iz singing *Over the Rainbow*.

"Val? It's Helen. I got your email. So, you really, truly, absolutely can't make it here to Painter's Creek before the inventory deadline?"

"I'm sorry, but no. They're simply not allowing any time off and I can't afford to use my sick leave." Valerie settled herself more comfortably, unbuttoning her coat and opening the window a crack. "However, I want to do my share. I have some friends who'll help me determine a realistic value on the furniture and antiques if you can get some digital photos made and sent to me. Be sure to get several photos of each piece and especially if there are any markings that show who made it. I'm really sorry I can't come down and do this myself."

"I guess if you can't, you can't." Helen was silent for a moment. When she spoke again, her voice sounded wary. "I've been looking through the place. You know, Dad never liked me to poke around in his house, not even to clean. There's an awful lot of stuff in there. A lot of weird things; I don't even know what half of them are or why he wanted them. And the barn loft is filled with all kinds of odds and ends. Honestly, I thought I knew Dad, but some of these things are just not making sense to me. Have you ever heard him mention paperweights?"

Val thought briefly about Dad and his ways. He'd inherited his magpie tendencies from his father. Granddad Hector always picked up bits and pieces, lugging home some treasure that some other fool had thrown away, and filling his pockets with everything from unusual rocks to stray keys. No wonder the house was crammed to the bursting point. "Don't stress out over it," she advised. "You've got better things to do. I suppose the Trips are done with classes by now?"

"Two more days, then exams will be finished. I think the girls will do fine, but I don't know about Devon. He's a little too relaxed about it all. I sure wish you could come home for Christmas. I realize it's just impossible, but I hate to think about you being alone. Seth will be here, of course."

"Oh, I'll be fine." Loneliness was a fact of life so ingrained that Valerie didn't even think about it anymore. A delivery van cut in front of the cab and the driver tore into a stream of colorful profanity, and Valerie had to cover her cell phone with her hand before Helen went into massive shock. The outburst over, she added, "And I'm glad Seth has your place to go to. He loves hanging out over there. Hey, listen, I've got to go. Give my love to everyone." She snapped the cell phone shut and stowed it in her bag. Seth did love being a part of Helen's family. Val was happy he enjoyed it, but just a tiny bit sad, too. In some ways, Seth was so much more like his father, Jack, than like his mother. He was outgoing and warm, and drew people to him like a magnet. Jack had always had that power, too. The cabbie pulled up in front of her building and, glad to stop the flow of thoughts, she paid him and got out.

Valerie's apartment was a third floor walk-up in a prewar building divided into tiny one-bedroom and studio apartments in the 1960's. She'd lucked into a sublet five years ago. Her sisters would faint if they knew what she paid for four hundred and fifty square feet of space, but it was a bargain compared to anything else on the upper west side and within walking distance of Lincoln Center and Central Park. Nearly anything she needed in the way of restaurants, dry cleaners or delicatessens could be found on Columbus Avenue, and there was a coffee shop on almost every block.

Coffee was her single main objective as she entered her apartment and dumped her coat and purse on the table. Coffee,

coffee, coffee. She had an old-style percolator, sized for two to four cups, and as she put in the filter and shoveled in the beans, ground fresh that morning, she thought about her conversation with Helen. It was classic; Helen worrying over something that didn't require it. Dad had been an odd bird, there was no question of that. Intensely private, he didn't voice enough of his thoughts to help anyone understand him. Mom, least of all. And he became more silent and more intense, the older he got. After Mom died when Valerie was seventeen, he began to develop noticeable quirks. He'd disappear on his boat for several days in a row, armed with just his fishing pole. 'Camping trips', the family learned to call them. Harmless, perhaps, but worrying when they didn't know how to reach him. Often, he came home with 'treasures' he'd found at a junk yard or flea market or by the road; oddball items like a hog snout puller or rusty tractor seats or, once, an old crank-style wall phone. Valerie had never known what to think. He didn't drink, didn't gamble. As far as they knew, he didn't run around. He just kept to himself all the time.

She had one heartwarming memory. Just one. When she was ten, Dad's brother Darwin made a rare visit east from his home in Oregon, bringing his wife and seven children. Valerie's family was living in Raleigh at the time, and the two families squeezed together in the three-bedroom brick home for several weeks. Two of the boy cousins delighted in teasing her mercilessly. They accepted Miranda, who could climb trees and balance on stilts with the best of them and were offhandedly kind to Helen, who was only four years old, but Val became an object to mock. One weary day, after being taunted, bullied, and chased with earthworms, she burst into tears in front of her father. To her surprise, instead of being told to behave herself, he took her on his knee and listened to a sobbing list of the miseries of life. "Now, darlin'," he said, patting her back, "don't let them hurt your feelings. They're just being boys, which means they're only one step up from crayfish and toads. If that."

This made her smile a little, and emboldened by his response, she asked, "Why do they have to pick on me? What did I ever do to them?"

"You didn't do anything, honey. Some people don't need a reason, they're just mean by nature. One of these days, you'll get back at them." He kissed her forehead and sent her on her way. She wasn't sure what he meant about getting back at them, but the next morning, as the boys loaded their Cheerios with heaping spoonfuls from the sugar bowl, her dad winked at her, and a second later the boys spat out their cereal, howling that someone had replaced the sugar with salt.

Valerie found herself smiling at the memory, but the smile lasted only a second. That one incident was the only time she could remember her father ever holding her tenderly or kissing her forehead in her entire lifetime. Surely, he must have done it when she was younger. There were photos of him smiling and holding her on his lap when she was a baby, but nothing within her remembrance. He was always busy, preoccupied, and silent.

The percolator began put-putting away. She stopped absent-mindedly rubbing the pale scar that ran from her wrist to her elbow and pulled out a mug, a packet of sweetener, and a bottle of Amaretto cream. Before the coffee finished brewing, she was interrupted by the intercom from downstairs.

"It's Alex," the visitor said. "May I come up?" His voice betrayed the depths of his depression once again.

Valerie sighed. Alex and his broken heart. "All right," she said, as she buzzed him in. "But remember I have a performance tonight."

A few minutes later, he arrived at her door, slightly out of breath from the stairs. Alexander Rippon, renowned character actor of stage and screen, winner of multiple acting awards, sexy villain of TV mini-series, *Parlor Games*, and quintessential Brit. *Parlor Games* was currently filming exteriors in an obscure corner of Central Park, the North Woods near the ravine. "I'm desolate," he said, leaning momentarily against the door frame and then wrapping her in his arms. "I need comfort." His lips pressed against her temple and then sought more warmth at her throat.

"Whoa," Val said, gently stepping back. "How about some coffee?"

"I come to you for tenderness and understanding." Alex muttered in his clipped tones, "And You. Offer. Me. Coffee. Where's the love?" He unwound a wool muffler and threw down his gloves and coat. "At the very least, you could make tea instead. I've been freezing my bloody arse all day."

45

Valerie stepped into the kitchenette and filled the kettle with water, set it on the burner and asked, "How much longer will you be shooting?"

"One more week." He slumped in a chair at the kitchen table. "Leila has gone back to Italy." He suddenly leaned forward and pillowed his head on his arms. In a muffled voice, he said, "I hate living alone. Have you anything to eat?"

She smiled. This was so typically Alex. "I have some tomato basil soup and a bit of leftover quiche. I could warm those up for you."

"I would be ever so grateful," he mumbled, still face down.

She fixed the meal and they ate in near silence, but the food seemed to revive Alex a bit. "Are you going to be alone on Christmas?" he asked as he refilled his soup bowl. She was glad to see him eat; after every heartbreak, he became rail-thin.

"Suddenly, everyone is concerned about my Christmas," she countered. "My sister, my son…"

"I'm not worried about *your* Christmas, I'm worried about *mine*. Colin and Roger are throwing a party and you know I hate to go to these things without a date. There's always some lone woman who thinks she's the answer to my prayers and she's never remotely close. Would you come with me? Nobody will bother me if you're there."

"Such an attractive invitation. I'm to be your bodyguard?"

"Well, no." He leaned his chin on his hand and looked sideways at her, raising an eyebrow. "Although that's an interesting thought. I see you now, with glittering breastplate and waving sword. A Valkyrie, out to avenge her man. Seriously, Val, I count on you to rescue me. You always do. One of these days, maybe, I'll return the favor."

Val sighed. "One of these days. I'll think about it. Going to the party, I mean."

After they finished eating, Valerie took their dishes to the sink, and washed them. Alex came up behind her and put his arms around her waist. "What is it that's so sexy about women doing dishes?" he said against her hair. "Turns me on."

"Caveman reflex, probably. Keeping the little woman in her place."

"I think it's the sight of a wriggling bum." He nuzzled her neck. "May I stay over tonight? I need the human touch."

"I have a performance tonight."

"So what's your point? You'll be home afterward." His lips moved to a sensitive spot under her ear. The man knew how to nuzzle.

"Not a good idea." Valerie dried her hands and attempted to move away from the sink. Alex just tightened his arms around her. "You do this every time you break up with someone."

"They always break up with *me*." He sighed and let go. "I have the worst. Luck. In the world."

Valerie put some space between herself and Alex by taking a wet cloth to the table. Wiping hard, she said, "You have the worst *taste* in the world. I mean, come on. Leila? Drama Queen of drama queens? It was doomed before it started."

47

"Yes, but what a start." He smiled, at last, and dropped back into his chair. "Let me stay over tonight anyway. For old times' sake? My bed is so cold." He reached out for her hand and pulled her closer. "I need to know somebody still loves me a little bit."

Valerie looked down at him. She'd met Alex in London, eight years ago, during her first heady year with the orchestra. Freed from the restraints of parenting, once Seth left for college, she decided to stay a little longer in Europe after they finished their summer tour. A friend of a friend, knowing she was in town, gave her name to Alex as someone who might be able to coach him for a movie role in which he would portray an accomplished cellist. As it turned out, not only did Valerie teach him how to authentically hold the bow and do proper fingering, she also ended up being hired to perform all the music that Alex's character would 'play' in the movie. Practice led to conversation, which led to dinner and wine and more conversation, which eventually led to bed. They had a lovely affair, lasting eight weeks, ending cleanly and without regret when Valerie returned to New York for autumn rehearsals. Over the years since, they'd remained friends and visited whenever they were in the same town.

She felt great affection for Alex. If he spent the night, it wouldn't change anything in their easy relationship but it would mean one night, at least, wouldn't be lonely and that was something to consider.

"Okay," she said, leaning down to kiss him. "For old times' sake."

Friday, December 19, 2008
"Woman Accused of Biting Man at NY Basketball Game", (New York Sun)

The weather outside was frightful, but inside it was so ... boring. Miranda stared out the shop window at a grey, sleety rain. Exams were over, most of the students had gone home, and traffic in the store was dead. It hardly seemed worthwhile to stay open. The only good thing about it was she'd been able to catch up on her paperwork—paying bills, doing the bookkeeping—nearly without interruptions.

Nikki-stix crawled around the window display, looking for the patch of sunlight that could usually be found that time of day. Miranda liked to avoid the expected, so her shop window held no Christmas greenery, no tinsel or ornaments mixed in with paint palettes, easels and tubes of acrylics. Instead, there was a small parade of metal sculptures—bronze elephants on stilts, some with baskets on their backs—in front of an abstract painting featuring shining grays and blues and an overlay of random twigs.

By tradition, Miranda permitted the students who worked for her to decorate the other window. This past week, it was an ode to duct tape. A 'wall angel' was created by fastening a mannequin to the back wall of the window with strips of tape that fanned out to the sides, making wings. An armchair and a bicycle had both been completely encased in the silvery stuff. Rolls of tape hung suspended like demented Christmas ornaments and, for a touch of color, smaller items such as a bucket, a toaster and several pairs of scissors were wrapped with electrical tape in blue, orange, yellow and green. One student had even painstakingly created a plaid lattice-crust pie, complete with crimped edge. Even though they took a lot of time to create, Miranda found her student-designed windows brought more attention—and business—than almost anything else she could do. For one thing, she'd sold a whole lot of duct tape that week.

However, nothing could make up for the fact that from now until Christmas, her only customers would be holiday shoppers, and it looked like there would be precious few of those. Sales of art supplies had gone up during the two weeks prior, of course, as students worked on finishing class projects, but now that was over and gallery sales were down more than thirty percent. Miranda toyed with the idea of closing the shop entirely until the new semester began, but she couldn't quite give up on the possibility of a tourist resurgence during Christmas week. Ordinarily, the last week of the year more than paid for itself.

She definitely would close the first week in January. This was always a dead time, until the students returned for the new semester. She decided to spend that week at Dad's, after all, inventorying his antique camera collection. Although she didn't want to credit Valerie for the idea, it could interesting and she had great plans for selling the cameras from her shop. This would make a great late-winter/early-spring campaign. She could tie in a gallery event with a photography slant, bring in some artists whose photographic work she'd only shown in a limited way before, and maybe make some good money. February would be the perfect time. Trade was always a little slow then but if she advertised properly, it could draw a lot of attention from serious camera aficionados and photography buffs, in addition to graphic artists. Maybe it would even kick-start her own stalled creativity.

Plus, going to Dad's house to inventory the cameras might give her the chance to run into Tim Heron again. She'd had such a crush on him in high school. It ended badly, but a lot of time had gone by since then.

Her thoughts were interrupted by the sound of a customer entering the store. "May I help you?" she called out.

"Ho ho ho. Merry Christmas!" a booming voice replied.

Oh yippee, she thought. Terry Chevchek, proprietor of the Jailhouse Diner across the street. She ate there frequently and he seemed to think this made them friends.

"How's it going, Miranda? Been caught under the mistletoe yet?" He leaned on the counter, all sunshine and affability. Terry had ten years on Miranda, and about seventy pounds. With twinkling eyes and a full white beard, he made a plausible Santa Claus, even without a costume. The only dead giveaway

51

would have been the numerous tattoos and the long gray pigtail hanging down his back. "You going to Portofino's tonight? Hawaiian luau and karaoke. A bunch of us are headed over there later."

"Probably," she replied without enthusiasm. It had become a tradition for many of the shop owners to have a holiday gathering once the students left. "For a little while."

"Don't wait too long. All the good pig will be gone." He gave her a jaunty wave and headed back to his diner. Terry was an alright guy, she thought, a bit begrudgingly, but sometimes his constant cheerfulness got on her nerves. Earlier in the week, she'd been looking forward to the party. Now, grumpiness had set in. Boone could be just a little *too* small-town. Too much a fishbowl where everyone knew your business. What made her think she could be happy here? It was nothing like Bennington.

After Ian's death, when she learned about the life insurance money he'd surprisingly left her, she decided to build a new existence for herself. Bennington was unthinkable without Ian. She searched for some other small artsy town where she could settle. Miranda thought about Sedona but decided it was too hot. Ann Arbor was too cold. Philadelphia too big, Driggs too small, and Cayucos too expensive. She'd even considered going back to Edinburgh. Then she happened upon Boone and it reminded her so strongly of Bennington that she rushed into buying before she could change her mind. And now she was stuck. Despite being in the beautiful Blue Ridge Mountains, and despite the advantages of the university, and despite the warm welcome she'd received from other local merchants, Boone had one major shortcoming. No Ian. No one even close.

Nevertheless, after she closed the shop that evening, Miranda went upstairs and changed into a flowing hand-painted skirt, black turtleneck and a necklace of three glass pendants suspended from a leather cord. She also wore her lucky orange satin underwear. Who knew? Maybe some new guy would show up and she wouldn't have to go chasing after Tim.

By the time she got to Portofino's, the party was in full swing. Plenty of eating, plenty of drinking, and the dancing had begun. Before she could down more than a single rum and coke, Terry swung by, grabbed her arm and had her out on the dance floor. It was a bit like being swallowed up by a cyclone. She got plastered across his hard round belly, nearly swept off her feet, flung out into the crowd like a yo-yo and reeled in again. "Haven't you ever learned to do the Carolina shag?" he shouted at her, above the music. "Gotta learn to shag if you're going to live in North Carolina. State law!"

State law or not, she needed another drink. Terry swallowed a beer in record time and tried to grab her hand again, but she scooted out of his way and got in the buffet line. "I have to eat," she warned, so he found himself another victim and danced away.

Jeez o'petes, Miranda thought as she made her way down the food line and found a seat. The bar got noisier by the minute. Glancing around, she saw a lot of familiar faces—Buzz and Nadia from the bagel place, Sharon and Eddie who rented

DVD's and video games, Smokin' Joe of Smokin' Joe's Whitewater Rafting. Every man she saw was spoken for, except a few who were unspeakable. Terry was currently single, but he was about it, and since he already enjoyed the favors of a number of women, Miranda wasn't too interested. Besides, he was a big ol' redneck, as country as they came.

She finished her meal, chatting with Myra Hunnesucker, who sold homemade jewelry and candles, and watched everyone else dance. Terry got wilder and wilder, twirling his partner in circles and attempting to dip. She laughed as his face turned scarlet and sweat began flying off in widely-scattered drops. "What a hoot," she said to Myra.

"Dwayne's a character, alright."

"Dwayne? I thought his name was Terry." She glanced at the big man who abandoned his partner to do an elaborate clog-step all his own.

"Terry Dwayne Chevchek, Junior. A lot of us call him Dwayne."

The music blasting from the sound system halted and Brewster Myers, owner of Portofino's, announced that the karaoke part of the evening was about to commence. "Who's going to be first?" he asked, jerking his thumb at the deejay. "Sign up and choose a song."

Terry dropped onto the seat next to Miranda, mopping his face with a huge bandanna. "Hot damn, that was fun. You gonna sing?"

Miranda rolled her eyes.

"Shoot, it's no big deal. It's just for laughs anyway." He watched as a giggling trio of women came up to harmonize their way through *Mama, He's Crazy*. As he settled down a bit, Miranda stole several glances at him. He wasn't a bad-looking guy, really. A bit beefy and red-faced, but he had good hands and looked like he knew what to do with them. Probably about sixty, gray as a fox and getting wheezy. He'd held up through those wild dances, so he could probably still go a round in bed. And if he needed a little Viagra to help out, so what? Viagra was God's gift to older women. Hell, she needed a little K-Y help herself, these days. He had nice forearms, she thought. Well-muscled and furry. Hmmm.

As the evening wore on, she warmed to Terry more and more. He seemed to appreciate it too, nudging her with his elbow, leaning close to talk. Each rum and coke made him a bit more attractive to her and she could only hope the many beers he downed were having the same effect on him.

Then he decided to sing.

The karaoke attracted some excellent singers and some real duds, but when Terry announced he would do an Elvis number, everyone applauded. His voice was pretty deep, Miranda thought, maybe it would work out. He climbed up onstage, stumbling a little on the microphone cord, clapped a Santa hat on his head, and started in.

I'll uh ha-ave a uh bluuuuue Christmas without you...

He began swinging his hips. The corner of his mouth dropped in honor of The King's sneer and a few women shrieked and pretended to swoon.

I'll be so bluuuuue thinking ahah-about you...

Terry grabbed the Santa hat and held it in front of his fly like some giant tassel, gyrating suggestively.

Miranda laughed until she cried. As Terry/Dwayne/Fat Elvis finished to thunderous applause, he turned to go down the steps and fell flat on his face. This was too much and Miranda put her head down on the table and howled, slamming the table top with her palm. She was in serious danger of wetting her britches. Oh my god, she thought, this is my life. Who else but me would have sex fantasies about a lewd Santa dancer, an old coot that I've tried to imagine into being something hotter, and now out for the count? Pretty soon I'll be humping the Easter Bunny. Yep. Everyone else will be doing all right with their Christmas of white, but I'll have a blue blue blue balls Christmas.

Wednesday, December 24, 2008
"Four Juveniles Accused of Urinating in Ice Machine", (Painter's Creek Chronicle)

Christmas Eve. Helen checked her list. She'd wrapped the stocking gifts already and finished the final grocery shopping. That left only items 3 through 11, including a quick trip to

Dad's house to collect the mail and check on things. The final weeks before Christmas had gone surprisingly well, without any major frustrations or snafus. Ordinarily, there would be at least one unresolved problem—a mail-order gift that didn't arrive, or someone's desperately-longed-for gift item that could not be found in the stores for love nor money—but that hadn't happened this year.

There'd only been one bad moment. A couple of days after Phil and Devon hauled down all the Christmas storage boxes from the attic and stacked them in the garage, she'd gone out to sort through them and begin decorating the house. She opened one Rubbermaid container, labeled 'Porch Decorations', and was assailed by a terrible odor. When she lifted up the top item, a Santa Claus pillow for the porch swing, it disgorged its innards like a mutant in a horror movie. Everything else beneath was disgusting with mold. Nothing in the box could be saved, and although none of the items were irreplaceable treasures, she found herself suddenly weeping.

"Silly," she told herself. "Don't be a ninny." It had taken several minutes of hard crying before she could stop, and hours before she could face any of the other boxes.

That was two weeks ago. Since then, she'd mostly been fine, especially after the triplets came home for Christmas break.

Today, Devon had gone over to Murph's house to shoot potato guns, and she didn't expect him back until later. The twins were still asleep, or so she assumed until she poked her head in their room and saw the empty beds. Devon had the car, so they couldn't have gone off anywhere else. Where could they be?

Helen headed up the stairs to the family room, above the garage. A faint buzz of conversation emanated from the far end, around the corner. She glanced down the length of the long room and saw…Barbies. Barbies on the pool table. Barbies on the carpet. Barbie dolls, Barbie furniture—the house, the store, the classroom. She heard a slight gasp as she rounded the corner and saw the twins sitting cross-legged on the floor, frozen in place with dolls in their hands and apprehensive expressions on their faces. They were both wearing footie-pajamas.

"Well, well, well," she said. "And this is how my grown-up college girls spend their break. A fine thing!"

The twins had the grace to blush. "We just wanted to …" Dee began.

"We'll clean it up," Erica said.

Helen laughed. "A little regression is not so bad." She examined the elaborate set-up. "Boy, I forgot you had so much stuff. Look at this store! Groceries for sale, jewelry, shoes, furniture. Must be a Walmart."

Dee giggled. "Remember the time we left all this stuff out and Devon came home and put one Barbie's head in the microwave and another one's in the toilet? And he made the cars wreck? Poor Ken went through the windshield."

Helen sighed, remembering the days. "Very nice. Just be sure it's cleaned up before our company comes this evening.

Well before. And here are your To-Do lists." A momentary vision of her girls at age seven swept over Helen and she resisted the urge to lean down and kiss them each on the top of the head. No real reason to resist, except she'd probably get all blubbery and they'd think she'd lost her mind.

Maybe she should go to Dad's next. She pictured herself, driving out of her two-street neighborhood, onto Cates' Island Road, following the road toward the end of the peninsula, where the land grew narrower and you could see the lake on both sides through the trees. Past large new houses, then smaller, older houses, until finally there were only a few cottages on each side. A narrow causeway connected the peninsula to the island and a graveled drive led between stone pillar gateposts to the house. She imagined driving up, parking the car, getting out.

No. First, she'd better go downstairs to Devon's room to change the sheets. Aunt Reenie always stayed over on Christmas Eve and Devon would have to sleep on the couch in the family room. This was an incongruous setting for Aunt Reenie. Two walls were pale gray, two walls were denim blue, and all four walls were plastered with posters—mostly fast cars and alternative rock bands—and one large cloth wall-hanging featuring Albert Einstein, for some obscure reason. Devon's guitars also hung on the wall and red curtains provided a punch of color. Helen fished under the bed for the ragged sneakers, linty socks and girlie magazines she knew were there, and piled them up on his desk so he'd be sure to see them and put them away somewhere more appropriate. Then she stripped the bed, remade it, and sprayed the whole room with Febreze. More, she could not do.

Seth would also spend Christmas Eve with them, and Christmas Day, but he'd stay at his own place overnight. He'd been doing this since he moved to North Carolina to go to college, eight years ago, and Helen wondered how much longer he'd choose to spend Christmas with them. One of these days, she thought, he would find himself a serious girlfriend and maybe start his own family. Oh, why did time have to pass and things have to change? She wished she could freeze everything to somewhere around three years ago, when the triplets were sophomores in high school, not driving yet, and Dad was still alive and active.

The thought took her by the throat. She missed him. Tears filled her eyes and she forced them back, going into the bathroom to make sure it was clean and well-stocked with soap, shampoo, and toilet paper. There was no use crying about it. He wouldn't have wanted to hang around, crippled by the strokes as he was. Unable to say the words he heard in his mind, blurting out 'comb' when he meant 'meatloaf'. Dribbling food off his spoon and onto his shirt. Knowing who everyone was, but unable to come up with their names. That was the worst of it, perhaps. He had lost so many abilities, but he hadn't lost his awareness of what was happening. He knew his mind was failing him, and the frustration and embarrassment made things even worse.

Things had been so different just six weeks ago. There'd been no sign of health problems before the first of the three strokes. She'd spent more time than usual with him that fall, since the triplets had gone off to college and she'd been fighting the empty nest syndrome. They'd gone out on the lake in the pontoon boat, enjoying the mild fall weather and the beginning of leaf change. She'd taken him with her to attend the high school football games and watch the Color Guard in action. They'd even talked about maybe making a trip to Asheville and the Biltmore House once it was decorated for Christmas.

Oh, it was no use to look back. Time to put it all out of her mind and concentrate on the tasks at hand. She cleaned out the fridge and made room for all the holiday food. Pulled the Christmas serving trays out from the back of the china cabinet. Checked to make sure everyone's clothes were clean and insisted the girls iron their own dresses. Vacuumed the living room. Finally, she could put it off no longer. She drove to the lake house.

In 1969, a hydroelectric dam was built across the river and gradually the low-lying farmlands upstream filled with water, forming an enormous lake. The steam plant was built to deliver hydroelectric power to the area, and farmland that had been in the family for five generations disappeared except for the hilltop which now formed Cates Island, fifteen acres of field and woodland.

The house stood on the far side of the island, carved into the hillside, facing the lake. She let herself in through the side door. As always, the quiet was unnerving. When Dad was alive, his TV was almost always on, whether he was watching it or not. Now the house was silent and fairly dark, with all the drapes pulled shut and only a few lights on timers. Helen walked through the main floor, checking to make sure everything was in order. It had been only six weeks since Dad's death, but already she'd realized that empty houses attract trouble. So she flushed the toilet, ran the taps in the sinks, checked for any signs of insects or mice. She went downstairs and checked through the basement rooms, including Dad's workroom.

Dad used to get uptight whenever she suggested giving the place a good clean. He took care of his home himself, until his stroke, and once he got sick, Helen was too busy to worry about the house. After he died, she checked to see if there were any important papers anywhere, and looked in the old wooden filing cabinet in the corner. The folders just seemed to hold magazine clippings, random photos from around town, and notes he'd made about some of his collections. The bottom drawer held an antique wooden music box that played *God Rest Ye Merry, Gentlemen*, and she decided now to pull this out and put it on the dining table. The house seemed so bereft without any Christmas ornaments. As she lifted the music box from its nest of yellowed tissue, she realized there was a large manila envelope beneath it.

She set the music box aside and opened the envelope. *Holy Hannah*. Unbelieving, she held the thick fan of twenty and fifty dollar bills in front of her eyes. Helen counted them out onto a desk top—five hundred, a thousand, two thousand. In all, there was seven thousand, six hundred and fifty dollars.

Saved! They were saved, at least for the short term. The property taxes could be paid, the power bills covered. She tipped out the rest of the papers from the envelope. Photos, similar in date to the ones in the upper drawers of the file cabinet—slightly discolored seventies-vintage, to judge by the hair and clothes of the subjects. However, these photos were enlargements, and as she glanced through them, she realized they were all candid shots. The people who'd been photographed did not appear to know they were being snapped. In fact, Helen realized as she looked closer, some of the pictures had been taken clandestinely—through uncurtained windows. Dad was...a *Peeping Tom*?

An icy chill thrill ran over her. Mechanically, she reached out and opened the top file cabinet drawer, and pulled out some of the files that held other photos and Dad's notes. She'd thought it a little weird at the time that he'd taken so many snapshots of people around town, doing mundane things like shopping, eating in a restaurant, driving a car. Some of the photos looked like they'd been taken with telescopic lenses. In one of the folders, she found a small ledger with entries that mentioned names and cash amounts. Luke Turbyfil - $780. Betty Burnette - $1,050. What did it mean? What had Dad been up to?

63

Christmas Eve. It was Christmas Eve, for heaven's sake, and she was standing there, possibly looking at evidence of her father's activities as either a Peeping Tom or a thief or something worse, who knew? Helen shoved the journal and photos back into the folder, threw it into the file drawer and whirled out of the workroom. She was not going to think about it right now. She couldn't. Her father couldn't be something so terrible and that was that. It was *Christmas Eve*, damn it, and she was not going to dwell on the possibilities right now. Maybe in a few days. Maybe in the New Year. Not right now.

*

In a daze, Helen finished her list of chores and before she knew it, Phil was home. He brought a big foil-covered pan with him. "Leftovers from the office party," he said. "I've got half a sheet cake out in the car and some other stuff."

Helen opened the fridge. Somewhere she'd have to find space for everything. Phil brought in a couple more items and slung his coat on the back of a chair. "Once everyone saw how small their Christmas bonus checks were, the mood got decidedly glum," he said, rubbing the top of his head. "I let them go early. We didn't have any work to do anyway."

Helen attempted to pull herself together and pay attention. "At least you were able to give them *something*. Do they know you and your family all passed up your own bonuses and took a cut in salary?"

"No. And please, don't go into that tomorrow when Mom's here. In fact, no shop talk at all." Phil's family all worked in the business, except his older brother, Don. His mother, Kat, had been the bookkeeper for many years, and although she was ostensibly retired, she still came in on nearly a daily basis to keep an eye on things. His sister Mary Louise was now the bookkeeper, and Jodi worked in sales. They and Mary Louise's family would all be coming over for Christmas day. Don, who lived and worked in Charleston, was taking his wife on a ten-day Caribbean cruise. "I suppose if we have to, we can break out the Skip-Bo or Mexican Train. That's about the only thing that can hold Mom's concentration. She's a Skip-Bo fiend."

"Uh, yeah. Whatever." Helen folded and refolded dish towels until she realized Phil was looking at her expectantly. "What?"

"I said, is there anything you need me to do?"

"Oh. Yeah. Um...bring out the extra table leaf and chairs for the dining room." She checked her list and glanced around the kitchen, looking for ideas. Alphabetize the spices? Color code the leftovers? Try to figure out if her father was a crook? Dear God, she thought. Help me through the next two days. Let things stay normal just that long. *Please.*

Chapter Four

Sunday, December 28, 2008
"Single Male Rhino, 20, Seeks Mate", (Fox News)

REENIE SAT IN THE RESTAURANT, THREE days after Christmas, feeling the activity and noise surrounding her, and stared at her menu without reading. They'd just come from a movie matinee—herself, Helen, the twins, and one of the girls' friends, a chatty brunette named Tina or Tori or something like that. She was still being chatty, bubbling on and on about the movie they'd seen, *Twilight.*

"This was my sixth time seeing it," she said, "and it just keeps getting better."

That seemed to be the consensus. Erica and her friend couldn't stop talking about the movie, the characters, the scenery, the actors, even the author who wrote the book. Helen joined in, too. She seemed to be nearly as familiar with the story as the girls were. Dee, on the other hand, was uncharacteristically quiet.

Whatever. Reenie enjoyed the movie, too, but she didn't see what the big deal was. Basically a Romeo and Juliet flick, with a different setting. Not really a horror film at all. So why did she feel so discontented?

"Not a lot of fangs," she said. The girls stopped yakking long enough to look at her. "In my day, it was all fangs and blood, fangs and blood."

"And coffins and capes," Helen added, smiling. She put her hand on Reenie's. "You can see why this one appeals to the girls more than the guys. So romantic. There's no romance in movies these days. Why is that?"

The waiter came by to take their order and Reenie allowed her sour feelings to continue as she watched them, one by one, respond to the waiter's flirtatious smile and good looks. Erica was the most eye-catching, with her long red hair and blue eyes. Her girlfriend—Toni? Tammy?—wore a skin-tight top that emphasized her boobs, something the waiter seemed to appreciate. Helen showed the effects of too much stress— circles under her eyes, pasty skin—the girl needed to learn to relax. Dee, ordinarily very attractive with her dark, tufty hair and edgy style, seemed to have all her lights turned out that day. She sat with eyes downcast, toying with the paper wrapper to her straw, mumbling her order.

When it was Reenie's turn to order, she decided to focus. She tilted her face up to lengthen her throat, leaned her chin on one hand to show off her rings, and asked the waiter his opinion. The fool answered her questions respectfully, speaking a little louder and enunciating carefully as if she was hard of hearing. To him, she was just an old lady. Practically invisible.

As soon as he left, the girls began talking again, gossiping about the principal actors in the film. Reenie had seen the photos on the cover of *Entertainment Weekly*, *Vanity Fair*, *Star*. She knew there was a lot of buzz. These young people, mere children, were on top of the world. A second movie was in the works, there was tons of interest in them.

And none in me, she thought. I had my time and now it's over. I can't expect fame to last. But damn it! I was *someone* once. I was a contender. It would be nice to have one last trickle of recognition before I die.

"Corn syrup," she said. "That's what they used to use."

Again, the girls stopped talking to look at her, polite but not really interested.

"With food coloring. It made for nice bright red blood."

A flash of understanding leapt into Erica's eyes. She turned to her friend—Traci? Tonya? Tallululah? Oh, phooey—and, arching an eyebrow, informed her Aunt Reenie had been an actress back in the 1950's and played a vampire in two movies.

"Get outta town!" the other girl squealed. "You really played a vampire?"

Reenie nodded. Graciously, as became a queen. "Of course, I didn't do just vampire movies. I also did *The Horror Comes at Night*, *Return of the Horror*, and *Horror's Re-Awakening*. Those were all with a mutant snake-man. That was when I was married to my first husband. He was the producer, and a real snake himself." She waited for Erica to tell the rest of the story, about her subsequent rise into other, more highly respected films, but their salads arrived then and conversation lagged.

The restaurant was only a block from Reenie's apartment, and after the meal, everyone walked back. When Reenie returned to Painter's Creek after fifty years of living in Los Angeles, she'd been full of foreboding that it would still be a horribly quiet backwater and she'd regret having left her beautiful condo in Beverly Hills. She *did* miss LA a lot, and so many of her friends—although they were fast dying off—but the Berkshire Village complex on the outskirts of Painter's Creek provided a saving grace. A 'mixed-use' development, it encompassed high-end clothing stores and specialty shops, numerous restaurants and coffee shops, a village green, bookstore, hair salon and spa, movie theater, dry cleaners and a variety of apartments and condos. Since she no longer drove, it was a real plus to be able to find so many destinations within walking distance. She went to the movies at least twice a week, and Helen came over every Tuesday to drive her to the grocery store.

Her apartment was in a dream location, directly above an Ann Taylor Loft store. Her bedroom window overlooked a side street, where an upscale Italian restaurant entertained a lively, but not noisy, crowd most weekends. Her living room window overlooked the main shopping street all the way down to the movie theatre, and Reenie loved sitting in a position of honor on the balcony, swathed in cashmere and comfort, surveying all the activity from behind her Roberto Cavalli sunglasses. Now and then, however, she got tired of just being a spectator.

The weather was sunny and fine, a Carolina blue sky and temperatures in the low sixties, but the beautiful day did not lift her mood. All the way back to the apartment, she brooded on dismal hopes for the future. Even if she lived to be Leland's age, what could she anticipate? Growing older, weaker. Maybe even losing her looks! Reenie was quite vain about how well she'd aged, so far. She had kept her figure, maintaining an erect posture. Only her feet were a disappointment. But to what end? What good did her appearance do her, if she only saw family and friends? They loved her for her personality, and generosity of spirit, of course. That wasn't what she craved. She wanted to exude mystery and drama, damn it. She wanted some mystique.

Reenie was usually not one to complain and whine. If something wasn't to her liking, she took action. By the time the whole group arrived at her apartment and she'd hugged everyone good-bye, her mind was made up. She'd find some way, by golly, to remind people of who she was. To make them notice she was *here* and she was *someone*. All it really took, she decided, was good PR.

"Thanks for taking me to the show," she told Helen. "It was fun. And yes, Erica, I'll read the book. IF I can find it in large text. And Dee?" She hugged her great-niece with one arm and tried to peer into her downcast face. In a gently teasing voice, she said, "Don't be such a chatterbox next time, huh? It's irritating as hell."

Dee finally smiled and hugged back. As Reenie turned to make the climb to her apartment, she waved to the group and thought, *Just you wait. You haven't seen the last of Reenie Cates yet.*

Wednesday, December 31, 2008
"World Markets Closing Out 2008 with a Whimper", (Wall Street Journal)

New Year's Eve afternoon and Dee still didn't have any plans for the evening. Erica had taken the car to go to her job at The Gap, but she'd be back after six-thirty. She was planning to go to a party near campus and just assumed Dee would go with her. They would spend the night in their dorm room afterward, so they wouldn't have to drive home in the wee hours, but Dee wasn't so sure she wanted to go.

"I'm headed over to Grandpa Lee's," her mother announced, brandishing her inevitable list. "You and Devon, come with me."

Devon, slumped on the couch, playing *Call of Duty* on his X-box, mumbled, "I don't wanna."

"Come along anyway." Mom went over and stood where she blocked his view of the TV screen. "I have to dig up some papers for the lawyer and I want you guys to go around and check stuff, make sure there aren't any problems creeping up." She continued to stand there until Devon sighed and put down his controller. "Wear a jacket; it's cold out."

Dee stared dully out the car window as they drove down the road. Her mother kept chattering away, like some squirrel on speed. Good grief, what was she on about now? Something about listening to *The Nutcracker* on CD. "I've been focusing on the cellos, trying to really notice what parts they play, imagining what it's like for Valerie. It's got to be a real workout. You can hear the intensity. Although I think the violins' part has to be worse. They have a much more fatiguing posture to hold, you know?"

Rattle on, Ma, Dee thought. How much caffeine have you had this morning?

Soon they were crunching over the gravel driveway. Mom parked the car and they got out. The air was cold and moist; it had been foggy all morning and even now, the sky was an opaque gray, nearly the same color as the lake which seemed flat and lifeless. A single fishing boat whined across the horizon.

"Okay, go around the outside first," Mom directed, "and be sure to check out the boat house and the barn." She let herself in the kitchen door and Dee and Devon walked down the stone steps that led in a curve around the house to the lake side.

Grandpa Lee's house was built into the side of a hill. From the front, it appeared to be only one story, but from the other side, the lower level with its heavy oak door and stone balustrade was exposed. As Dee came down the steps to the flagstone terrace, she glanced back at the house. It seemed such a magical place when she was a little girl with its strange Gothic touches and unusual features. Today, though, she felt more drawn toward the lake and she strolled downhill to the shoreline.

Everything was quiet now compared to the summer when the lake rang with the sound of boats and jet skis, people splashing around in the water. In winter, especially on overcast days like this, noises were muted and yet, somehow, even more distinct. Water slapped against the rocks lining the shore. A creaking sound came from the ramp connecting the pier to the floating dock, and a different, higher pitched creak came from the pontoon boat's metal frame flexing as it rode on the waves. Dozens of seagulls rested on the water, flotilla-style, with a couple of birds lifting off every so often but otherwise simply floating along. Dee walked out to the end of the pier and leaned her arms on the railing. "I can't believe we might lose this," she said.

"We *can't* lose it," Devon replied. "There's got to be a way to raise enough money to keep it in the family. I mean, isn't it basically the property tax, insurance and stuff like electric bill that need to be paid? How much could that be?" He tried skimming a couple of stones across the water. As usual, he aimed poorly and the stones sank immediately. "One of these days…" he muttered. Turning to Dee, he said, "Hey, want to hear something funny?"

"Not really."

"Murph and I went to the movies in Huntersville. You know, at that new mall? The minute we walked into the theater,

I said, Dude, this place stinks. It really did. It smelled like the poopy truck. Murph said, Nah, that's just your breath blowing back in your face. But it got worse as we climbed up to the top level of seats and just before I sat down, I looked, and man, there was a *turd* on my seat."

"No shit!"

"Yes, shit!" He laughed and leaned against the railing, his curly hair standing up in the breeze. "It was just sitting there. Not smeared or anything. A perfect torpedo of a turd. So I went to tell an usher and the guy said, oh no, not again."

"Again?" Dee finally had to crack a smile. "It happened before?"

"Yeah. The guy said it's the third time this week. I'm like, Dude, you're telling me there's a *serial crapper* running around loose?"

He laughed again and Dee shook her head, grinning. "Devon, you've got some kind of strange relationship going on with Number Two. It's not natural. Last summer, the turd that looked like Keanu Reeves. And the dog turd you tracked all through the house. And now this."

"Yeah. Guess it means my life's going down the commode."

Dee laughed and headed back up the pier. "We better make sure no one crapped in the boat house or barn. You go first."

As they checked the structures for any sign of roof leaks or mice or other problems, and Devon drooled over Grandpa Lee's old cars, Dee thought about last night.

Bryan had called. She'd been in bed, reading *New Moon* for the second time, when her cell phone went off. Erica, fortunately, had been in the bathroom shaving her legs. "What do you want?" Dee asked, rather grumpy at the interruption.

"I miss you," he said. "When can I see you again?" She immediately pictured him, that look he could get in his eyes, all soft and tender.

"What about Jessica?" Her voice had been harsh, but what the hell? He'd already stomped her heart to mush once. What made him think she was willing to go through with it again?

"I know," he sighed. "I'm a bum. But I can't stop thinking about you. Can't we get together for coffee or something?"

"I hate coffee."

"Coke, then. Or we could go to Drake's for old times' sake. Get a Loaded Sprite."

She sat up in bed and let her book slide to the floor. "We can't go backward, Bryan. Loaded Sprites and Drake's Restaurant are from high school. You have a girlfriend. If you're such a horndog, go bother her." She snapped her phone shut. Jeez! Who needed this?

Every time she remembered the day she found out, it made her sick all over again. Sitting in English class, still in shock from seeing the photo on Carrie Leatherman's cell phone— Bryan making out with skanky Jessica at Carrie's boyfriend's eighteenth birthday party, a party she hadn't even known Bryan was going to attend. To make things worse, they were studying *Oedipus the King* in class that day, and she had to listen to Mr.

Solomon ranting on about it, going into nauseating detail how Oedipus poked out his eyes with a pin. It was all she could do to keep from spewing lunch all over her desk.

Her cell phone chirped again and she saw he'd sent a text message. *I just want to be with you*, it said.

She couldn't return to her reading. Lucky Bella, with two guys fighting over her, instead of the other way around. Of course, one was a vampire and the other a werewolf, but still. Bryan's voice kept going through her mind all night long. "I miss you," he said. What if it were really true? What if she was throwing away a chance to be happy?

Well, that had been last night. Today, Dee needed to figure out what she wanted, and what she was willing to do to get it.

Mom's voice called from out front. "Come on, kids. Time to go!"

Devon caught Dee's eye and they began trudging up the hill to the front of the house. "I keep thinking," he said, "maybe we could make some money renting out the woods for paintball parties."

"Oh, please. Paintball is so last century." How could he think of mundane things at a time like this?

"Or maybe restart Great-Granddad Hec's bait stand down by the water's edge. We could sell bait and fishing supplies, maybe offer sandwiches and beer. A lot of fishermen come by this way all the time."

"While we're at it," Dee snapped, driving her fists into her jacket pockets, "why don't we start raising chickens and selling the eggs? Granddad Hec did that, too. Get real."

Devon flipped her the bird and ran on ahead.

"I *said*, it's time to *go!*" Mom yelled again, like there was a tornado coming or something. Jeez, she was so uptight.

What would happen, Dee wondered, if she took the upper hand? If she called Bryan, if she made the next move? And what would it feel like to steal him back from slutty Jessica? Tonight was the last night of the year. Maybe tomorrow was a good day for new beginnings.

Saturday, January 3, 2009
"Police Officer Assaulted with Bible", (Painter's Creek Chronicle)

"So anyway, my boyfriend went to this reflexologist? Because he's been feeling real puny? And the guy had him take off his shoes and socks?"

Miranda's assistant, Evadena, had a habit of speaking in questions. She followed Miranda around the store, haphazardly sweeping as she went on with her tale. Miranda tried to close her ears and get on with her inventory.

"So the guy keeps massaging Robby's feet? And pushing on them? And on his hands too? Robby said he got real ticklish when the guy did his feet. But it felt good, you know?"

Evadena worked her way into a corner and stayed there, bumping the Swiffer against the floor molding but never quite capturing the final bits of scrap and dust. "And he come home and took a nap afterward? Said he was wore out. And then you know what?"

Miranda, her hands full of sales slips and receipts, didn't answer right away so Evadena stood there, Swiffer in hand, and just waited. The silence was deafening. "I give up," Miranda said, finally. She put her two handfuls of paper down on the desk. "So what then?"

"He peed?"

This was said to another silence so profound even Nikki-stix complained. She thumped down heavily from bookcase to chair to floor, permitted herself one evil snarl, and disappeared up the back stairs.

"He peed," Miranda echoed, resigned to her fate.

"Yeah. Said it smelled real funky?" Evadena recommenced her sweeping. "I told him it was all those toxins? Leaving his body? I bet he had ten years of junk in there. You ought to try it. Might make you feel better? Just don't worry about the funky pee."

Miranda shook her head and returned to her papers. She was leaving in an hour for Painter's Creek and it was *so* reassuring to know the store would be in Evadena's capable hands.

At least it would be a quiet week at the store. Students weren't back yet, and most of the visitors were gone. She probably should just close down. Hell, even last week was pretty sleepy, and usually the week after Christmas was a nice finish to the year. The way things were going, she didn't need any financial pundits on television to suggest that the recession was here to stay. She could cover her rent, just barely, but how she would make her health insurance payments, Miranda didn't have a clue. Maybe a week in Painter's Creek would bore her to death and then she wouldn't have to worry about old age.

It didn't take long to pack a few things, entrust the key to Evadena—oh, Lordie—and be on her way. She decided to take the slightly shorter route to Painter's Creek that followed Highway 321 across the mountains, even though it meant driving through ten miles of heavy construction. Just south of Blowing Rock, a wider new road was being clawed out of the mountainside to replace the narrow two-lane. It gave her a thrill to look up at sheer rock walls with dangling trees and crumbling rock threatening to slide at any moment, and to look down on the other side of the road at precipices and vistas newly exposed. Whatever gets my ticker jumping, she thought. Takes more these days than it used to. Helen wouldn't even drive 321 anymore. Said it gave her the willies. Well, Helen always was a big chicken.

Miranda had plans. She would inventory those cameras right away and then do a little snooping around the place to see what else might be worth displaying at her store. She didn't ordinarily handle antiques, but Dad had been such a magpie, finding things and tucking them away. Who knew what might be hiding at his house, just waiting to be discovered?

Her five-year-old Jeep Wrangler threaded its way down the mountainside, through Hickory, and along the final stretch to Painter's Creek. She grabbed some carryout from Drake's—man, they still sold those Loaded Sprites, stuffed with maraschino cherries and pineapple tidbits and chopped strawberries—and headed down the home stretch just at dusk. The steam plant chugged away—thick billows of white against the purpling sky, shot through with orange rays of the setting sun. It made her think of Maxfield Parrish paintings with thick cumulo-nimbus clouds and nymphs in flowing drapery.

She drove past Helen's road. No need to announce her presence tonight. It could wait until morning. After all the fuss Helen made at Thanksgiving about everyone pitching in, lately she'd been surprisingly quiet on the subject, even suggesting that maybe she should do the whole job herself after all. Helen was a born flip-flopper, Miranda decided. Never sure of what she wanted, even after she got it.

Miranda drew a deep breath. Nearly there. Across the causeway to the island, up over the brow of the hill, swerve to a parking place on the gravel drive. She got out of the car, faintly daunted. The house was completely black, not a light in sight, and she had to use the faint illumination from her cell phone just to find the key to the side door, hidden on the framework above one of the windows.

The side door opened to the kitchen, and she switched on the light right away. Now it didn't seem quite as creepy. The big front doors opened directly into the main living area, across from the fireplace, but no one used those. They were enormous and heavy, Gothic-looking oak things with elaborate iron hinges and an antique key the size of a Pekingese. Family lore said Granddad Hec rescued the doors from a demolition site in Salisbury, but Miranda had her doubts. More likely, he made the doors himself with red oak, dyed with india ink to look black, aged them by wholloping them with a couple of tire chains, and then swiped the iron hinges off an old Victorian-era church or something. Yeah, he'd built the house almost entirely out of 'found' items, but sometimes the items he found hadn't exactly been lost in the first place.

The main floor was mostly one huge room. The ceilings had heavy beams and there were four pairs of curve-topped windows flanking the fireplace, their view of the lake obscured at the moment with heavy curtains. A hodge-podge of antique furniture and the merely old and outdated filled the room to a point of disguising some lovely architectural details. This was one of the things that always drove her crazy about Dad. He had great taste when it came to individual pieces, but then he threw them all together in a jumble that made the house look like a none-too-tidy junk shop. And there was never enough light. At least the stacks of old newspapers and magazines were gone, and the place smelled better than before.

Miranda checked out the fridge to see if Helen had stocked any food for breakfast. The house had been built during the late forties, and the kitchen was small in the style of those days. It had been updated in the 1980's, and the results were discordant to the rest of the house and, by this point, out of date anyway. The only good thing she could see was a half-full bottle of Bailey's, which she immediately opened.

Swilling directly from the bottle, Miranda wandered around a bit. Over in one corner of the living room were the built-in cabinets that Granddad Hec designed, almost like a puzzle. They reminded her of a Louise Nevelson sculpture—an elaborate combination of different shapes and dimensions. Some individual sections were short and wide, others tall and narrow. Some had plain doors, some had doors that were carved and pierced, some sections were open. Each knob was unique—brass, silver, blue glass, clear glass, cloisonné. She opened the door to one space, about four feet tall and only a foot wide. Inside, as she remembered, an almost-life-size Shirley Temple paper doll from the 1950's, carefully preserved with a thin wood backing and shellac. The shellac had yellowed over the years so that poor ol' Shirley looked like the victim of an overly enthusiastic spray tan. The doll's paper dresses, fragile as cobwebs, leaned alongside, protected in an artist's portfolio. Miranda closed the cabinet, smiling, remembering the time she got caught playing with the doll, which was strictly off-limits. How difficult it had been, living surrounded by Granddad Hec's treasures and not allowed to touch any of them!

Well, she called the shots now. She tipped the last of the Bailey's down her throat and went out to the car for her things. For once, there was no one to lay down the law, no one to give disapproving stares, and she laughed. This could be fun.

Around the corner from the massive staircase that led to the lower floor, were two bedrooms and a bathroom. She could see Helen's influence in the guest room. Cleared of clutter, it exuded relaxation and refined taste. Dad's bedroom, on the other hand, while scrupulously clean and minus the evidence of his final illness—aluminum walker, potty chair, tray of medicines—hadn't changed a lick. Too many pieces of unmatched furniture of different periods, too many framed prints on the wall—everything from Harrison Fisher and Norman Rockwell to Boris Vallejo and Klimt—beautiful leaded windows covered with hideous olive green drapes, gorgeous wood floor boards hidden by worn carpet. Why, why, *why* was he so obtuse? He was an intelligent man, for chrissake. How could he not see what was right in front of his face?

A TV sat on one of the dressers and Miranda switched it on, fiddling with the channels. Oh, good, a *Dr. Who* evening, with back-to-back episodes until midnight. She pulled the combs out of her hair and let it slide down, heavy and rippling, almost to her waist. Glancing in the mirror, she smiled. Valerie might be scrupulous about holding back the gray, but Miranda liked hers. Besides, it wasn't really gray. More of a creamy white, pale against the red. Mostly, for some reason, on the right side of her hairline, but streaking throughout.

She pulled off her clothes, letting them drop where they would. She was still a damned fine-looking woman, she decided, looking in the mirror. She'd never had children, so her breasts weren't as droopy as many women her age, and her waist remained relatively small. Yeah, her butt was bigger than it used to be, but she had great legs. All the Cates women did, right down to Dee and Erica. Her legs might not be as long and lithe as Valerie's, but they were well-shaped and unmarked by varicose veins. Not many women her age could say that.

Miranda pulled an old cigarette case out of her purse, one of those metal compacts that movie stars used in the old days. She found it perfect for holding joints and she padded barefoot out to the kitchen, located an ash tray, and came back to her father's room, where she settled down, lotus-position, on the rug in front of the TV. She proceeded to light up and watch as the Doctor took Rose back through time.

I am smoking pot in Dad's bedroom, she thought. Hot damn. I'm a grown woman and can do what I want, and this is it. She took a long drag and watched the smoke spiral up. Here's to you, Dad, ya old fart. You never got one thing right. I'm sitting here butt- naked and smoking pot in your bedroom. How you like them apples, Dad? I'll tell you what. I like 'em just fine.

The phone rang and she languidly stretched out an arm to pick up the cordless receiver. "Yowza," she said with all politeness.

"Uh, Miranda? It's Helen. I wasn't expecting you. I thought we agreed you didn't have to do the cameras after all. Why are you at Dad's? Phil saw you turning onto Cates Island Drive when he was driving home from work."

"Yep. Decided I'd like to sort the cameras anyway. Do my bit, you know? So, how ya doin', Helen, old pal, old chum?"

A moment's silence. Then, "I guess it's okay. By the way, Tim is coming over there tomorrow. He's going to work on the roof of the barn. You were right to suggest him. He said he's glad to help."

"Good."

"Now, he won't need to bother you for anything. He knows what needs to be done. So please, don't get in his way. He's doing this as a real favor to us—you know, he's a very successful contractor now."

"Oh, yeah. Like there's tons of new buildings going up these days. Thass okay, let him come on over." Miranda smiled again and closed her eyes, remembering. "Yeah. He'll be real welcome. See ya." She hung up and leaned back against the heavy quilt folded over the foot of Dad's bed. Good. She'd see Tim tomorrow and decide if it would be worthwhile to take a trip down Memory Lane.

Well, the next few days were going to be quite an adventure after all. She took another hit, savoring the undertones and feeling the high begin to build. "Yeah, Dad," she said aloud. "Might be some high times in the home tomb this week. Won't that just send you spinning, Father dearest?"

Chapter Five

Sunday, January 4, 2009
"New Jobless Claims Jump to 26-Year-High as Layoffs Spread", (Detroit News)

THE NEXT MORNING, MIRANDA WOKE and felt absolutely fantastic. She'd anticipated bad dreams and restlessness, but instead, she'd slept like the dead on ice. With thoughts of Tim possibly arriving soon, she showered and dressed in jeans and a clinging turquoise jersey, and did her hair in a loose braid.

Two years of experience in running the store had left Miranda with plenty of knowledge in the art of taking inventory. There were two cameras on display in the living room—a National Graphlex from 1933 and a 1958 Voigtlander, but most of the cameras, she knew, were downstairs.

The wide wooden staircase with elaborate banisters led to a landing and then turned 180 degrees to continue to the lower level. At the foot of the stairs there was one door to the left and three to the right, and straight ahead was a hallway they called The Tunnel. It was called that simply because it had an arched ceiling and stretched a long way forward to the huge double back doors. There were no ceiling lights, so it was always dark. A couple of small niches, displaying artwork, could be lit but usually weren't. A stone floor made the tunnel aspect complete. The grandchildren used to love to scare themselves sick, playing there.

The basement level consisted of four rooms—two more bedrooms, a bath, and Dad's workroom, a huge space thirty feet square, with a large work table in the center and plenty of storage for his 'treasures'. Along three walls was a motley collection of glass-fronted bookcases, curio cabinets, an old pigeonhole desk and other antique office furniture. The fourth wall had a counter built all along its length, with windows above and a couple of architect's flat file cabinets underneath, the drawers full of rock samples and other small items. Dad's collections were varied and large, and Miranda couldn't believe there wasn't money to be made there. An old wooden filing cabinet took up one corner of the room, but when she checked the drawers, they were all empty.

Of his collections, the cameras were the most valuable. He'd been interested in photography all his life, starting with high school where he learned to develop his own film, and later when he worked with the Civilian Conservation Corps. After he retired in 1990, Dad began frequenting antiques fairs and collecting old cameras—first, inexpensive models like old Brownies and Kodaks and then later, as he "swapped up", he came into possession of Graphlex and Pentaflex models, and even some old stereo cameras with multiple lenses, used for making stereopticon cards.

She began by setting up a spreadsheet on her laptop and worked her way through the cameras, which were stored in the glass-fronted bookcases. Some of them had wooden cases and clearly dated back to the late 1800's, others made her think of the kind used in old movies like *Rear Window*, with bright reflectors behind the flashbulbs. Many were the folding type. She had to admit a grudging respect—Dad certainly had accumulated a wide range. She became so engrossed in what she was doing, she didn't notice the time pass. She'd just listed the thirty-eighth camera when she heard a rapping at the window and about jumped out of her skin.

Tim stood on the other side of the window. "Hey," he shouted through the glass. "I've been knocking on the door upstairs for twenty minutes!"

"Oh, sorry! Didn't hear you." Rattled, she gestured for him to go back up to the door. She pounded up the stairs and let him in at the kitchen, slightly out of breath by then. So much for good first impressions.

Some men are good-looking from birth. Some begin to draw admiring glances when they're pre-adolescent, and some men grow into their looks. Tim was a member of this last group. When she'd first met him back in high school, he'd been a rotund, clueless nerd, hanging onto his popular older brother's coattails. She liked him anyway, despite his looks. Maybe too much. He was such a sweetheart, and the fact that he had a hopeless crush on Valerie only made him more of a challenge. Later, Miranda had seen him again at Valerie's wedding to his brother Jack, and he'd slimmed down by then, lost the glasses and become cute, but remained clueless. After that, she'd seen him only once, at Seth's college graduation four years ago. By then, he'd married a beautiful blonde, was the proud father of a pre-adolescent girl, and should have been the happiest of men, but he looked miserable that day. She always wondered what happened.

He did not look miserable today. Tanned and fit, bigger and more muscular than his brother had ever been, he exuded health and confidence. "How ya doin'?" he asked and smiled, laugh lines jumping into view. "Sorry I startled you, but I left my drawings here and needed to get them."

Miranda found herself uncharacteristically tongue-tied. Seeing him brought back so many memories. She opened the door wider and invited him inside. He walked into the living room and took some graph paper drawings from a drawer. "The barn roof has a leak, and while we're up there, we're going to shore up the rafters." He paused and discreetly eyed her up and down. "You're looking well."

She put her hands into her back pockets and glanced down at her ice-cold bare feet. "Yeah, I'm great." Flipping her braid over her shoulder, she straightened her back. *Knockers up*, Aunt Reenie always said. "Would you like some coffee? I think there's some around here somewhere."

"Nah." He shook his head. He wore an old quilted baseball jacket and jeans, heavy work boots, and a faded plaid flannel shirt. "I've got a thermos. But hey, maybe we can grab lunch together later and catch up on things."

She nodded and he left. Suddenly feeling giddy as a schoolgirl, Miranda scampered downstairs to do as much as possible on her inventory and still leave time to slap on a little mascara and lipstick before they went to lunch.

When the clock said twelve-twenty, she walked out to find him and saw that Dad's old cars had been pulled out of the barn. "Took me all morning," he said, looking a bit harassed. "Didn't dare do any work on the roof, with these sitting below, but before I could move any of them, I had to charge the batteries and put air in the tires."

"I'm amazed you could move them at all," Miranda said, glancing at the old wrecks. A 1969 Cadillac convertible in pale yellow with a ripped top and plenty of rust, a 1977 Buick Nighthawk covered with dust, and a '98 Chevy Lumina. "Dad never could bear to part with a vehicle, but he stopped driving more than five years ago and these have just sat since then. Look at the size of that Cadillac. A refugee family of five could live in that trunk."

"Yeah, well, there might be a couple of families of mice living in there now." Tim dusted off the knees of his jeans and wiped his hands on a shop towel. "Let's eat. I'm starved."

Over a couple of hamburgers at McDonald's, Tim told her of his plans to reinforce the barn roof. "Phil and I figured out the barn is nearly a hundred years old. At least, the original parts are. A lot of it has been replaced, bit by bit, over the years. Parts of the current roof go back to the late eighties, early nineties, but it's a patchwork and not a very successful one."

Miranda nodded, remembering. "Yeah. The old one got ripped up during Hurricane Hugo, in 1989. I was in Italy at the time but I heard about it and Helen sent me photos."

"Italy, huh? Italy, Paris, Scotland… you've been all over." Tim added some sweetener to his coffee and stirred it. "I was so blown away when you ran off to San Francisco that time. Didn't see that coming. I was envious as hell."

Miranda smiled and glanced down. Obviously, he still had no clue what set her off that time in the first place. If she'd only known he felt that way. Damn! She sighed and said, "San Francisco was great. But Europe—now, that was heaven! Sometimes I wish I was still there. I felt so free, backpacking all over, picking up work here and there when I needed to, and then moving on. Now, I feel stuck in Touristville and no way to leave."

"Your store?"

"It seemed like a good idea at the time. That should be my epitaph, actually. *It seemed like a good idea at the time.* I sank all my money into inventory. Now, with rent, utilities, insurance, payroll, and new stock bought on credit, I can't afford to close and I can't really afford to keep going."

"I hear you. I have similar problems—loans for equipment, payroll and benefits for my crew—but work has slowed to a

91

damn crawl. Just renovations, no new construction at all. I'm happy to do this job for your family, but it won't keep my crew together. I hate to lose good men but I can't keep them working." He leaned back and ruffled his hair, and then locked his hands behind his head, a wry expression on his face. "Listen to us. Solid citizens. What the hell happened?"

"It's a damn shame," she replied, smiling. Leaning forward on her elbows and keeping her voice low, she added, "I've got a coupla joints back at the house. What say we blow this pop stand and forget our problems for an hour or so?"

Tim chuckled and dropped his hands into his lap. She was delighted to notice a blush spreading up his neck. So, the teenage nerd lurked beneath the confident surface. How cute was that?

"I don't mind," he said, grinning down at his tray. "Sounds like old times."

"You bet it does." Miranda slowly stood up, winding a long cobalt-blue scarf around her throat, grateful she'd put on a good bra that morning as his gaze traveled up her body. Once, long ago, she and Tim had had a moment. A very nice moment, never repeated. Until now.

Still Sunday, January 4, 2009, an hour later
"As Networks Cut Back, Soap Operas Feel the Pain", (Soap Opera Digest)

Miranda stretched and purred, feeling contentment all the way to her toes. "That was lovely."

Next to her in the rumpled bed, Tim folded his hands behind his head. "Thank you, Ma'am. You've learned a few things along the way, haven't you?" He turned on his side and regarded her, a quirky smile on his lips. "Now how am I supposed to concentrate on work the rest of the day?"

"You don't. That barn will still be there tomorrow. Why work on Sunday, anyway?"

"Because I have another job to do on Monday." He threw himself back on the pillows and rubbed his chest. "I'd better get moving. I have to be done by five. Hayley's got a 'thang' that I need to attend."

"Hayley? I thought you and your wife were divorced." Miranda rose up on one elbow. "Shit! I don't get involved with married men." She threw off the blankets and pulled on a caftan. "Damn it! I swore never again."

"Hey, cool down," he said, laughing as he pulled her back into bed. "Hayley's my daughter. Relax." He curled his arm around Miranda, settling her against his chest, and smoothed back her hair. "My wife and I divorced two years ago. Do you mean you haven't heard the gossip? Lord, I gave Painter's Creek more credit than that. People here are usually so happy to spread bad news."

"What's so gossip-worthy about being divorced these days?" Miranda grumbled, secretly relieved. She cuddled up closer and stroked his jaw.

93

"My wife is also in jail."

His voice was soft and bitter. The corner of his mouth turned down and his gaze went to the ceiling. "Embezzlement. Not only had she been cheating on me, she'd been cheating her employer. Took everyone in with those big innocent blue eyes. The trial finished a couple of weeks ago. She was convicted and got three years. Eighteen months with good behavior. Hayley's pretty devastated so I spend as much time with her as I can. Tonight she's got a presentation with the Winter Guard—you know, the flag team. Some kind of kick-off thing that I said I'd go to."

With obvious reluctance, he rolled Miranda off himself and crawled out of bed. As he began dressing, he asked, "How long will you be in town?"

Miranda watched, sighing as Tim covered all his good bits. "Only this week. Students will be returning to campus Friday and Saturday, so I'll probably go back Friday morning." She rolled over and mushed her face into the pillow. Her muffled voice continued, "My one good chance to make a little money as they buy supplies for the semester. And then, I expect major drought."

Tim sat on the edge of the bed and rubbed her back. "Can I call you later? Maybe we can get together some time tomorrow." He leaned down and kissed her neck, stroking her hair and pinning her briefly with his weight. "Sure is nice to see you home again, Miss Cates. Good friends like us shouldn't lose touch for such a long time." He patted her rump and left, and Miranda thought, as she had many years ago, *what a nice guy. Valerie was a fool.*

It was difficult to get back to work. Miranda would have preferred to just wallow in the sheets, reliving the past hour and catching a few zzzz's, but with the help of some hot coffee and P!nk's *I'm Not Dead* on her I-pod, she was finally able to concentrate.

First thing she did was phone Helen to ask about the cameras. "Didn't he have some kind of list of these things? Identifying them, or what he paid, or anything at all?"

"Yes, I found some hand-written notes he made over the years. Sketchy, but they're all we have. There's a folder in the center drawer of the desk in the workroom." Helen said. "I hope you had everything you needed in the guest room."

"Actually, I slept in Dad's room. It was fine."

"But why sleep there? That's what a guest room is *for*, for guests. Why would you want to sleep in Dad's room? I'd have thought that would be the last place you'd feel comfortable."

"Jeez, don't worry about it! No biggie. I'm gonna go find that folder now." Miranda was ready to snap her cell phone shut when Helen spoke again.

"Okay, it's fine, no problem." Helen said in a more conciliatory tone. "I just assumed … anyway, I'll come over to help. I would have been over sooner, but I've been working on writing a new ad for my business, trying to build up my client list."

"Your *client list?*" Miranda stifled a laugh. "Well, if you're so *busy*, don't worry about coming over here. I'm doing fine." When Helen didn't respond, she added, "And I'm having dinner with Aunt Reenie later, so I won't be here after six o'clock." The call over, Miranda heaved a sigh of relief. It was a good thing Helen wasn't coming over to 'help'. She was so damned left-brained, it was a wonder she didn't tip over. And always so anxious to please, no matter how rude you were to her. She could drive a person nuts.

The camera collection was amazing. Dad owned some really old stuff, a 1920 Speed Graphic, a century-old Rochester Camera Cycle Poco No. 3, a Hasselblad 1000F that ought to be worth a pretty penny or two, some Japanese and German cameras whose names she didn't even recognize, and tons of Kodak, Zeiss and Argus. He even had a 1960's era "spy" camera, tiny for those days, which made her think of early James Bond movies. There was a half-used roll of film still in it. She'd have to see if she could get it developed. Might be interesting. There were also a couple of movie cameras and a movie projector. She could probably be finished with the initial task of listing and photographing the whole collection within a day or two. Then she'd have to talk to a couple of experts before she could get a guess on their value.

*

The evening with Aunt Reenie didn't exactly go as planned. She'd hoped to get the old bird on her side before the expected showdown with Helen over how to sell the cameras. All Reenie wanted to do, however, was watch old BBC episodes of *House of Elliott* on DVD.

"I can't believe I missed this show when it originally ran," Reenie said. "What a fantastic series! Look at the dresses—the beading, the chiffon, the jewelry. They had real style in the 1920's. Not like now. Oh, yeah, Vogue puts on a display, but who can really wear those things? Carolina Herrera is the last fashion designer left who knows how to dress a woman instead of a fourteen-year-old child. And maybe Stella McCartney." She sat entranced, chin on hand, curled up in the corner of her couch. Her two cats deigned to join them. The big white one, Meany Mouse, lay on the mantel, green eyes languidly surveying the scene. The black and white cat, Hungry Bogart, curled himself over Reenie's shoulders, looking like a particularly ratty fur stole. He was old and arthritic, protesting loudly every time Reenie moved an inch.

"I wondered if you knew anything about Dad's cameras." Miranda asked, after waiting impatiently for the episode to end. "He's got them all listed, including where he bought them, but I don't know whether he actually used any of them. I haven't seen any photographs."

Reenie simply pointed the DVD remote control at her set and selected another episode, her attention strictly on the TV. After a second, she said, "I don't know what you're talking about. There are a zillion photos in the albums in the living room. I ought to know, Helen has forced me to sit and admire each one. Some beautiful pictures of your Mom when she and Leland were courting, back when she danced with the ballet. And all the pictures of you kids." She watched as the program ran through its opening credits, and hit Pause.

"There are some more photos somewhere," she added, peering over the bifocals she wore when no one of consequence was around. "You know how Lee liked to bring home all kinds of strange and unusual items. Well, whatever he couldn't actually obtain, he'd photograph. Like, old buildings and tombstones and weird trees and clouds. He had all kinds of special long-range lenses and cameras that took pictures in the dark, and special film and all that jazz. Kept the film in the refrigerator. The first year after I moved here, before he had his stroke, I would go with him sometimes. A little adventure. Like that old round barn out on the back road behind the school? The owners didn't want anyone on the property, so he found a way to photograph it with a telescopic lens from up on a hillside. Or we'd go out at night and he'd get pictures of the Methodist church by moonlight. He'd take me because I could drive better in those days, especially after dark." She clicked the Play button on the remote and her show began. With that, she was off in her own world, suffering through more problems with the Elliott sisters, Beatrice and Evie. "Evie reminds me of you,"she added. "Terrible taste in men."

Miranda felt her mouth twist. Not wanting to be the image of her own constantly-dissatisfied mother, she decided it was time to say goodnight. "Any ideas where those photos could have ended up?" she asked as she bent to kiss Aunt Reenie good-bye and avoided, just in time, an evil swipe of the claws by Hungry Bogart.

Reenie shrugged, her gaze never wavering from the TV screen. "I dunno. Never saw the developed film. Might be in the old file cabinet in his workroom. Once when I stopped by, he dropped some big envelopes in there real quick and locked it up. You know how paranoid he could be about his privacy."

Big fat lot of help that was. Miranda had already verified the file cabinet was empty. God, what she'd give for a drink, and a bar peopled with *people*, not the idiot rednecks in Painter's Creek. At this rate, she might as well work some more on the cameras, so if Tim ended up having some free time in the next couple of days, they might be able to take advantage of it. Then she could blow this pop-stand.

And she did *not* have terrible taste in men.

Wednesday, January 7, 2009
"City Council in Uproar Over Budget Cuts", (Painter's Creek Chronicle)

Helen had opened her fledgling business, *An Organized You*, during the brief interval between the triplet's high school graduation and her father's illness. She'd come up with the idea nearly a year prior to that, when the mother of one of Erica's friends had commented on how Helen always seemed so organized and serene, and could she bottle a little of that? It was a jolt to realize she actually possessed marketable skills and, ever after, whenever her busy little brain got worn out trying to imagine the empty days ahead, the idea of starting her own business had been a lifeline.

No one took it very seriously. Phil smiled and urged her to go ahead, his attitude the same as when he watched the girls perform in endless dance recitals when they were younger. Nothing would probably come of it, but they had a good time pretending and it kept them out of trouble. The triplets' attitude was even worse—they thought their mother's little job was *cute*. And obviously, Miranda thought the whole thing was a joke.

Nevertheless, she'd pursued the idea, turned it into reality. She studied up on how to run a successful home-based business, fitted up a corner of the family room to be her office, sent out flyers, and advertised in the Painter's Creek Chronicle. And she had actual clients. Women who were trying to juggle job and family or who, like Helen, were part of the sandwich generation, needing someone to help them organize their house, their garage, their basement or attic, their calendar and their lives. She never had more than a few clients at a time, but it was enough to keep her busy. More than enough, after her father got sick.

The holidays had brought extra clients, people who were desperate to get their homes organized before guests came to visit, or who needed help dealing with all the extra work that Christmas shopping and party planning entailed. But since then, things had died down.

On Wednesday, January 7, Helen finished her housework and sat down at her desk. The appointment calendar was empty. A recent ad in the paper had brought not a single enquiry, which was surprising. January was usually a time of fresh intentions to make *this* the year things finally got organized. WalMart and Target were filling their aisles with storage containers and closet organizers, and all the magazines carried titles like *Clear that Clutter* and *Hoard No More*, so why wasn't she getting any phone calls? Even old Mr. Mullen, her first and perennial client, seemed to have decided at last that every detail in his 1920's bungalow had been arranged to perfection. Phil used to tease her about the old gentleman, claiming he just wanted a pretty face in his life, and perhaps to some extent this was true. Helen realized Mr. Mullen was more lonely than disorganized and introduced him to a couple of members of the local Toastmasters club. Since then, the old guy had perked right up, begun giving speeches and now was acting with the theater guild. He'd been a great client, but he didn't need her any more.

Neither did the triplets, apparently. They were all ready to move back to their dorms early, tomorrow, instead of the weekend. Classes didn't start until next Monday, but their friends were starting to trickle back to school and the Trips wanted to be there.

So, she looked at the empty calendar. What she really should do was go over to Dad's house and check on Miranda's progress. Or if Miranda was snarly as usual, she could work in some other part of the house. Maybe it was time to clean out Dad's closet. She couldn't face it earlier; going through his clothes, deciding which items to throw away, which to give to Goodwill, and which, if any, could be used by someone in the family. Clothes were so personal.

At that thought, she felt her chest simply lift her right out of her chair and instead, she grabbed her purse and headed to Phil's office. He could jolly well have lunch with her. Mitchell Furniture Specialties was located on the highway leading to Painter's Creek. When Phil's dad started the business, back in the late fifties, he bought an old brick building from the 1920's and modernized it with showroom in front, offices upstairs, and production area and warehouse in back, with a loading bay handy to the railway tracks that ran behind the town. In the old days, access to the train system had been crucial; now, not so much. When Helen arrived, the showroom area was empty. Phil's younger sister, Jody, sat at the long counter, listlessly paging through a *People* magazine. Helen smiled at her and headed up the stairs to the offices. "Mind the bullets," Jody said.

As she got to the top of the staircase, Helen realized why. Another family 'conference'—a polite term for the bickering that had been commonplace lately—was underway.

"Just rip off the bandage. That's my opinion." Phil's mom, Kat, said, following him around as he organized some papers into his briefcase and grabbed his coat from the rack. "Putting it off just prolongs the pain. The new year is not going to bring us any relief, believe me."

"I still say let's wait and see. I'm not laying anyone off right now, Ma, and that's that." He brightened up when he saw Helen. "Hey, what brings you here?" His relieved smile and shoulder hug told Helen volumes. Kat finally stood down, frowning, and nodded briskly to Helen without saying anything. Phil said, "I can't have lunch with you today, Helen. Just heading out to a meeting, but walk me down." To his mom, he added, "We'll finish talking about this later, but I'm not going to change my mind. We'll just have to think creatively and come up with other options." Helen feebly waved to her mother-in-law and left with Phil.

On the way down the stairs and out to the car, Phil kept his arm around her shoulders and talked about inconsequential items with suspicious cheerfulness. He stowed his briefcase in his car and, smiling, turned to Helen, and pulled the collar of her coat up against the wind.

"What's going on? Are things that bad?" Helen whispered, feeling as though Kat could still hear them.

"No. Mom's just getting her britches in a snarl, that's all." His gaze left hers and his expression became bleak as he looked over her head to the horizon. "Things will get better. It might take a while…"

"But in the meanwhile, will the company go deeper into debt?"

Phil smiled down at her again. "Let me worry about that. Look, I've got to go. How about something especially good for dinner? I'd like to come home and just relax later. Okay?"

"It's all about you," she joked. He gave her a peck on the cheek and climbed into his car. As Helen watched him drive off, she wondered, how long can he keep playing this game? Keeping it to himself, pretending everything was fine. She knew how Kat could be—pessimistic even when times were good— but conflict within the management team didn't bode well. Phil never wanted this job. He got it by default when his father died three years ago, and his brother Don walked out of the business after demanding his twenty percent ownership in cash. It put the company in financial straits even before the economy tanked. Phil's passion was in the design and production of the furniture, not in crunching numbers and making hard-core business decisions.

Well, this obviously wasn't going to break Helen's depressed mood. She got into her car and headed over to Dad's house. Might as well get some work done, and make sure Miranda wasn't poking around in anything she shouldn't. She could concentrate on sorting Dad's clothes. Then the task wouldn't be hanging over her head like some big black cloud, like the big cloud hanging over the steam plant this morning, heavy and sodden and oppressive, allowing no glimpse of blue sky.

Ten minutes later, she pulled up in front of the house, tires crunching on the gravel, next to Miranda's car. She knocked on the side door, but there was no answer. Miranda was probably in the basement, so she let herself in.

As might have been expected, the living room was a mess. Miranda had been there only four days but already, clothes hung draped over the couch and chair, several pairs of shoes were scattered across the floor, plates and glasses and carryout bags crowded the coffee table. Helen sighed. Miranda had always been a force of nature, a tornado leaving debris in her path. There would be a lot of cleaning-up to do after she left for Boone, no doubt.

"Miranda?" she called, pausing at the top of the stairs. A soft thud caught her attention and she turned toward Dad's room. The door was open and she saw a shadow move against the light from the window. "Sorry. Did I catch you indecent?"

There was muffled laughter, and then Miranda's voice. "Um, yeah. Give me a minute." And Helen, frozen in place, realized she could hear a man's voice, very low, murmuring something to more muffled laughter. Holy Mother of Pearl, she thought, I've walked into a mare's nest.

"Uh...just stopped by for a second to get something," she said. "I have to go downstairs for a minute." She hurried down the steps, face flaming, knees shaking, and practically dove into

Dad's workroom, her fingers over her mouth. In Dad's bedroom, for God's sake? In his bed? It wasn't right.

And who the hell was the guy?

By the time Miranda sauntered downstairs, smiling and relaxed, damn her, Helen's embarrassment had mutated to steaming rage. She managed to gather a few shreds of dignity and sat at the long counter, theoretically looking over Miranda's notes. "Lot of stuff here," she said, casually off-hand, gesturing toward the shelves. "How are you coming along?"

"Oh, I'm just great," Miranda said, smiling more widely with an assessing look in her eye. "I'm just hunky-dory. How are you?"

"Good. Fine." She'd be damned if she'd give Miranda the satisfaction of seeing how upset she was. Helen gathered her purse and coat while managing to avoid meeting Miranda's eyes. "Just dropped by to say hello and see if you needed anything."

"Mind if I come over for dinner tonight?" Miranda's voice was an absolute purr, a self-satisfied catty meow that made Helen want to smack her.

"I think we're going out. Phil has a Chamber of Commerce meeting later. Maybe tomorrow." Helen inched toward the doorway but Miranda remained in her way, leaning against the doorjamb. No bra, Helen noted, nipples brazenly sticking out through the thin fabric of her shirt. Finally, as Miranda held her ground, Helen raised her gaze and met the slap-in-your-face expression she'd expected. Some things never changed. Rigidly, she lifted her chin and said, "Yes. Come for dinner tomorrow instead. It'll be the triplets' last dinner at home before they go back to their dorms. Maybe we can invite Seth, too."

"Fine." Miranda shrugged. "Oh, and maybe I can bring a guest? Tim's been here, you know, working on the barn roof, and it's been great catching up with him. Just like old times. You know?" She smiled once more, walked over to the table and picked up her clipboard and notes. "He's such a nice guy." She began flipping through the pages, effectively dismissing Helen who turned and fled up the stairs and back to her car. From the driveway, Helen could now see Tim's truck parked by the barn, and even got a glimpse of him, whistling as he carried lumber on his shoulder through the open doors.

Trust Miranda, Helen thought as she started the engine, aggravated beyond belief. Trust Miranda to start stirring things up the minute she got home. And Tim! Didn't he have sense enough at his age to recognize trouble and steer clear? More than thirty-five years ago, there had been a scene of epic proportions between Miranda, Tim and Valerie. Was that likely to happen again or had Time produced any kind of maturing effect? Tim should have known better, but then, he never did show much sense when it came to women. And Miranda was still Miranda. She stirred things up for the fun of it and took off, running away in one fashion or another, again and again. Helen was tired of the whole mess. Why did she ever think that it would be great to promote more family togetherness? Why hadn't she left well-enough alone?

One thing for sure. She'd be damned if she was going to cook dinner tonight. Who could concentrate? It would be Domino's instead and Phil could like it or lump it. She already felt like she was trying to build a house of cards. One more card and the whole thing would collapse.

Chapter Six

Friday, January 9, 2009
"Most Asian Markets Decline on Worries About U.S. Jobs Report", (Evening Standard, London)

"SO WHAT BROUGHT YOU TO PAINTER'S CREEK?" The magazine writer, Freddie Hightower, leaned forward, his attractive and youthful face belying the less attractive, not-as-youthful figure straining the seams of his navy slacks and yellow shirt. The camera man, standing behind his tripod, was even less prepossessing—beard, scruffy jeans, stained t-shirt. He remained silent and motionless, almost forgettable except Reenie never forgot a camera in her vicinity.

"I have family here," she said, waving her hand. She'd worn a few of her favorite rings and they caught the light. "And I grew up here. Yes," she smiled nostalgically, "I went to high school right here in Painter's Creek during the war. Graduated in '45." At this point in her life, telling the truth about her age was way more impressive than lying to make herself appear younger. "I left for Hollywood a year later, after all my brothers and my sister came home. I had five siblings in the war, but they all survived, thank goodness."

Freddie glanced at his notes. "I know about your early movies, but tell us about your later career, especially the commercials." He smiled, finally a sincere expression. "I loved those coffee commercials. They were a hoot. I was only a kid, but I remember."

Reenie preened slightly. "I won a Clio for that series of commercials. Best Actress." She tipped her head at the statuette standing on her mantel.

"I can believe it. And no lines. Everything was conveyed with just your facial expressions." He chuckled, remembering. "The whole idea was brilliant, especially with the popularity of shows like *Bewitched* and *The Addams Family*. I loved it—the guy making coffee early in the morning and then the sight of your crypt in the basement, and a tiny peek at your hand drifting up the banister, your foot, your cobwebby gown. And his nervous voice, 'Honey, I think your mother's awake', and then your eyes, looking at the coffee perking and finally, one eyebrow lift. Perfect. What was the tag line? *Coffee good enough to wake up for*."

"Grammatically imperfect, but it did the trick. I got the job through sheer serendipity. I was married to my second husband at the time, Lou Hersch. He produced TV commercials, but I never thought about acting in them. I'd just about retired by then. I was thirty seven—that's old for an actress. Can you imagine? Washed up. I didn't care. I was having the time of my life, throwing big parties for my friends, schmoozing with his clients. We had a wonderful house out in BelAir, great views of the canyons, enormous flagstone terrace. Anyway, Bob Beecham of Beecham Coffee was at one of our parties and we hit it off. He suggested a vampire-y kind of commercial and thought it would be great fun if I did it, given my old movie roles."

Reenie paused to allow some photographs. She knew exactly how to place herself in the best light, how to show herself at the best angle. Never from the left. Never. Her left nostril did not photograph to any great advantage.

" So there you have it," she continued, "advertising history. We did six commercials in that series. I finally got some lines in the fifth one, and it jump-started my career again. I did all kinds of guest appearances on TV. *The Munsters, Batman, The Brady Bunch, The Love Boat*, you name it. And then got back into movies."

"And was nominated for Best Actress when you did *Carefully*. For which you should have won."

"Oh, no. I was up against Cher and she was wonderful in *Moonstruck*. Her timing was absolutely impeccable. I still enjoy watching that movie. Olympia Dukakis was fantastic too."

They talked some more about movies she'd been in and, while Reenie enjoyed that, none of it would to get much attention unless she threw in some tidbit on which he could hang the story. Otherwise, it was simply some old gasbag reminiscing. "And now I'm getting ready to start a new film."

"Really? I had no idea! Tell me more." Freddie's eyes brightened and he hitched his chair a little closer.

"It's in the early stages," she said, thinking quickly. "An independent film. We're hoping to show it at Sundance." So what if there was no such film actually planned? After all, projects were begun and abandoned all the time. "And my niece, Valerie Heron, is composing the original music. You know, she composed the soundtrack for several documentaries, including *Vision*, which was nominated for the ACE Eddie award two years ago."

"No kidding. I'm not familiar with the film or the, er, Eddie, but clearly talent runs in the family." He made a note and Reenie wondered if she'd made a mistake—skewed the article in Valerie's direction. That would never do.

"And we hope to get Alexander Rippon as the male lead." A whopper of a lie, but his name came to mind because of Valerie. Well, now she'd have a good excuse to go visit Val in New York and maybe wrangle an introduction to Alexander, at the very least. Get some photos taken with him.

"That's huge! Can you give me a hint of the story line?" Freddie was nearly panting now. "Alexander Rippon! I loved him in the music video, the one where he dances the tango with what's-her-name, the singer. Oh, I'm getting fraught."

Reenie smiled, and slowly, graciously, rose to her feet, offering her hand to the writer. "I can't reveal anything more right now, but perhaps during a second interview?"

Freddie momentarily looked as though he wondered if he was supposed to kiss her ring, but settled for a heartfelt handshake, both of his hands clasping hers, and a semi-bow. "Absolutely! Well, let my photographer here get a couple of still photos before we go, and I'll get back to you as soon as I hear from my editor."

Reenie was well-prepared for posing. She'd seen her facialist every day since the phone call setting up the appointment with Freddie, and knew she looked youthful. Not a day over seventy. Good bone structure, that was what mattered. You couldn't fake it.

After the two men left, Reenie felt exhausted, more from the passing flood of adrenaline than from concern about her fabrications. Those were small details, easily handled, and maybe she could even make them come true. Stranger things had happened.

She kicked off her shoes and removed the green suede jacket that always reminded her of the beautiful suit Tippi Hedren wore in *Marnie*. Sitting on the couch with her cats, she flipped on the next episode of *House of Elliott*. She hated to see it coming to an end. Only three seasons. What had the BBC been thinking?

Later, she'd have some leftovers from last night's dinner at Helen's. Reenie had the makings of a salad and Helen had given her a good-sized container of lasagna. It had been a strange evening. Miranda was there, and the triplets and Seth, and Phil, of course, and Tim Heron, Valerie's ex-brother-in-law. Helen seemed to be flustered. Not that Helen wasn't almost always flustered over something, but it seemed worse last night. It got weirder when she, Reenie, mentioned Valerie. But why? Everyone knew Val would be coming down to Painter's Creek soon to work on the inventory. There had never been any awkwardness before when Tim came to family functions. He was Seth's uncle, after all. So why did that simple announcement send such an odd vibe through all the adults? The triplets seemed oblivious to everything except their return to college, but Miranda, who'd been highly cheerful all evening, suddenly got downright snippy. She couldn't *still* be jealous of Valerie after all these years, could she? Of course, she'd had quite a bit to drink at dinner. Maybe that explained it. Miranda never could hold her liquor.

Oh well. It wasn't worth thinking about. Reenie scooted down a little lower on the sofa, stretching out full length. With Meany on her stomach, and Bogey purring next to her ear, and the memory of Freddie Hightower's very gratifying respect and admiration fresh in her mind, it was time to take a nap. She was sure she'd have pleasant dreams, maybe featuring herself and Alexander Rippon. Dancing a tango.

Tuesday, January 13, 2009
"Computer Geeks Learn to Flirt", (Berlin Morgenpost)

"You told him what? Oh, Reenie, you didn't!" Valerie groaned and shifted the phone to her other ear. It was after midnight and she had just gotten home from a performance of *Coppelia*. Reenie knew she didn't go to bed right away and often called at this hour, but she usually didn't have anything so outrageous to report. "What were you thinking?" Valerie continued. "You tell whoppers like that and people are going to assume you've gone around the bend."

"What if it's not a whopper? Why shouldn't I do an independent film?"

"Oh, for crying in the sink." Valerie pulled the pins from her hair and let it swing to her shoulders. "I didn't say you *shouldn't*, but the fact remains, you're *not*. You'll look like a fool when the truth comes out."

"Maybe not. Maybe I *will* do a film. Why not? Gloria Stuart was eighty-seven when she did *Titanic*. And got an Oscar nod. I'm just as good as her." Reenie sounded quite irritated. "And lots younger."

Valerie sighed. There was no point in riling up the old bird. "Well, fine. But wishing won't make it so." She picked up a hairbrush and began the traditional hundred strokes. She felt herself beginning to relax, falling into the nightly routine before bed. These rituals were as necessary to her as air and water.

"That's what I want to talk to you about." Reenie's voice took on a cajoling tone. "See if you could back me up a little. Agree to do the music. Talk to Alexander Rippon. I know he probably has other commitments, but maybe he could at least do a cameo."

"Reenie! You don't even have a film! You don't have a script, you don't have a producer. Why would someone of his caliber even consider it?"

"Well, silly, that's why I want *you* to ask him. I can find a script and I'll produce it myself. I'm loaded. Might as well do something with all my cash before I kick off. Come on, it'll be fun. Hey, maybe we can make it a family affair. Get Miranda to do the sets, be all artsy-fartsy. I'm really getting excited now. Oops, wait a minute…"

Val filled the kettle and put it on a burner, pulled out her favorite blue mug and put in a chamomile tea bag. Still waiting for Reenie to return to the phone, she went to the bedroom and pulled down the blankets, sprayed the sheets with lavender-scented aromatherapy spray, selected a CD of sleep music with low chimes and rain. It took a lot of effort to fall asleep after an intense performance. Reenie hadn't come back on the phone yet so she pulled on the wrist splints she wore every night to combat carpal tunnel syndrome while she slept.

Finally, Reenie spoke up. "Okay, I'm back. Sorry. Bogie was having trouble with a hairball. What was I saying? Oh, yes. So I'm thinking of flying up to New York in the next week or so. Do you think you'll have a chance to speak with Alexander by then?"

Valerie glanced around at all her carefully prepared sleep inducers and knew they didn't have a hot dog's chance in hell now. She'd be awake all night, thinking about Reenie and the would-be film. Trouble was, she couldn't just dismiss her aunt's crazy ideas. Reenie had a way of making crazy come true.

Thursday, January 15, 2009
"Pink Slips Pile Higher Amid Deepening Recession", (Wall Street Journal)

Alex had gone back to London after Christmas, but Valerie heard from him two days after her conversation with Reenie. He called to say he was mad with boredom and could she get away? They could go to the Amalfi coast, maybe Capri. Somewhere with sunshine and lots of wine.

"I can't. I really can't," Val replied. "Why don't you fly here? Do you remember me telling you about my Aunt Reenie? She's coming for a visit and would love to meet you."

"Sorry. I don't do aunts."

"You'd be missing out. She wants to make a business proposal to you." Valerie was in the midst of her pre-performance ritual, fixing her hair and make-up before she headed over to Lincoln center. "You remember, I've told you about her acting career. She's thinking of producing an independent film. She's a huge fan. Has all your stuff on DVD."

After a moment's silence, he replied, "She might not be *too* dreadful. Oh Val," he added in a sulky voice, "everything's so dead here. It's all come to a complete halt over the economy, thank you very much to the United States. Why can't you people manage your finances better? Your economy burps and all of Europe develops indigestion."

"Don't blame me! It's no picnic here, I can tell you."

"Well, it makes me mad."

Valerie took a deep breath, set down her mascara wand, and stared at herself in the mirror. She hadn't wanted to tell anyone, hadn't wanted to admit her fears, but then again, telling Alex wasn't the same as telling someone who'd expect to rescue her. She didn't need to be *rescued*. "They're letting me go," she said. "Basically, I'm being retired."

"What?"

"As of next Monday, I'm out of work. They're buying me out of my contract."

"Bugger. How long have you known?"

"Since this morning." All of a sudden, she realized how much she'd longed to unburden herself, even though Alex was not the most sympathetic listener in the world. "They've cut ten percent of the orchestra, mostly among members who are within ten years of retirement age, with the exception of the principals. I understand, of course. Ticket sales have fallen way down. They're in a fix." Her voice started to wobble, and she stopped to clear her throat. After a second, she continued. "I've got some savings, I can survive a while. I'm a bit worried, though, about finding another job, especially in these times. I'm fifty-six. Too young to retire, but not exactly an attractive package when there are younger performers out there."

"It's. An. Outrage," Alex pronounced. "How dare they? You're in the prime of your career. Beautiful, strong. Retirement! You're a mere child. A babe. Practically *in utero*. Those bastards. I hate them." And his voice, familiar and always impressive, did make her feel better. "Bloody hell. They'll suffer for it! Look, all the more reason to go on holiday with me. Keep me company, I've nothing to do. Soak in the sun and forget your troubles."

Oh, she thought, if only it were that easy. Just put everything out of her mind, as if she could. But she wasn't about to go sponging off Alex and she really did have to plan what to do next. She *needed* to perform. It was lifeblood to her. She could get some work composing, probably—well, that depended on the economy, too—or she could even teach, but nothing was the same as actually performing, surrounded by a full orchestra. How could she leave it all behind her?

"I'll think about it," she promised, "but you consider coming here, too. Aunt Reenie will be here in a week or so. I have to go now. All Ballanchine dances tonight, with music by Hindemith, Strauss, and Gluck. Wonderful pieces. I figure I'd better enjoy them while I can." She hung up after promising Alex she'd phone him later, and went back to her preparations. Hair, make-up, jewelry. She chose her favorite black evening gown, a copy of a Giorgio Armani with a draped crystal-edged panel at the waist and a flared skirt which allowed room for the

119

cello between her knees. She called a cab and traveled to the Lincoln Center with Baby. How many more trips like this would she make?

In the rehearsal room, warming up, she listened to the instruments around her. Scales and arpeggios, snatches of melody, a roll of beats on the kettle drum. She tuned up in alignment with the first violin, feeling the strings beneath her fingers vibrate and come to life.

Playing the cello had always been such an intimate act. A cellist physically embraced her instrument, wrapping legs and arms around it in a way no other musician did. She felt the vibrations throughout her body. The bow became an extension of her arm, her fingers. Val bought her cello, Baby, during her senior year of college, replacing an inferior-quality student cello with a restored 1903 beauty by an Italian maker, named Celeste Farotti. It cost all her savings and monthly payments for the next ten years, and she thought of it as her child, to protect and love. The cello had become nearly a living entity to her, something that breathed and sang, was sometimes obstinate, sometimes giving and forgiving.

Playing in the orchestra was more than a way of life; it was her community. Not only the people, but the instruments—the flutes like young children with their piping voices, the 'hen talk' of clarinets, a French horn's warning tones, strident brass and booming percussion, and then the first violin or oboe coming in with a melody and message that caught everyone's heart.

This was her village, and leaving it would be like moving out of the only home where she found comfort and acceptance.

She felt ashamed. Maybe that was the worst part. They considered her expendable and she felt so *ashamed*. She was past her prime. The carpal tunnel problem had become a major issue and nothing she did seemed to make a real improvement. She'd tried physical therapy, shots, heat treatments and massage, but the final verdict was always the same. The doctors wanted her to cut back, practice the cello fewer hours per day, and that was like a death sentence to her career. To add to the problem, there was intense competition for every slot in the orchestra. Fred Zimmerman, the lead cellist, was big league, a major element in the New York musical scene and internationally, and younger, more ambitious musicians were always pushing up from below. Rostropovich performed well into his seventies, Pablo Casals into his eighties, but it was beginning to look like Valerie would be washed up before her next birthday.

Ageism was subtle in the orchestra, but it certainly existed. Val had seen other musicians leave because they could no longer handle the pace and she'd worried about when her time might come. There was always a bit of pressure to seem as youthful as possible. Last year, she'd had her eyes 'tweaked', a mini-lift to reduce a tired look. When she told Miranda about it, Miranda huffed something about how sexist it was, that women were required to maintain their youth, while men could age and be considered distinguished.

"Don't you believe it," Valerie had replied. "There are so many guys in the orchestra who belong to the Men's Hair Club, they could form their own chapter." But there was also an element of truth. When her wrists began aching again last summer, she kept secret her visits to the specialist. Sometimes, by the end of a performance, she was in agony, but that remained a secret, too. Now she had to wonder, even if she *could* find a job, how long would she be able to keep up?

Oh, too many thoughts! Val resolutely put everything from her mind and walked out with the rest of the orchestra to the pit. As always, a few people gathered at the upper railing, staring down as the musicians took their seats, settled their sheet music, and warmed up again. After a few minutes, Mr. Canon, the conductor, entered and the audience applauded. The lights went down, the magic began. *Chaconne*, with the wonderful Peter Boal and Melinda Roy dancing. Val put her heart and soul into playing, letting the next couple of hours be a respite from all the whirling thoughts in her head. When the evening ended, she had tears in her eyes.

Chapter Seven

Tuesday, January 22, 2009
"Shoplifter Gets Run Over Twice by Her Getaway Car"
(Painter's Creek Chronicle)

"HEY, DUDE, IT'S A SET OF WHEELS. Better than nothing." Murph walked around the Lumina and kicked the front left tire. "Besides, it's almost old enough to be retro."

Devon looked on glumly. "I'd rather have the Nighthawk."

"No, you wouldn't." Seth investigated the Lumina's engine and dropped the hood back down. "Looks cool, drives like crap. Grandpa always told me he'd never been so disappointed in a vehicle before. Even the fancy paint job didn't make up for the rubber band motor. The Lumina's in good shape and it'll run forever. Make up your mind, boy."

His mind had been made up long before. Devon was desperate for a car. His sisters' domination of the Malibu put a severe crimp in his social life. The Lumina would need an infusion of cash—tires, battery, maybe a radiator flush—but as Murph noted, it was better than nothing. And since he only had twenty-seven hundred dollars in the bank, nothing was what he'd have if he didn't take it. Nevertheless, nobody could expect him to be thrilled about a Granny car. "Doesn't even have a CD player," he pointed out.

"Dude, you've got an I-pod, what do you care?" Murph glanced into the barn. "Can we ride the go-carts now?"

Devon felt Seth's hand on his shoulder. "Seriously, it could be a lot worse. My first car was a Volkswagen *Rabbit* my mom made me buy. The happiest day I had was when some drunk totaled it in a parking lot. Grandpa let me have his old pick-up after that. Look, you'll feel happier once you're behind the wheel."

Maybe. Devon and Murph got the two off-road go-carts running and headed over the brow of the hill and down into the woods on the north side of the island. Well-worn paths led through the trees, and the go-carts' studded tires plowed through the rough terrain, but still managed to skid satisfyingly around turns where dead leaves, wet with last night's rain, slid on the red clay mud. The boys humped up and down over old fallen trees and defied gravity riding the sides of ravines. The go-carts were another reason why Devon and his sisters didn't want to give up Grandpa's house. Where else could they have the freedom to goof around this way? Grandpa's house was where they went for swimming, boating, fishing. It had been the site of many family celebrations, including the triplets' big blow-out graduation party with all their friends. The family just couldn't let it go.

After a while, starving to death, the boys rode back to the barn. Tim Heron must have arrived while they were gone; they could see his truck parked near the Lumina and when they drove closer, Devon saw him up on a scaffold, shouting down to Seth on the ground. As Devon climbed off the go-cart and hit the switch to silence the motor, Tim's daughter Hayley walked out of the barn.

Hayley. She was a sorta kinda cousin, niece by marriage to Aunt Valerie. But since Aunt Val was divorced, that made Hayley a former cousin, but not a cousin now. Right? But it felt like she was, since they'd practically grown up together and she was still a cousin to Seth, who really *was* a cousin to Devon. Gahhhh. It made his head swim.

Hayley made his head swim, too. Petite, curvy, cute. He had never thought much about her until a year ago. Before that, she was just this kid who sometimes tagged along with Seth and hung out with the twins, but was mostly a noisy brat. When she started high school and joined the marching band, he'd become alert to the fact that she had breasts now. Nice ones.

They were both in the percussion section—him on lead snare, her on cymbals—and as Drum Line Captain, Devon was required to keep his section toeing the mark. Even though she was a lowly sophomore, she'd been an asset to the line— determined, a fierce competitor—and he absolutely fell for her bouncy boobs and her grin and the way her ponytail stuck out the back of her baseball cap during summer band camp. Not to even mention, her seriously cute butt.

"Hey," she said, ambling toward them. She'd colored her hair, he noticed, a big magenta streak slicing through the blonde, and cut it off short in a kind of wedge angling toward her jaw. "You guys going back out?"

"Not right now," Devon replied.

Murph introduced himself and actually reached out to shake her hand. "We're going to Taco Bell," he said. "Want to come along?" Oh crap, Devon thought. Murph hit on all the girls.

"Bring us some carry-out," Tim called from the roof. He reached into his back pocket and tossed his wallet down to Hayley who caught it with barely a glance. "On me."

Murph drove them to the Taco Bell, flirting all the way, and Devon became aware that Hayley did not mind in the least. She did occasionally look back at Devon. With a little smile on her face, she kept asking Murph to tell more about himself, which he did with greater and greater exaggeration. "And so my mom and my stepdad live in Atlanta now, in this big house with a pool and a huge 'entertainment' room with one of those massive flat screens, and my stepdad gets tickets to all kinds of football games and stuff 'coz he works for the stadium, with all the VIP's. It's really cool. Devon and I go down there on breaks. Maybe you could come."

"If we live long enough," Devon said. "You might want to look where you're going," he snapped, as Murph's attention lingered too long on Hayley and the car wandered across the centerline.

When they got to the Taco Bell, Hayley handed over her dad's cash and gave her order before excusing herself to the Ladies' Room. "Very nice," Murph noted as she walked away.

"Jeez, what I could do with a cousin and two sisters like you have."

"How about you shut up now?" Devon asked, with no sense of humor whatsoever.

"Don't taze me, bro! I'm just saying, you're the luckiest bum I know. All those good-looking women in your family. How'd *you* end up so ugly?

"Pure luck, I guess." Devon placed his order with the clerk and looked at Murph. "Besides, the day you find me attractive is the day I move out. And Hayley's not really my cousin."

By the time they returned to the barn with the food, Hayley and Murph were exchanging teasing elbows, gentle pushes, slaps. Devon finished his Taco Supreme platter quickly, and went into the barn.

Grandpa Lee had all kinds of junk in there; old farm equipment that belonged to his father, Granddad Hec, equipment from the machine shop Grandpa Lee had owned in the eighties, fishing tackle, dead car batteries, leftover floor tiles, stacks of unused lumber. You never knew what you'd find if you poked around long enough. A patch of sunlight fell on the floor and he looked up. Old shingles had been removed and Tim was nailing in some support boards before putting in new shingles. The whole roof probably needed to be replaced. Devon knew his parents had talked about putting on a metal roof, one of the new kind that were going on a lot of buildings, but the price had been out of reach. If only they had some money.

Devon kicked aside some trash and climbed up the ladder to the loft. When they were kids, he and his sisters loved to play up there, especially on rainy days. The place was filthy with dust and dirt, which had been part of its attraction. There was a lot more trash up there, too, some of it hung on the walls. An ancient harness for a plow horse, metal tractor seats, farm implements, and all kinds of crap Grandpa found when he was rummaging around flea markets and yard sales. There were a couple of old humpbacked trunks in a corner, under a tarp, and a big crate full of wooden steering wheels. Devon lay back on an old pew Grandpa Lee bought when some church got half-burnt down, and stared up at the patch of sky visible through the barn roof.

School sucked. He'd started out as an engineering student but chemistry was a bitch. Trouble was, he didn't know what else he should study. Nothing really interested him, except maybe video games, and every third guy he knew was hoping to make a killing as a game designer. Not going to school, though, would suck worse. At least in college, he could go to the basketball games, hang out with his friends between classes, and have a little free time. If he quit school, and went to work full-time, the fun would be over. He'd seen it with some of his high school buddies who worked nights at Walmart and spent all their paychecks on some lousy rented trailer and groceries.

"What are you doing?" Hayley appeared at the top of the ladder. "Cripes, you go off and leave me all alone with your idiot friend."

"You seemed to like him okay."

"On a limited-time basis. Which ended ten minutes ago." She found a seat on an upturned barrel. "Something's going on between your Aunt Miranda and my dad."

"Whoa." Devon sat up. This was news. "What do you mean?"

"I think they slept together while she was here."

"Oh crap. Don't even go there." He got off the bench and looked at Hayley. She didn't seem to be upset, just stating facts as she saw them. He always liked that about her—she didn't get emotional. "They're way too old."

"Don't believe it," Hayley warned, her eyes darkening a little. "Women are always trying to date my dad. It's disgusting. They're so obvious." She stood up and stretched and Devon enjoyed for a second the sight of her breasts swelling against her shirt. "Let's go treasure-hunting. There's gotta be *something* in your Grandpa's house that's worth selling, so y'all can keep the place. I'll bet he had all kinds of secrets."

As they turned to go, Murph's seemingly decapitated head leered at them from the top of the ladder. "Hey, boys and girls. What's this about secrets? I love a mystery."

"Yeah," Devon replied. "A mystery. As in, it's a mystery to me how you keep from getting your ass kicked constantly."

"Genius and charm," Murph answered, smiling. "Nothing but genius and charm. Too bad you don't have any."

Murph lowered himself back down the ladder, but just before Hayley climbed over the edge of the loft to follow, she whispered to Devon, "I mean it. I've always been convinced there are *loads* of secrets here. Let's dig them up. You wanna?"

And Devon, staring helplessly into her brown eyes with their fringe of curly dark lashes, nodded. Anything that would buy some time alone with Hayley was fine by him.

Sunday, February 1, 2009
"Sister Beats Up Bride at Wedding Reception", (New York Daily News)

Right, right, left, left, block. Left, left, right, right, block. Helen kept her gaze glued to the TV screen as she followed the exercises. Ever since Christmas, she'd been doing the Wii Fit program daily. It seemed to help work away some of the stress. Everyone in the family had their own personal Wii Mii, and for some reason, the sight of Devon's Mii doing the step aerobics exercising alongside her own Mii was oddly cheering.

The rhythm boxing was her favorite. Helen threw her all into the movements, aiming her fists right at eye-level on the boxing dummy. At first, all she'd earned was a "You can do better than that" from the Wii instructor, but recently he'd admitted, "Good job!" I am strong, Helen told herself. I am invincible. I am Wii-Woman.

"What the heck are you doing?" Phil stood in the living room doorway, dressed only in rumpled undershorts, squinting in the light.

"Um, boxing." Helen stepped off the balance board and unstrapped the controller from her wrist. *Hey, where'd you go?*, the Wii instructor asked.

"At two in the morning?"

"I couldn't sleep." She looked at him, his hands on his hips, shaking his head, and burst out, "So I'm not on the same timetable as everyone else! What's the big deal? I had the sound down real low."

"Helen, you're losing it." Phil rubbed the back of his neck and sighed. "What's going on with you lately? You snap at me whenever I open my mouth, you're disorganized, you run around in circles accomplishing nothing. No wonder you can't sleep at night." He paused and in a gentler tone, he added, "I know you're uptight about finishing the inventory…"

"That's right!" Helen flipped the off switches on the game consol and the TV. "I have all these things to worry about. The inventory, my business, *your* business, Devon's grades."

"Worrying never got anyone anywhere. *Do* something. Every day you talk about going over to the house to finish it, but every day, you don't. Why?"

"It's not that easy!" Helen stalked a wide berth around Phil and marched down the hall. "Everybody thinks it's so darned easy. Well, it's not."

She locked herself in the bathroom and bent over the sink, breathing hard. Nobody understood. Phil was right that she was dithering, but he had no idea how difficult it was for Helen to be in Dad's house for even a few minutes. What was she

131

supposed to do? Choose a few pieces of furniture they might want to keep, and plan to dispose of the rest? She tried to imagine the house picked bare, just empty rooms, but that was impossible. Most of the furniture had sat in the same place for years. Every time Helen sat in a chair or put something on a table, she was repeating the motions of her mother, her grandmother, and her great-grandmother. Her father Leland, and Granddad Hector and Leland's brothers built the place in 1946, but some of the furniture came from *Great*-Granddad Virgil's farmhouse, which had originally been further downhill on the property, near the river's edge. The farmhouse had been torn down, but the furniture lived on.

The house was so full of stuff, and maybe it *was* a jumbled mess, but she loved it. Everywhere she looked, she saw something that made her think of Dad or Granddad and she missed them more than ever. The fact that she was usually alone in the house didn't help. She preferred seeing it as a place full of lively, quirky people, and the quiet, dark rooms felt surreal.

But even these problems weren't the real cause of her sleepless nights. What really kept Helen awake was the circling of her thoughts, coming to no resolution. Secrets, she decided, were like rats nibbling at your soul, eating away at your inner peace. Well, she was tired of it. Heck, they weren't even *her* secrets! Why did she have to pay the price?

Phil tapped softly on the door. "Hey," he said, "I'm sorry. I know it's hard for you. Look, you want me to go over there with you tonight? I'll help. We'll get this damned thing over with."

Oh, for pete's sake. Helen jerked the door open so quickly he nearly fell into the bathroom. "Stop being so darned nice! If I want to be in a bad mood, then for crying out loud, let me be in a bad mood! All I want is a good fight. What kind of husband are you?"

He laughed. "Well, it's all about me, you know. Besides, I don't even know what we're fighting about."

"NEITHER DO I!!" She burst into tears and Phil put his arms around her. "I just want to scream!"

"Okay, okay, okay," he crooned, rocking her back and forth. "Go ahead, there's just you and me in the house. It's all about you, right now." Hunching his shoulders, he waited for the scream that didn't come.

She sighed instead. "Phooey. Why do you have to always be nice?" She rubbed her wet face against his shoulder. "I'm so tired."

"I know." He walked her over to the side of the bed and they sat down. "Look, why don't you take a sleeping pill, just for tonight, and get some rest. It will all look better tomorrow."

No, it won't, she thought. You don't know everything that's going on. And I can't tell you. I've never kept secrets from you before and I hate this, hate this, hate this. Helen lay down and pretended to go to sleep, but behind closed eyelids, her mind whirled madly.

Ever since she found Dad's secret stash, she'd been petrified at the thought that someone else would find out. She could hardly bear to examine the loot more closely. The money seemed to burn her fingers, she felt so conflicted about it. The answer to a prayer, or the door to a nightmare? The more she tried to figure it out, the crazier things seemed to be. Photos, lists, that darned journal. She found a stash of letters in with everything else, old-time carbon copies on onionskin paper.

Dad was a blackmailer.

It was difficult to imagine her father doing such a thing. He'd been a strict disciplinarian when she was young, and then later, had mellowed into a warm and loving grandfather. The Trips loved him. They'd spent tons of time over at his house, playing, exploring, learning from him about planting watermelons and identifying constellations and catching fish. How could that man be the same one who spied on his acquaintances and friends, caught them in questionable actions, and sent threatening letters? And how long had it gone on?

She wished she could ask. Dad had always been very private with his thoughts and feelings. He never explained any of his decisions, and although he could show warmth and tenderness, his reserve always kept an inviolable wall between him and everyone else. The contents of the file cabinet revealed a side of him that was completely unexpected. Helen found herself unwilling to expose it to the rest of the family, so she emptied the cabinet, making trip after trip to carry the contents up to the barn loft, and stashed everything in a couple of old trunks.

Now she thought about the trunks, covered with a tarp. Their heavy locks were surprisingly easy to jimmy, so although she kept the keys hidden in Dad's workroom, she buried the incriminating items under some stuff already stored in the trunks and hoped for the best. The problem was, what to do with all the evidence? It couldn't stay in the trunks forever. The photos could be shredded or burned; the letters too, but what about the money and the other things? A bunch of glass paperweights. She remembered hearing about a robbery when she was young—this collection belonged to Dwight Canfield, the county commissioner. There were some stamps going back over a hundred years, and even some jewelry. She hadn't the stomach to figure out the values. So, now everything just sat there like an unexploded bomb, ticking away. Sometimes, Helen wished it *would* explode and vanish in a cloud of smoke. Why had he done it? If he never used his ill-gotten gains, what had been the point? Oh Dad, she thought, why did you leave this mess behind? Didn't you know I'd find it some day?

Wednesday, *February* *4,* *2009*
"Painter's Creek Schools Closed Due to Snow; Nearly One Inch Accumulation Expected", (Painter's Creek Chronicle)

"So, like, I had three papers to write this week and no computer. My laptop just died right in the middle and I had to go to the library and work day and night to finish. The guy at the writing lab said I could probably apply for residency, I spent so much time there." Erica hurtled the little white Malibu through traffic on I-77 without breaking a sweat. Val surreptitiously curled her right hand over the door handle in an effort to remain calm. "And then, what happens? They call off classes today because everyone's so convinced there's going to be big snowstorm and what do we get? About three flakes. Gahhh."

The twins had offered to pick Valerie up from the airport, since they had no classes. Val was glad to see them when she arrived but now she began to have doubts. Erica hadn't stopped talking for the past forty minutes.

"Oh, did I tell you? I'm on a new diet, it's so great. You drink two glasses of really cold water, first thing in the morning, and then you eat your regular meals but cut them in half, and then you don't eat anything after 6 pm. I feel like I'm starving all the time, but I've lost ten pounds already."

"Don't forget about the bitching and moaning," Dee put in from the back seat. "That seems to be a crucial main component."

They shot off the expressway and headed out the main highway through Painter's Creek and into the countryside. As they turned onto Cates' Island Road, Val glanced at the steam plant. There were at least a hundred huge turkey buzzards perched on the railings or circling the stacks. It reminded her of the scene in the Hitchcock movie, where a flock of crows waited on the playground equipment for Tippi Hedren to finish her cigarette and the children to get out of school. Val wondered what these particular turkey buzzards were waiting for. They were exceedingly ugly birds.

"The girl in the dorm room next to ours is so weird; she doesn't eat anything, only drinks this gross dark green stuff with herbs and things floating in it, and she doesn't talk to anyone, not even her roommate, and she doesn't go anywhere except to class or else late at night. We think she's secretly a vampire, except with acne and a bad attitude." Erica pulled up in Dad's front yard with a flourish and a spray of gravel. "Well, here we are. Hey, I just realized—what are you going to do for a car while you're here? You probably should have rented one at the airport."

"I don't drive," Val said, smiling, as she pulled her luggage from the back seat.

"You don't drive?! How do you live?!"

"She walks, you idiot. She takes cabs." Dee sighed and grabbed Hopalong, Val's electronic folding travel cello. "Haven't you ever watched *Sex in the City*?"

"Thank you, honey," Val said, as Erica ran ahead to unlock the door. "I know it seems strange to anyone not living in Manhattan, but I don't even have a driver's license. Never needed one."

Together, they carried Valerie's luggage into the house. The twins began to place it in the guest room, but Val took one look around and said, "Can't I sleep downstairs instead?"

"No one ever wants to sleep in this guest room. Why is that?" Dee murmured, but obligingly picked up the cello case again. They trooped on downstairs to the bedroom usually used by the twins when they stayed overnight. Every time Val saw the colorful, attractive room, she couldn't help remembering how plain-Jane it was when she and her sisters shared it so long ago.

"Uh, sorry about all the junk," Erica said, moving quickly to clear a pile of magazines and CDs off the desk and remove several pairs of flip-flops and a beach bag from the easy chair. She opened the closet to reveal, unfortunately, plenty of clothes on the floor but few on hangers. "I guess Mom didn't have a chance to clean this up. She thought you'd sleep upstairs."

"Don't worry, I'll be fine. At least there's a bathroom down here now. When I was in high school, the whole family had to share the upstairs john."

Eventually, reassuring the girls she'd really, truly, be okay without a car, Val ushered them to the door and closed it behind them with a sigh of relief. Wow. Probably she and her sisters had talked that much when they were young, but it was an onslaught when one wasn't used to it.

After she unpacked, Valerie dressed warmly and went outside, down the slope to the gazebo. She sat in the swing and gazed out on the water. After weeks of hectic activity, she finally had time to unwind and have a moment of silence. Or maybe she would just start screaming.

Seth had heard something on the news about layoffs in the New York music community. He called Val, she admitted the truth, he immediately went into action. "I'll be fine," she had insisted. "I'm putting the word out. Surely I'll hear something any day now." That day had not come. In fact, not only did none of Valerie's friends have work for her, most were searching for jobs themselves. Manhattan was in meltdown.

So, naturally, since she wanted to keep it quiet, Seth blabbed to Helen, who immediately phoned with sympathy and suggestions, and finally Valerie agreed to come work on the inventory just to shut her up. One complication after another, and there she was, the place she least wanted to be, surrounded by relatives who only wanted to offer loving support. She felt like a squirrel on the highway, not knowing which way to jump, or which doom was worse.

Val sat and stared at the water and it was there that Phil found her, two hours later, when he came to pick her up for dinner.

"Good grief, aren't you freezing?"

"Just my nose," she laughed, cupping her gloved fingers around it. "This is nothing, compared to home. I mean, New York."

They walked companionably back up to the house, where she picked up her handbag and then rode to Helen's with Phil.

"I'm glad you're here," he said as they drove. "Helen has been having a hard time. She's grieving."

Val couldn't think of anything in particular to say. Phil knew how she felt.

"They were close," he added, squinting in the late-day sun. "And Leland was awfully good to the Trips. Seth, too. From what Helen says, he changed a lot after your mom died."

"Too bad he didn't change before." Her voice came out more harshly than she'd meant. She felt a little ashamed; it was all a long time ago.

Phil, ever the diplomat, didn't respond until they were almost pulling into the driveway. "All I'm saying is, Helen's having a hard time. You and she have always gotten along, though, so I'm glad you're here."

*

They enjoyed an excellent dinner—chicken and dumplings, squash casserole, sweet tea—real comfort food. Seth and Reenie joined them, along with the kids, so there were eight at the table. Helen seemed to be her usual self, Val thought. She looked a little tired and uptight, but other than that...well, yes, probably she was grieving. All those dishes had been Dad's favorites.

For Val, Dad's passing didn't seem to touch her the way it should. Maybe it just didn't seem real. He hadn't been a part of her life for a long time. She'd always been more of a Mama's girl anyway. Mom was the one who encouraged her to pursue a career. "Don't let anything stop you," Mom said. "Don't set aside your dreams like I did."

Mom had been a ballerina. She'd been a star in a small Detroit-area company, and even though the budget was small in the post-World War II years, she'd danced a number of key roles, including Odette in Swan Lake. Like most women of her era, she gave it up when she got married, but always urged her children to think beyond the normal limits, to 'make something' of themselves.

Dad thought differently. For him, life was what happened within the limits of your own home. Valerie could understand the philosophy, but she always wondered why he married Mom, if that was how he felt. Their goals were so different.

After Mom died, Valerie couldn't leave home soon enough. She was afraid, for one thing, that Dad would change his mind about allowing her to continue her music studies. She didn't want to get caught in a trap of being the 'woman of the household', taking over the cooking duties, the cleaning, the laundry. It was different for Helen. She was only eleven at the time, and Grand-dad took her under his wing, spending time with her out in the garden and on the boat. Dad just turned inward and Miranda, of course, ran away. Valerie's grief had to be submerged and controlled, or she'd have drowned. Maybe that was why she couldn't feel any grief now.

After dinner, Phil offered to do the dishes, so Valerie and Helen went for a walk. Helen's street led to a community boat dock, past a couple of dozen large and beautiful homes. Three of them had For Sale signs in their front yards.

"So, what are you going to do now?" Helen asked as they walked, her hands stuffed deep into the pockets of a blue car coat.

"I figure I'll start tomorrow with photographing everything, and then I have some friends who deal in antiques whom I can contact."

"No, I mean, about work. What will you do?"

Val pulled a strand of hair out of her eyes. The sun was going down and a cold wind snaked down her neck. "I'm not sure. Under any other circumstances, I could probably find some freelance work, but now...Besides, I need a regular gig, not just freelance, so that I can be sure of covering my health insurance and rent. In fact, I've been talking to an agent about subletting it. Find myself a cheaper place in Brooklyn."

"You could stay on at Dad's."

"And end up like Mom? No thanks."

"Oh gosh, don't even *joke* like that."

Helen's voice sounded so startled that Val glanced down at her sister and threw an arm around her shoulders. "Sorry. I guess I'm freaking out a little. Being home, staying at the house, it's all a bit unsettling. Things will work out, sooner or later." She hugged Helen, marveling at how it was always something of a shock to realize how much smaller she was, at least five inches shorter. The youngest and the littlest. "I've put some feelers out through my friends, to see if there's any work out there. I'll figure something out, don't worry."

Helen didn't look very reassured. They reached the community boat dock, and leaned against the railing, staring out across the cove. The day was beginning to darken, and a breeze ruffled the water's surface. Valerie pulled the collar of her coat up higher and was about to suggest they headed back when Helen said, "Actually, I understand what you mean about being freaked out at the house. It's funny, I never felt that way before, not even after Mom died. As long as Dad and Granddad Hec were there, I felt perfectly fine. Safe. The lake house always felt more like a real home to me than our house in Raleigh. I don't know why."

Valerie shook her head, remembering. "All the rest of us hated the move, except you and Dad. I guess you were something of a daddy's girl, even back then." She closed her eyes and just listened for a moment to the sound of the water lapping at the pier and felt the breeze against her face. "For him, it was coming home. For Mom, it was just another step into Purgatory. That's when she really began urging me to go to the music conservatory."

"Well, she was so proud of you. I'm afraid I was a disappointment."

"Oh, you were not."

"Yes, I was. She didn't know what to make of me. I *hated* to perform, hated to be the center of attention. And since I didn't have any talent anyway…" Helen looked sideways to grin up at Valerie. "Can't sing, can't dance, can't play the accordion."

"You have other skills."

"Oh, I balance a mean checkbook, I'll grant you that." She gave a big sigh and shook her head. "Doesn't matter to me. I like what I do. But I'll be glad when all this stuff about Dad's estate is finished. I miss him, and being at the house with him gone does freak me out a bit. And it's just plain depressing." Helen shoved her hands in her pocket and added, "Let's go home. I'm freezing."

As they headed back up the street, Valerie tried to think of something cheerful to say. She told Helen about Reenie's visit to New York and subsequent meeting with Alexander Rippon. "She totally charmed him, of course. They became a mutual admiration society. Started their own little café society right there in my apartment. Reenie has all these girlfriends from TV and movies, like Ruta Lee and what's-her-name from Hollywood Squares. And Alex has tons of stage-actor friends, all of them older than God, getting half-blitzed on those lethal Irish coffees Reenie makes. I'd come home and they'd be passed out all over my couch or laughing and arguing until four in the morning, shouting over each other and telling all their old stories to whoever would listen. It was a side of Alex I've never seen before. He was actually *chipper*. It was kind of frightening, really."

Helen grinned. "Aunt Reenie constantly amazes me. She can even get my mother-in-law to smile and that's saying something."

Phil called to them from the front porch. "Hey, are you two ever coming in? There's a red velvet cake in here and it's calling our names!"

Helen waved to indicate they were coming and Phil went back inside, but she stopped Val before they walked up the driveway. "Listen, I found some stuff at the house that bothers me. I wonder if Dad was a little off his beam at times."

"Honey, we all get off our beam at times. Don't fret about it. Everyone has secrets." She looked down at Helen's anxious face. "And don't personalize whatever you've found. Just sell it or throw it out or give it away. Let him rest in peace and move on. That's my advice. *I* sure don't want to deal with it." And, boy, that was the truth. She had problems enough of her own.

Helen looked down at the ground and slowly nodded. Then she pulled herself together. Linking her arm with Valerie's, she turned toward the house. "Okay. Maybe it's just as well," she said. "Besides, you only have a few days here and there's so much to do. Best to concentrate on that." They went up the front steps and just before she opened the door, Helen added, "The important thing is we actually have some time to spend together. That's worth celebrating. So let us eat cake."

Chapter Eight

Monday, February 9, 2009
"Competing Stimulus Bills Divide Congress", (The Charlotte Observer)

OVER THE NEXT COUPLE OF DAYS, VALERIE went through the house, room by room, taking inventory of the furniture, making digital photos and sending them to a couple of friends back in New York. One of those friends, Teddy Payseur, called her with some advice.

"Manhattan is the wrong market for what you've got, Sweetie," he told her in his raspy voice. Teddy liked to cultivate a faint physical resemblance to Freddie Mercury, but he sounded more like Joe Cocker. "Here, it's strictly high end or funky. You've just got farmhouse antiques; not worth much even when new. Your best bet is to sell them locally. I'm betting even Charleston would be too high end."

"I was afraid of that," Valerie sighed. "I know he picked up most of these pieces locally, so it makes sense. What about value? Do you have any idea what they're worth?"

Teddy chuckled, a low rumble that turned into full-strength heavy bronchial coughing. "Oh, honey," he said when he finally caught his breath, "they're worth whatever someone will pay for them. And right now, nobody's paying anything. I haven't had a serious customer all week. Just bargain-hunters. No one has any money, and if they do, they're holding out for the lowest possible price, knowing some of the dealers will be getting desperate."

"Jeez, Teddy, really? I had no idea. Sorry to be making you look at all this stuff when things are so slow." Valerie glanced out the kitchen window, waiting for the coffee to finish doing its thing in the percolator.

"Ah, what the hell. What else am I going to do all day? Watch the soaps? Do the dusting? At least, the pieces are interesting. Your dad had an eye. Each one has some small detail that's unusual. Not real valuable—you're not going to retire on 'em—but unusual. Like that dresser with the three drawers and the square mirror. It's made of American chestnut. You don't see much of that—the American chestnut tree was pretty much wiped out about a hundred years ago and now all you see are pieces of reclaimed wood from old barns, but this is an original piece from around 1830. Worth about $800 or so. It's the only chestnut piece I saw, but like I say, each item has something unusual about it. I'll email you a list with estimated values. The thing is, babe, you'd be better off if you could wait a few years to sell these. Right now, it's going to be hard to get their real values."

"Oh, great."

"Look at it this way, doll. Until they sell, you get to live surrounded by the past." He coughed some more, mumbled that one of these days he'd have to give up smoking, and promised to get the list finalized and emailed by that afternoon. "Take care of yourself, angel. Give me a buzz when you're back in the city."

Valerie flipped her cell phone shut and poured herself a cup of coffee. *You get to live surrounded by the past.* He said it as though it was a privilege, but she sure didn't feel that way. The past was getting on her nerves. Nearly every night while she stayed in Dad's house, she had disturbing dreams. This morning's had been the worst.

She'd been in Great-Granddad Hec's farmhouse, as it was when she was a child, an old white, two-story frame structure on a foundation of handmade bricks. It used to stand downhill from the house where she now slept, closer to the river's edge. She remembered the wide front porch and the elaborate Victorian screen door. In her dream, the river was rising. Not slowly, week by week, the way it really had after the dam was built, but rapidly, flooding the house. Furniture began to float and fish swam in through the windows. She ran upstairs to the bedroom, dragging an eleven-year-old Helen behind her by one arm.

The water rose higher and Valerie tried to hack her way through the ceiling, to get them out on the roof, but the only thing she could find to work with was a small spade, highly inefficient. Terror filled her lungs and she jabbed harder and harder, making only a tiny hole in the ceiling, until she threw the spade away and tried to break through with her bare hands. At that moment, she realized she'd let go of Helen's hand and looked back to see her sister floating away, like a rag doll caught in a current, eyes wide open and staring up in a sort of calm confusion. Valerie swam after her and suddenly they were out in the garden and she was swimming through stalks of corn. Watermelons, bobbing on the surface, tethered by their vines, got in her way and kept her from seeing where she was going. And Helen just kept floating away, spinning faster and faster and faster. Valerie had woken with a gasp, sweating, heart pounding.

Even now, just remembering the dream, she felt hot all over and breathing hard. She lunged over to the side door and flung it open, allowing the cool, misty air to envelop her. Jeez! Who needed *this*? She grabbed her cup of coffee and went to the living room, to sit in the rocking chair by the big window.

Although it was mid-morning, fog still covered the lake. The sky was overcast, an unbroken grey. There was really nothing further to do. Once Teddy sent his list, Helen should be able to meet her ninety-day inventory deadline with reasonably accurate evaluations and Val could go back to New York.

During the past week, Valerie poked into some of the crannies and corners of the house and came across an old record collection Miranda left behind when she ran away the second time. The old stereo was there too; horribly cheap-sounding but somehow it made listening to the records more evocative. Among the albums were two by Cat Stevens—*Tea for the Tillerman*, and *Jake and the Firecat*. All this week, Valerie had been playing them over and over, the music taking her back to the early seventies, when she was at the conservatory. Now she pulled out Hopalong, assembled the folding travel cello, and turned on *Wild World*, playing along, her cello a perfect mimic for Cat Stevens' voice.

> *Now that I've lost everything to you*
> *You say you want to start something new*
> *And it's breaking my heart you're leaving*
> *Baby, I'm grieving*

Life at the music conservatory had been a magic time, a golden era in which music wrapped around and completely encompassed everything she did. It was probably the happiest time in her life, when every dream remained a distinct possibility. It was a time of uncertainty, too. She could be lifted to the highest exhilaration and the deepest, darkest despair all within the same few hours. During classes, she and her fellow students concentrated on the classics—Bach, Kodaly, Elgar— and after-hours, they jammed on the hits of the day—Cat Stevens, Simon & Garfunkel, Carole King, The Who's *Tommy*—blithely disregarding the fact that this music was written for guitar and piano instead of cello quartets or quintets. It certainly hadn't surprised Val at all many years later, when a cello quartet named Appocolyptica developed a huge fan base playing covers of heavy metal hits by Metallica. After all, there were an awful lot of band and orchestra nerds out in the world. They ate that stuff up.

Proceeding from *Wild World* to *Sad Lisa*, Valerie lost herself in the music, ignoring the clock. She didn't hear the discreet knock at the door, didn't notice when the door opened. It wasn't until the music stopped and someone began to clap their hands, that she became aware she wasn't alone.

"Very nice." Tim Heron applauded for another second, and smiled at her. "Takes me back."

Val, surprised but not embarrassed, smiled back. She had always liked Tim. He was a good guy. And although she wasn't dressed yet, she was still quite respectable in a pair of men's silk pajamas and a Chinese-print robe. "You're early," she said.

"No rest for the wicked."

"Oh yes, you're so very wicked."

"That's a wild-looking contraption," he said, his gaze on the travel cello. "Looks like a praying mantis."

Valerie lifted the needle off the record. She'd never cared much for *Miles from Nowhere* anyway. "So, aren't you finished with the roof yet? I thought you guys had it done."

Tim's face reddened and he cleared his throat. "Yeah. That's not why I'm here." He glanced back over his shoulder and another man entered the room. Tall, handsome, as fit as ever. Jack. Tim's brother. Her ex.

Val set the cello aside and stood up. "Jeez, haven't you guys ever heard of phoning first?" It was totally unfair for him to stand there, cool and calm, his hands in his pockets and a little smile on his face, while she was in her pajamas, with bed-head and no make-up. Irritated, she whirled for the stairs. "One of y'all make some coffee." she called back. "I'll be at least thirty minutes." Oh my god, she thought. I just said *y'all*. Staying in this house is making me revert to childhood. Might explain the fetal curl I've been sleeping in lately.

Thirty-two minutes later, Val emerged from the basement, her hair clean and shining, wearing enough make-up to feel human, dressed in charcoal-grey herringbone slacks, an Elie Tahari blouse buttoned to the throat, and a pale gold sweater. She held herself very tall.

Jack stood at the windows overlooking the lake, holding a mug of coffee. He looked good. Maybe a little more gray in his hair, but of course, even that was coming in attractively. It figured. He turned to her and smiled, his dark brown eyes gleaming under quirky brows, a cute little crinkle thing going on at the corners of his eyes. The legendary charm remained. "You're looking good," he said, at the exact same moment that she said the same.

"Well, now that we have *that* out of the way," she said, with half a grin. "What brings you here, Jack?"

"Hey, Legs," he said, and took a sip of coffee. "I hear they've cut you loose." Oh, *grrrrr*. Who told him? "Nice way to repay your long years of devotion."

Willing herself not to show annoyance, Valerie merely smiled and lifted one shoulder in an almost-imperceptible shrug. "Shit happens."

He glanced across the room toward the kitchen. His brother stood in the doorway, a coffee mug in each hand. With an embarrassed look on his face, Tim crossed to Valerie and offered her a mug. "I remembered the cream," he said. "A double shot, right?"

"Thanks." She took it from him gratefully. Too bad the double shot had not been whiskey; she could have used it right then.

"I'll be outside," he added, and immediately left through the side door.

Valerie took a seat at the table. There was no way she was going to stand there as if playing a game of Statues. "What do you want?" she repeated, wearily running a hand through her hair. "To gloat?"

He smiled again and shook his head, remaining near the window, and cast a glance at the record player. "Cat Stevens, eh? Takes me back." When she didn't respond, he added, "Seth's worried about you. Being let go, and all. He didn't want to upset you, so I said I would say something. I don't know how you're fixed up—"

"I'm fine."

"Well, good. Great. All I'm saying is, if you need some cash, or a place to stay—"

"Thanks, but I don't need rescuing. I'm perfectly fine."

A slight frown passed over his face, and he finally walked over to the table and sat down. "Wilmington's not a bad place, you know. There's still work going on there. Filming, special

153

events. I'm willing to bet there would be interest in having someone of your caliber composing, performing. Whatever. Or even if you just want to get away from it all and sit on the beach." When she didn't respond, he leaned back in his seat and looked out the window. "Look, if you don't need it, fine. I'm making the offer. For Seth's sake. If you don't want it, then I suggest you should reassure him. Lay out your plans."

Valerie relented a bit; maybe he was sincere. She just didn't like the idea of asking anyone for help, and especially not her ex. She had never wanted to lean on him in the first place and she wanted it even less as the years went by. "I expect to line up some interviews when I get back," she said.

His gaze came back to her then, with one eyebrow raised. "Interviews? Or do you mean auditions?"

"Interviews, at this point. Mostly with music directors who already know me. They know what I can do." She allowed a brief smile to flit across her face. "I'll wear my lucky panties."

"That ought to do it," he grinned. "Always worked before, didn't it?"

"All except once," she responded and the smiles faded from both their faces. Valerie got up from the table and walked to the door. Holding it open, she shrugged her shoulders slightly.

Jack got the message. He walked over and dropped a light kiss on her temple. "Best of luck, then. I mean that. And like I said, if there's anything you need, just say so. I'd like to think we're still friends." His eyes met hers for just a second, and for just a second, she almost believed him. Then he left, with that walk of his that was so graceful, yet purely masculine. He was still the best-looking man she'd ever known, but what the hell good was it? You could never lean on a man; that's what she'd been learning since she was sixteen years old. They all eventually centered in on their own needs and left you in the lurch, and when you needed them the most, that was when they betrayed you in the worst way possible.

The answer was, don't ever get yourself in a position where you needed them, or anybody. Rely on yourself and no one else, baby. You're all you've got.

Sunday, March 1, 2009
"Rare Snow Blankets South as East Braces for Storm", (AP)

"And so all the judges thought there was some kind of symbolism in just one white flag among all the blue ones. It was lucky for us Dara stands in the center of that formation." Hayley had found an old rake handle in the barn. She flipped it in the air, watching it swing end over end, and neatly caught it before it hit the ground. "So we won."

The winter guard's final performance of the season resulted in a triumph despite the fact that one member had grabbed the wrong flag in the final pass. Devon and the twins had gone to cheer the team on at the competition in Rock Hill. "I saw Dara crying after the show," Devon said. "Jeez, if she knew how many times Dee or Erica screwed up." He sat on an old bale of straw and watched Hayley's curvy figure as she sent the rake handle through a series of spins and tosses. There were certainly worse ways to spend a winter afternoon.

"All's well that ends well," Hayley intoned as she performed a final tricky maneuver. "Now, did you find the keys to those trunks?"

They turned their attention to the two humpbacked trunks in the corner of the loft. Devon had already pulled a tarp off them and they stood in dusty glory. He produced a couple of old keys from his back pocket. "I don't know if any of these fit," he admitted, "but they were in Grandpa Lee's workroom, so I guess we can give them a try. There's probably nothing good in there—those trunks have been up here as long as I can remember."

"Nevertheless," Hayley said, a determined frown on her face. One by one, she attempted the big old-fashioned keys, but none worked. Sitting back on her heels, she thought a minute. "I just bet there's something valuable in there. Why else would they be locked?" She rattled one of the latches. "This one's kind of loose. Maybe we can pick it."

"Hold on," Devon said, "Maybe I can pry it up." He bent over awkwardly, hoisting up his saggy jeans and pulling his oversized t-shirt down over his butt, and forced the blade of a screwdriver behind the metal plate. Hayley leaned to one side to give him room, but he was very aware of her nearness and the scent of her hair.

"Oh, let me," Hayley sighed, elbowing him out of the way. "You've got to do it from *this* angle." With a final violent effort, the shackle suddenly gave way and flipped up, and Hayley landed on her ass. Laughing, she held a hand up to Devon for assistance and he pulled her up and into his arms. Seizing the moment, he tried to plant a kiss on her lips but missed her mouth almost entirely and managed to bump heads at the same time. "What are you doing?" Hayley exclaimed and pushed him away. "Don't be a jerk." She pulled loose and turned her attention to the trunk, lifting the lid. "Here we go…"

Devon stepped back. God, he *was* a jerk. What stupid timing. And she hadn't responded at all. Acted like it didn't matter, had never happened. All she cared about was the stupid trunk. He didn't even care what was in the damn thing now. It could be filled to the brim with gold doubloons and he wouldn't give a shit.

Hayley lifted out a big cardboard box the size of a sheet cake, tan with reinforced corners. She set it on the old pew bench and dusted off her knees. "This is getting exciting," she whispered and waggled her eyebrows. Then, getting a glimpse of his face, she said, "Oh, get over yourself. I just don't think of you that way, that's all. It's not a big deal. Don't you want to see what's in here?"

No, basically he wanted to punch a hole in the wall. Instead, he jerked the lid off the box to reveal an army shirt, neatly folded, with a flattened canvas hat sitting on top.

"Whose is that?" Hayley asked, peering over his shoulder. "Grandpa Lee's?"

"No." Devon lifted one shoulder of the shirt to reveal some camo-print trousers and a canteen beneath. "We'd better not poke around in here anymore; this all has to be Uncle Gary's stuff."

"Who the heck is Uncle Gary?"

"Mom's brother." He replaced the lid and went over to the trunk. Inside were a number of smaller boxes, taped shut, and several manila envelopes. He opened one; nothing but some old photos inside, slightly faded. "This is old memento stuff," he said, too dispirited to care or even look closely. Devon put the carton back on top of the other things and closed the trunk. "He was the oldest in the family. I think about two years older than Aunt Valerie. Died in Viet Nam." Throwing the tarp back over the two trunks, he told Hayley what little he knew. "I think he was only twenty or something. Mom told us all about it when we were kids and there's a photo of him on the wall in the family room. Haven't you ever noticed it? I guess he was pretty popular in high school. Lettered in basketball and baseball. Played drums in a garage band. That's all I really know."

"Oh, yeah. I think Erica mentioned him once."

"We don't seem to talk about him much. I mean, I never knew him and it was right after he was killed that Grandma went nuts, totally whacko, so...Anyway, I'm not messing around in those trunks any more. Doesn't seem right." And

158

besides, all the fun had gone out of it anyway, he thought. Not caring whether Hayley followed or not, he climbed down the ladder to the barn floor. Snow covered the ground outside, a rare late snow for North Carolina. He could see his and Hayley's footprints leading from the Lumina to the barn door. They'd figured it was the perfect day for investigating since everyone else would be staying indoors, and the roads hadn't been too bad except for the causeway between the peninsula and the island. That had been icy as a witch's tit and he'd steered the car along the edge of the paving, leading the right-hand tires along the gravel for better grip. Now he'd have to drive her all the way back home with the memory of that failed kiss between them. Damn. She'd probably act like nothing had changed, like they were still friendly near-cousins, like he was some kind of neutered dog. It sucked.

A vintage Mustang pulled into the driveway. Devon called back to Hayley, "Seth's here."

"Seth? Were you expecting him? I wonder why he came." She hurried down the ladder and smoothed her hair quickly. When Seth walked into the barn, she launched herself at him with a high-pitched squeal and an exuberant hug.

Startled, Seth caught her with one arm and swung her around a little, so that her feet left the ground. In his other hand, he carried a camera. "Hey, kid, I love you too, but let's not go crazy." He set her down and turned to Devon. "What are you guys doing?"

Devon felt a sudden dart of jealousy. What the hell?

Not waiting for an answer, Seth added, "I've been talking to one of my friends on campus about this place. Do you know Professor Ericksson, of the School of Architecture? I've been telling him all about the house, some of the neat features, and he wanted to see photos. It's possible we could get some kind of grant or something to preserve it, because so much of it is really unique." He paused, noticing the lack of response from Devon and the keyed-up expression on Hayley's face. "You guys aren't up to something, are you? You're not smoking weed or anything?"

"Get real," Devon muttered. "I'm not completely stupid."

"We were poking around," Hayley admitted, shoving her hands in the pocket of her hoodie and practically bouncing on her toes. "We keep hoping we'll find something valuable, so the family can keep the house. I guess we're all on the same page, there. You need any help?" She had this big cheesy grin on her face and the jealous dart Devon felt suddenly spread like a flame. Get a grip on yourself, he thought. Seth was her cousin, a *real* cousin, not just an ex-cousin-in-law. She couldn't seriously be flirting with him. Besides, he was practically middle-aged, nearly thirty. Still, she looked like she was getting awfully cozy, leaning close to Seth to look at the photos already on his camera instead of taking her hands out of that damn pocket to hold the camera herself. She flashed Devon a mischievous glance and he thought, yep. She *is* flirting with Seth, and all just to make him feel even worse. He knew how it worked. There'd been a lot of girls who acted all flirty around him before, getting his hopes up, only to realize they'd done it to make some other guy jealous. What the hell *was* it about him that made girls just want him for a friend all the time? Did he seem gay or something?

He didn't need this, for sure. The hell with her. "I gotta go," he muttered and walked out of the barn before anyone could respond. Seth could damn well take Hayley home. And to think, he used to look up to Seth, thought he was cool. Damned if he would now.

It happened this way all the freakin' time. Girls always seemed to like him as a friend, but never as a boyfriend. Why? Did he seem gay? Was he ugly? It wasn't just looks—he'd seen some rat-faced jerks with pretty girls—but then, they had something else going for them, like a hot car or money or they were jocks. I don't have anything going for me, Devon thought as he drove away. Coming to the causeway, he abandoned his previous caution and sped up, hitting his brakes halfway through and sliding the rest of the way on black ice until he came to the other side where his tires finally caught some traction and stopped. I can't stand it. I can't stand going on like this, on a treadmill at college, taking classes I don't care about and coming back to the dorm to play X-box because there's nothing else to do or losing money at poker because I suck at cards, and watching Murph and the other guys pick up cute girls practically at will. Life sucked. It sucked major butt.

Hours later, Devon stared out his dorm room window at the darkening sky. It looked like it might snow again soon. Good. He hoped for a real ice storm, something that would close everything down for a week. Ten floors down, he could see a couple of kids shivering at the bus stop. He hoped they froze to death.

He was about to turn on his X-box when there came a volley of knocks at the door. "Hang on, hang on," he muttered and opened the door to find the twins. Erica and Dee pushed their way past him, chattering about how cold it was outside and saying they needed his bedroom window. Giggling, they switched off the overhead light and walked across the room to stand by the window.

"Can you see him?" Erica asked. She craned her neck to peer around Dee's head. "Is he out there?"

"What's up?"

"Nothing," Dee said. "Well, that is—"

"Old Bryan-boy is about to get punk'd." Erica pointed down at the bus stop. There was no shelter, just a bench, and Devon saw Dee's ex-boyfriend, Bryan, his shoulders hunched against the cold. A sleety rain was beginning to fall.

"Dee told him to wait there and she'd meet him."

"You're not dating that jerk again, are you?"

"I was." Dee's grin was wicked. "Only a few times. He thought I didn't know he's still going steady with slutski Jessica. He *told* me they broke it off, but I know for a fact he went to Winston-Salem last weekend to see her. His own sister said so."

"And now he's waiting down there for Dee to pick him up. A very *special* date, she told him. He thinks tonight is his big night." Erica was practically bouncing up and down in excitement. "Oh goody, it's really coming down now."

A very unhappy-looking Bryan was clearly getting soaked and pelted with freezing rain. "What a tool," Dee commented, her tone suddenly serious. "He totally deserves this." They all watched as Bryan pulled out his cell phone and an instant later, Dee's phone rang. She snapped it open. "Yes? Yes, I'm on my way, hang on." She kept her voice low, just above a whisper. "Erica's being nosy. I need to throw her off the trail. Hang on a few more minutes and I'll be there." After she hung up, she snapped several pictures with her cell phone of Bryan's cold vigil.

"He's going to be so pissed off when he finds out." Devon loved his sisters' deviousness—Bryan really was an ass—but he felt a bit worried, too. "He's the kind of creep who might try to take it out on you later. You'd better not play with fire. Call him in a minute and tell him you can't make it."

"No." Dee's eyes narrowed to green slits. "I *want* him to realize what's going on. He has lied to me again and again, so just once, I want him to know what it's like to be lied to."

"Could backfire."

"I don't care."

Erica sighed and looked around Devon's room. "Jeez. Could it get any messier?"

"Yes, *Mom*, I guess it could." He kicked at a pile of clothes. "What do you care?"

"You drop your clothes where you step out of them. They look like filthy laundry cow-pies, plopped everywhere. Complete with skidmarks."

"Hey, there's method to my madness." He indicated one particular heap of clothes. "See? Everything I need is there, including shoes under it all. If I'm late for class or there's a fire in the middle of the night, I can step in and pull them up like a fireman and I'm ready to go. These cow-pies might save my life someday." He bent over to pick up a pair of jeans. "Probably two perfectly good wearings left in these."

"Oh crap, don't bend over like that again," Erica laughed, covering her eyes. "It's a horror movie."

"F.U." Devon sat on his bed. "Well, if you're done torturing Bryan, how about leaving? I have things to do, you know. Junk food to eat. Hours of mindless TV to watch before I sleep."

Dee hadn't moved from the window, but she glanced over at Devon. "You're crabby tonight. What's your problem?"

"I got my period."

"No, really." She looked out the window again, with a grim smile of satisfaction. "He's still there. What an absolute shitwad. I can't believe I loved him so much back in high school."

Erica dropped down beside Devon. "Some girl dump you?" She went to tickle him but stopped cold when she got The Look. "What you need, my boy, is a makeover. No wonder you have no love life. When was the last time you washed your hair? Or shaved? Or scraped the moss off your teeth?"

"Ahh, eat my shorts."

"I'm serious." She jumped up and pulled at his arm. "Come on, let me do a makeover on you. I'm a genius at it." When he resisted, she yanked harder. "Believe me, there are tons of guys who'd pay big money for my advice."

"So go bother them. *Stop*." He jerked loose. "I have plenty of girls chasing me. I have to beat them off with a stick."

"He's calling someone," Dee said, still glued to the window. However, this time her phone didn't ring. "Probably some other stupid girl. After all, a good boner's a terrible thing to waste."

She turned her attention to her brother and sister. "Have Mom or Dad said anything to you guys about the dorm situation for next fall? I'm worried they'll decide it's too expensive and make us live at home. Mom hasn't said anything to me, but she's awfully uptight and Dad's been spending a lot of evenings with a notepad and a calculator, growling to himself."

This had a sobering effect. None of them wanted to give up the relative freedom of living at school. "No one has said anything to me," Erica replied. "You can never tell with Mom.

She gets uptight over some strange things. And Dad's always growling about something."

Devon considered mentioning Seth's idea about getting a grant but that brought up memories of this afternoon with Hayley, so he kept quiet. He noticed Erica looking at herself in the mirror, checking out various enigmatic smiles. "Oh, no. Don't tell me. You have a new boyfriend."

"I do not." She grinned suddenly. "Okay, I do."

Devon groaned. "Not the cheesy charismatic guy, I hope."

"Worse." She caught Dee's eye and giggled. "It's so embarrassing. I'm totally crushing on Latham Forrester."

This brought a shout of laughter from Dee. "From the computer center? He's such a nerd!"

"Yeah!" Devon added. "How can you rag me about *my* hair when his is so bizarre?"

"It gets even worse than that." She covered her face with her hands. "Do you know what his other part-time job is? He's the *Chick-Fil-A cow*. He wears a cow costume and dances out by the highway near the restaurant."

Dee slammed her hand on the desk. "Oh my god, I've seen him! He does the moonwalk and that snaky arm thing. Holy crap, I didn't know that was Latham under the costume. Erica, how could you? You've always dated such smooth guys."

"I know, I know. I'm so embarrassed." She pulled a lock of hair over her red face. "I just can't help myself."

They all laughed until Dee's phone rang again and she snapped it open. "Hey, look." Dee showed them the screen. Bryan had sent a text message. *I'll get you for this*, it said. *Bitch.*

"Something tells me he's peeved," Erica said, pushing her hair back and looking out the window. A car had pulled up and Bryan got in. "I hope we haven't made a serious mistake."

Dee watched impassively as the car drove away. "We haven't. After all, what could he do? He's a jerk. This threat is meaningless. Like everything else he says."

Was it? Devon hoped so. Some guys absolutely could not *stand* being made a fool. Bryan might be one of them.

Chapter Nine

Monday, March 9, 2009

"Octo-Mom's New Publicist Quits; "This Woman is Nuts", (US Weekly)

YOU KNEW YOU HAD TOO MUCH TO DRINK the night before when you couldn't find your car in the morning. Miranda awoke late, with a terrible headache and a tongue like Velcro, and would have slept later but for her cat's insistent meowing. She had no memory of how she'd gotten home last night. Her car was definitely not in the driveway. Had it been stolen? Had she walked home? And if so, where had she left the car?

All she could remember clearly was heading out the door in a huff after an argument over the phone with Tim. Determined to put the incident behind her, she'd gone to Portofino's for scotch and sympathy but had a dim recollection of heading somewhere else after that. But where?

Meanwhile, Nikki-stix was growling into her bowl of Friskies, still bitter over her late breakfast. Miranda took a couple of aspirin, washed them down with a little *vino* and made herself some instant coffee. Her reflection in the toaster told her she looked like crap.

Damned Tim. She was sick of him. Always so *nice*, so reliable. You could carry a virtue too far. The conversation had started out fine, trying to figure out when they could get together again, her telling him how the camera sale had gone.

"It was great—I'd done a good job advertising it and we had a ton of customers. Even a couple of bidding wars over the best cameras. I made over fourteen thousand dollars."

Tim gave a low whistle. "That's fantastic. I know you can use it."

"Well, you have to remember, it's not *my* money. Fourteen thousand sounds like a lot until you divide it by nine people. But, yeah, it's nothing to sneeze at."

Then he said, "I know Valerie can sure use it. I'm worried about her."

Something clicked inside her brain and she felt a surge of adrenaline. "Oh, when did you talk to her?"

He back-pedaled a little but soon enough it came out he'd been talking to Val on the phone regularly. He'd wormed out of her all the problems with her lease, filing for unemployment, job-hunting. "She's kinda shell-shocked," he added. "Drifting."

"Oh boo-hoo-hoo," Miranda replied. Either anger or a badly-timed hot flash was making heat sear through her face and scalp. "The goddess has tumbled to earth. My heart bleeds for her. About time she knew what it's like for the rest of the human race."

"Jeez! Don't you care about your own sister?" His voice sounded shocked, and Miranda could feel him pulling back. Damn it! Why did Valerie always have to come between them?

"Why should I? Does she ever give a flip about me? Besides, looks like she's got plenty of people tripping over themselves to offer help. You. Jack. Seth. Even that pantywaist actor, what's-his-name. All *men*, I notice. And she doesn't even *want* their help. Or need it! When did I ever have someone to worry about me?"

She couldn't believe it, couldn't believe the whole situation was playing itself out the same way again, all these years later. For a moment, she saw red as a vivid memory flashed in her brain. Herself, hiding outside in the dark, looking through the living room window at Valerie and Tim back in high school days. Supposedly studying, ha ha. Val tutoring Tim in Spanish, and him looking like a lovesick bullcalf while Miss Priss was completely oblivious, gave him even less importance than a dust bunny out for a stroll. And Miranda all the time eating her heart out with jealousy. She'd *slept* with Tim and he still liked Valerie best.

Nobody knew how hard it was to follow Valerie through life. Not even Helen, who'd been so much younger that direct comparisons had never been made. But Miranda had *always* been contrasted with her sister and found wanting. By their mother, by their father, by every teacher. And by every boy who followed Val like puppies on a leash. Miranda had never been as pretty or graceful or smart or talented. All she had was a determination *not* to be compared, to be as different as possible. Better to be a complete opposite than a pale replica.

I'll be damned if I watch this play out again. She spewed every hateful comment she could think of into the phone. Tim stayed silent, and then, in that freakin' calm detached voice he could summon, said he was sorry she felt that way and hung up. Miranda grabbed her keys and purse and headed for the nearest bar. And then the next, and then the next. No wonder she felt like puking this morning.

The sudden ringing of the phone made Miranda jump. "Hey, sweetheart, how you doing this morning?" Terry/Dwayne/Fat Elvis drawled. She could almost hear the twinkle in his eyes. "I was kinda worried about you last night."

Miranda thought hard. "I don't remember much," she admitted. "I guess I drank a lot."

"No kidding."

"Did I do anything stupid?"

"Nah. You did a little karaoke. *Under my Thumb.*"

Oh, crap. "I can't sing worth beans."

"Tell me about it."

God, she really did need to puke. "Did I drive myself home?"

Terry chuckled. "Oh, that's why you're so confused. No, babe. I drove you. Your car is still at the bar."

171

Miranda shook her head. Gingerly. So okay, problem solved. Well, she probably made a fool of herself last night, but what the hell. "Thanks, Terry," she said, "for getting me home. I appreciate it. Oh, and one more thing?"

"Yeah?"

"Um, which bar?"

*

Miranda finally managed to pull herself together and go to work. There were still a few cameras left for sale and she decided she would go down to Painter's Creek one day soon and look for any other camera equipment. There were some supplies for photo developing, and some of Dad's better pictures might be worth enlarging. He favored shots of strange things—antique farm implements and crap he found at flea markets—that might work up well into a small collection if she took a little time with it.

And maybe...she couldn't help toying with the idea of watching Tim a bit. Old memories were turning up now like bubbles coming to the surface in a heated pot of water. The night long ago, when she'd spied on Tim and Val, had been just the start of a seductive habit. It became a sick fetish, sneaking out at night to peer through windows. At first, she'd spied on people she knew, especially Tim and his brother Jack; later, any girls she hated, still later she spied anywhere that promised something of interest. It was a dangerous obsession, fraught with dangers beyond simply getting caught. A fourteen-year-old girl had no business being out at night, skulking around where she shouldn't be.

In fact, peeping in windows was what ended her short sojourn in San Francisco when she was fifteen. When the police learned she was not only a voyeur, but a runaway, they were happy to send her home and wash their hands of the whole affair. Her dad wired money for airfare and met her in Charlotte. For once he didn't scream and yell, or even lecture her. He just listened to her surly explanations as they drove and then patted her once on the knee. "You can't blame other people for your own misery," was all he said. "And you can't outrun your problems, no matter how hard you try."

It was the only time in her life Dad had shown the faintest glimmer of understanding her and, Miranda reflected, the only time she'd understood him. Life with Mom hadn't been easy. Maybe there was a reason he'd always been so bad-tempered and distant.

Maybe if she'd had more moments like that with her dad, they could have become friends, but as it was, she ran away again the following year and never really came home. Listening to advice had never been Miranda's strong suit. Then or now.

Monday, March 16, 2009
"Millions in AIG Bonuses Draw Outrage", (Associated Press)

Reenie popped her bubble wrap. Sitting at the little table by the front window of her apartment, she sipped bergamot tea, watched the March rain fall, and popped bubble wrap. It helped her think.

Valerie wasn't doing well. That much was clear (pop pop pop). Immediately after returning to New York, all the bravado she'd exhibited while here doing the inventory had leaked away and she simply went berserk. Freaked out. Insisted there was no way anyone could help; all was lost. "What can I do? I've asked everyone I know for a job, made myself look pitiful. I don't want the family to know how bad things are. It's humiliating." Val said over the phone. "New York's in a panic. Everyone's gone into protective mode. No new projects. Budgets slashed. The ballet has a five and a half million deficit and they've laid off *eleven members of the corps de ballet*. That never happens! Orchestras all over America are in financial despair. Some are folding."

"Yes, darling," Reenie had replied. "It's the end of the world as we know it." Then, feeling impatient, she'd added, "It's *temporary*. You just have to get through the next six months or so and things will pick up."

"Will they? And if they do, who's to say *I'll* be picked up by anyone? In six months, I'll be fifty-seven years old. Who wants an over-the-hill cellist when there are young, hungry ones out there with tons of talent and no carpal tunnel? Face it, Reenie. It's over for me. Over. The doctors keep telling me my wrists aren't getting any better because I'm too uptight. So, why am I so uptight? *Because my damned wrists aren't getting any better!* Oh my God, Reenie, what am I going to do?"

That conversation had been two weeks ago and since then, so far as Reenie could tell, Valerie had gone to bed and pulled the blankets over her head. She just folded like an old card table. Silly girl. Life was full of obstacles; you couldn't crumple up when you hit one. Leaping Lizas, if Reenie had thought that way when she was young, she'd never have made it in Hollywood. Probably wouldn't have even made it *to* Hollywood. She'd still be working at Granddad's gas station and bait shop.

Well, there was no other choice for it (pop pop). Reenie would have to step in and get things moving (pop).

Later that day, Miranda came into town and drove Reenie out to Cate's Island. They walked around the place, snapping photos of various views. "Location shots," Reenie explained. "I'm thinking of shooting part of the film here."

"Do you even have a script yet?"

"I'm working on it. But I do have a cinematographer. Wonderful young guy I found through YouTube. He's done a few independent films already and I think his work is lovely. He's from Indianapolis. An indie from Indy. And a real bargain."

They'd already visited the barn and Miranda had obligingly climbed up to the loft. "There's a couple of old trunks here," she called down. "One is Gary's stuff. And a bunch of old photos beneath it ...hey, wait a minute." After several moments of silence, Reenie yelled up to remind Miranda she was still down there. "Yeah, yeah, okay. I just wanted to see what these were. Old photos from the seventies. I...I'm gonna borrow them. You never know, maybe Dad took some good pix at some point." She made several trips, each time carrying three or four large envelopes or boxes. "I'll look these over at home," she said, dusting off her hands after loading the boxes into her car. "I'll let you know if there's anything useful."

After that, they made their way across the yard to the "playground", where the kids had always gathered to climb on Granddad's contraptions—a gate mounted on a post so they could swing around on it, an old buggy seat on springs, a wooden wagon wheel set horizontally so it made a one-person merry-go-round, the World War I-era canon. A few forsythia bloomed at the edge of the woods. Reenie sank gratefully onto the buggy seat. "I want to make something really special," she said. "With quirky characters and a positive message. Something like *Little Miss Sunshine*, or *Breaking Away*. Great dialogue, you know? Not heavy, but meaningful. And funny. I've got a definite bent for comedy."

Miranda perched on the wagon wheel and treated herself to a few twirls. "Hey, I say go for it. Why the hell not? And if you need anything in the way of set decoration or artwork, give me a call. I've done that for stage presentations, you know, in Edinburgh for the Festival Fringe. That's where I met Ian."

"I never knew I could do comedy until those commercials. They were my break-through moment." Reenie sighed with

176

nostalgia. "You never know when you're going to hit one of those, but they can change your life."

"Ian was doing a scene from Hamlet with some friends. Fencing. You see, he'd been on a fencing team in college. He and his friends were in Edinburgh for the Fringe Festival and got this gig doing the scene simply because they were the only ones who could fence and spout dialogue at the same time, and look gorgeous while they did it, of course."

"And then, I got all those jobs on TV comedies after that. Totally revived my career." Reenie smiled. "People suddenly discovered they *loved* me."

"I had done this big mural for a background for my friend, who did a solo act, and Ian saw it and asked who painted it…"

"And then the real irony is, after getting all that attention for doing comedy, I wind up being nominated for the Oscar for a drama. Another of life's little turns and twists…"

"After we were introduced, I showed Ian some of my other work, and he asked if I would illustrate his book and the rest is history…"

"…so when Valerie tells me her life is over and she can't go on without an orchestra to perform with, I tell her she's being ridiculous and closing her eyes to all the possibilities out there…"

"…and we were so happy in Bennington. Who would have thought a man his age would have a heart attack? I couldn't believe it. My one true love…"

"…that's why I have to get Valerie out here and away from New York. Alexander agrees with me; he's a lovely man, we had the nicest chat on the phone this afternoon and he's gotten her out of her lease…it seems Val has reached the point where she's positively helpless. Spends all day playing Free Cell on the computer or watching *Live at Lincoln Center* and crying."

"…not that I'm bitter. I'm so glad to have had that time with Ian, but I miss him so much…"

"…so he's going to persuade Val to come here with him at the end of April and I hope to begin shooting…"

"*What?*" Miranda hopped off the wagon wheel.

"Alexander Rippon and Valerie will be here for all of May and maybe June. Haven't you been listening?" Reenie glared at Miranda who looked at her with an expression of complete astonishment on her face. "Good golly, Miss Molly. Try to follow along."

"Oh, I'm following, all right." With some venom, Miranda hauled Reenie up from her perch. "Throw out the lifeline to Valerie, yessiree. Never mind *my* life is crapped up right now. Sales are flat, flat, flat, but don't worry. I'll survive. I always do." She hustled Reenie unceremoniously to the car. "Just be sure poor old *Valerie* gets aid and affection. We can't let anything bad happen to *her*. As if she'd thank you for it."

Dumped into the car seat, Reenie snapped, "Hey! Easy on the old lady. What's eating *you*? All I said was…"

"Yeah, I know what you said. Got your seatbelt on?" Miranda hopped into the car, jerked it into reverse and backed out of the driveway, with the tires spitting gravel all the way.

"Jeez Louise, take it easy." Reenie grabbed the armrests. "I was going to ask if you wanted to get together tonight, but—"

"I got plans," Miranda muttered.

"You going to see Tim?"

"Maybe. Very possibly. Chances are fair to middling I will *see* him."

The rest of the ride was in silence. Later, when Reenie recounted the tale to Hungry Bogart and Meany Mouse, she had to say, "Miranda's getting more and more irritable the older she gets. Maybe it's because she's never had one special man. It makes a girl bitter. I, at least, can look back and know I was loved. Now, what do you two want for dinner? Chicken Tuscany or Tuna Primavera? Hmm? Mummy's widdle wuvsies?"

Friday, April 10, 2009
"County Jobless Rate at 14.8%", (Painter's Creek Chronicle)

Helen sighed as she climbed off the chiropractor's table. Third visit this week.

"Seriously, Helen, I thought things were getting better," Dr. Lewis said, making notes on her chart. "What happened?"

"Oh, too much lifting, I guess," Helen replied airily, although she knew perfectly well it wasn't physical stress that had her all kinked up.

"Uh huh," Dr. Lewis responded. "What are you lifting? Refrigerators?"

Helen attempted a smile and went off to schedule another appointment for Monday. At this rate, she and Phil would meet their insurance deductible by June. As she left, she bumped into Cindy Lineberger, the indefatigable Events coordinator for the Painter's Creek Chamber of Commerce, just walking in the door. "Hey, are you going to be at the Networking Luncheon next week?" Cindy asked. "Great way to meet everyone and we have a real nice goody bag for newcomers!"

Helen nodded and murmured something about how she couldn't wait, and made her escape. She'd probably never attend another Chamber function for the rest of her life. Last week's After Hours social at the Sweet Dreams Mattress Shop had nearly done her in.

Helen's organizing business had gone from bad to worse throughout March. She'd had exactly one customer in the past few weeks, despite a new, larger ad in the Painter's Creek Chronicle. Nobody had any money to spend on organizing, even though there were probably loads of people who needed to get their home, business or life organized better during such stressful financial times. Helen had finally joined the Chamber in hopes of making new contacts. Armed with a new set of business cards, she'd coerced Phil into attending the After-

Hours with her for moral support, and bravely made her way through the crowd.

It wasn't so difficult. Helen knew quite a few people from ordinary activities with her kids and church. John & Melvina Terry, who ran the Va-Voom Video shop, Lisa Erlinger from King's Office Supply, Ryan Colvin who owned the tire store. Of course, there were also a lot of people she didn't know, including a scary tall woman with spiky hair and a loud voice. The setting at the mattress store was pleasant enough. Once you'd snaked through the line at the finger foods table—courtesy of Showmars, down the street—you could mix and mingle among the showcased king, queen and double bed mattresses.

She'd lost Phil almost immediately, the bum, when he got deep into conversation with Gordon Allen, editor of News at the Creek, the Chronicle's rival, who had been raising questions about the city manager's increase in pay at a time when health benefits were being cut for almost all other city employees. Nevertheless, she was mildly enjoying herself when suddenly Boyer Nalley, one-time pharmacist at the Rite-Aid, grabbed her elbow and propelled her around a corner and down the small hallway leading to the employees' rest rooms.

"Uh, Boyer, how are you?" She had to look a long way up. Boyer stood a lean 6'3". Years of bending over his pharmacy counter had turned him into a standing question mark. An angry one, apparently, to judge by the look on his face.

"I'm not having it," he muttered, bringing his pointy old face down at her. His eyebrows looked like wooly-worm caterpillars. "I'm retired now, you can't do a thing to me."

"What are you talking about?"

"Don't get smart with me, missy!" He shook an arthritic finger in her face. "I didn't fall off the turnip truck. Your daddy mighta been pretty slick, but you're just second-rate. Knocking on my walls and windows, leaving your little photos under the door. I saw you out there, hiding behind the trash cans the other night. You stay away from me, you hear? I ain't payin' no more. I'm on a fixed income these days, and it's fixin' to get worse, so don't even think about coming down on me. Them days is *over.*"

He turned and stumped away before Helen could ask a question, grab a breath or do more than cross her legs tightly and hope to stay dry. He saw her out by the trash cans? What trash cans? What the heck?

Then she thought, oh my lord. His face was among those in the photographs in Dad's secret stash. The blackmail photos. Money changing hands for unprescribed medications; at least that was how it looked. Ultimately, Helen had hoped she'd never need to know any of the details of Dad's spying and blackmailing activities. It sounded like Boyer thought she was trying to revive things, as though he thought she'd been out there in the dark at night, spying on him. Ewww. That gross old man? How could he think that of her? Good grief, she hardly ever went out alone after dark in the *car*, let alone

182

skulking around the neighbor's trash cans. Why would he assume it was her?

She had to clear this up. Helen hurried after Boyer. He wasn't difficult to see, moving through the crowd. His white hair had a beacon effect. Before she could reach him, though, her arm was grabbed again. Why always the arm, right above the elbow? Was there some protocol about making threats that had evaded her until now? This time it was Luke Turbyfil, former mayor. All he did was lean close and whisper, "Knock it off, Helen. I ain't falling for it this time," and then he gave her the stink eye.

It was right about then that Helen's back had begun to hurt.

*

Despite the chiropractor's best efforts, Helen felt herself tensing up during dinner and afterward. It didn't help that Miranda was in town again, grousing about the economy and commenting unfavorably about nearly everything Helen had been doing over at Dad's house. "Seriously," she complained, "why go to the effort? No one's going to want that weird old house. We should just burn it to the ground. It's the land that's valuable anyway. Over fifteen with a 360 degree lake view. Whoever buys it is going to tear down the old house anyway and put up something gorgeous. They'd be crazy not to."

"We haven't even decided if we *are* selling yet," Helen reminded her. "Meanwhile, the Trips will be home from school for the summer pretty soon, and they'll want to go over there to swim and jet-ski. So why not give it a spring-cleaning? I don't mind."

"That's because you're crazy," Miranda said, giving a light laugh as if she were teasing, when Helen knew perfectly well it was a dig. "You and Dad, both. That old guy was one sly fox, I'll tell you. Had all kinds of secrets, didn't he."

Helen shot her a glance. What was Miranda up to? Could she possibly know about the blackmail photos? Why the heck did Miranda keep showing up anyway? Usually they didn't see her for months at a time. Helen had originally thought it was because of Tim, but come to think of it, he hadn't been around the last few weeks.

"Dad didn't seem like a sly old fox to me," she said slowly. "A loner, sometimes. Private. But mostly, we got along okay." It was true. He'd changed, over time. Especially after the grandkids came along. He had finally relaxed and seemed to enjoy puttering around the house and barn, going fishing, working in his garden. He'd finally seemed at peace. Tears threatened to fill her eyes and she grabbed a broom and began sweeping the kitchen floor. Miranda, thoughtfully for once, dropped the subject.

Later, though, worries came back to haunt Helen. She lay beside her sleeping husband and kept telling herself Miranda couldn't possibly know about the photos. She just couldn't, and that was that. Sleep evaded her and finally Helen got up, dressed, and crept out of the house. It wasn't very late. Phil

184

always fell asleep by ten o'clock because he got up so early. She could sneak over to Dad's and be back before he missed her.

This is stupid, she told herself as she drove to the island. *Everything is safely locked up.* Nevertheless, she would feel a lot better once she'd gone into the barn and made sure all the stuff was in the trunks, undisturbed. She convinced herself they were fine until she drew back the tarp and saw the latches hanging loose, one of them nearly broken off. Damn! Helen knelt to examine them when she suddenly heard a noise below, someone coming into the barn. Nearly peeing herself with fear, she peeked over the edge of the loft railing.

And Miranda, arms folded, big grin on her face, strolled toward the ladder. Helen reluctantly stood up and they stared at each other for a moment.

"Well, well, well," Miranda said. "What are *you* doing out so late? Got secrets?"

Chapter Ten

Monday, April 27, 2009
"Swiss Heartland Voters Ban Nude Hiking in Alps", (Yahoo! News)

HELEN SAT ON HER BACK PORCH AND watched the rain come down. She loved this porch. It had become a habit for her and Phil to sit out here after dinner whenever the weather was reasonable and look out across the back yard, the swimming pool, and the woods beyond. Tonight, though, as with every night lately, Phil elected to stay indoors and watch the news on TV, even though it obviously gave him severe heartburn. She'd tried curling up under his arm and encouraging him to share his problems, but he didn't want to open up. "I'm fine," he insisted. "Don't worry. I'm handling it."

"Is your Mom still hassling you to let people go?"

"Helen, don't go there. I don't want to be rude, but this really doesn't involve you." He pulled loose and moved to the end of the couch. "I don't tell you how to deal with *your* family."

So she left him alone and rocked on the swing, watching as the soft rain watered the lawn and flowerbeds for her. Over the weekend, she'd planted a small garden with tomato plants, radishes, squash and peppers, so it was great to see the 'east forty' getting its liquid refreshment. Phil had his demons and was determined to fight them himself, but she sure wished he'd let her help. What good was it being married if you couldn't both bear the burdens? She might be small, but she was wiry. She had Tiny Fists of Fury waiting to be unleashed, if only he'd let her.

As Helen propelled the swing back and forth with increasing vigor, she thought about last night's session with Miranda. Ever since the discovery of the secret stash, Miranda had taken to driving down from Boone whenever she had an opportunity, to sit with Helen in the workroom and go through the envelopes and boxes. When Helen packed them, she'd thrown everything together, trying not to see too much. It had been horrifying enough to know these items existed, let alone examining them more closely. Miranda, on the other hand, was completely methodical.

The photos provided the impetus. When Miranda found them, and checked them out thoroughly, she knew there had to be more to the story. And there was. More photos and hundreds of slides, some of them enlarged to bring up details, many of them in duplicates. In the boxes, there were copies of letters, notebooks with handwritten details, clippings from the newspapers, and, of course, the loot. Cash, paperweights, collector stamps, jewelry. It took a while to figure out exactly what had happened.

Miranda was persistent. While Helen kept trying to figure out the *why*, Miranda focused on the *who*, the *what* and the *how*. Who did Dad focus on, what did he blackmail them with, and how did they respond?

Many of the photographs he'd taken had led nowhere. People doing ordinary things, nothing to raise any questions. Most of the faces, they were able to identify. Various teachers, storekeepers, town officials, neighbors. Valerie's cello coach. The guy who ran the coffee shop. Nearly everyone who lived along Cates' Island Road.

"Dad had a thirst for knowledge," Miranda laughed one night when she came across a picture of Mrs. Trask bent over, setting out food for her cats. From behind, you could see the old woman wore knee-high stockings under her flowered dress and had pasty white thighs. Fortunately, her skirt covered everything else. Not a pretty sight.

Eventually, they could see he'd focused particularly on a handful of people—including Boyer Nalley, Luke Turbyfil, and four others. Two of them, Mrs. Penn, who lived down the street from Dad, and Margie Linden, the church secretary, did not appear to ever have been blackmailed. Hundreds of photos showed them doing ordinary things—washing dishes, hanging laundry, driving through town. Apparently they had no vices. But the others—Boyer, Luke, Betty Burnette, and Dwight Canfield—had all been caught in activities that were questionable at best. Blackmailable. Betty Burnette, for example, despite being the wife of the town sheriff, liked to shoplift. Luke Turbyfil, married to a wealthy wife, had a couple of girlfriends on the side. Very young girlfriends.

While Miranda pursued these lines of thought, Helen kept wondering why. Why had Dad done this? He hadn't even used the pay-offs, apparently, just kept them packed away like trophies. What had he wanted to accomplish? The journal shed a little more light: lists of names, starting with those six, and a starting date—June 22, 1970. Little more than a month after Mom died.

And that's when it hit Helen. Sitting on the porch swing, all of a sudden, she remembered Mom's funeral.

It had been a nightmare. Helen practically sleepwalked through the whole process, unable to comprehend that only six months after Gary's death in Vietnam, they'd also lost Mom. Only eleven years old at the time, Helen was on the periphery of the arrangements, doing as she was told, spending much of her time curled up in bed with her dog, Toby, or walking silently through the woods with Granddad Hec. He didn't say much of anything at all, just held her hand and occasionally pointed out something of interest—a bird, a plant, a sun dog. If it hadn't been for him and Toby, she probably would have cried for days.

Valerie was the one who found Mom first. It was supposed to be Dad who found her. That much was clear from Mom's suicide note. Mom had sent the three of them to the movies to see *Airport* and Dad should have been the one to enter the bathroom and find his wife curled up on the floor of the shower, her wrists slit, the letter nearby. But that evening, Dad decided to surprise everyone with some Kentucky Fried Chicken, a real treat in those days, and he came home late to find an ambulance in the driveway, his dead wife on a gurney, and Valerie in hysterics.

There was so much blood. Miranda tried to stop her from seeing it but, for a long time, the image was burned into her brain—Mom's grayish naked skin, the red blood against the white porcelain, a pink stream of shampoo meandering through the red. It was no wonder cleanliness became her obsession for years after that.

And then, the funeral. It was a devastating dream in which a few recognizable figures came and went. Mom's parents and Aunt Kathleen from Chicago, Aunt Reenie and her husband from L.A., a few school friends. The ritual brought back too many memories of Gary's funeral before Christmas, even though it didn't have the military trappings. Her sisters were nearly unrecognizable in their dark dresses, with no makeup. Until Gary's funeral, she'd never seen her sisters go out in public without their mascara and eyeliner, but now, with eyes too swollen and tears too frequent, they showed their bare faces to the world. Somehow, at eleven years of age, Helen found that small aspect loomed nearly as large as everything else.

She'd had a splitting headache. Well, they probably all had, but it forced her to lie down for a while on the couch in the funeral director's office. Aunt Kathleen sat with her, but eventually Dad arrived and told Helen she had to make at least one appearance in the visitation room. People were talking. She didn't want to do it. She couldn't bear to look at her mother in the coffin, but the habit of obedience was strong and she took his hand.

A long line of mourners crowded the visitation room. She and Dad walked up behind a small knot of people talking eagerly to each other in the hallway. Helen had been too full of her own grief to notice what they'd been saying, but it was *this* particular knot of people that Dad set out to destroy. Boyer, Luke, Mrs. Penn, Margie, Dwight and Betty. It must have been something they said that set him off.

Helen came back to the present from her thoughts. Her hands were ice-cold, even though the rest of her felt on fire. She went into the house. Phil was still watching the news, his shoulders hunched forward, his hands gripping each other. "Broyhill and Thomasville Furniture announced today they are downsizing and consolidating their distribution network in view of the downturn in the economy..." the newscaster said. Helen threw Phil a glance of compassion but he didn't even notice her passing through the room. She grabbed her cell phone from her purse and went out into the yard to phone Miranda.

"That's got to be it," Miranda agreed after Helen told what she remembered about the funeral. "Something nasty they said about Mom, I bet. Or no, more likely something nasty about Dad. Probably gossiping about how they'd known all along she was too depressed to leave alone. Well, they'd have been right. Dad messed up big time with the way he handled Mom after we left Raleigh."

"Oh, for crying out sideways," Helen snapped. "How was he supposed to handle her? Lock her up? Gary died and Mom went a little nuts, that's all."

"A *little nuts*? She tried to kill us all!"

"No she didn't."

"Yes, dear, she did. How much of this have you wiped from your memory banks? She went after us with a *carving knife*, you idiot. Don't you remember? Mom slashed Val's arm, we all thought her cello-playing days were over. She knocked me down the stairs and broke three bones in my foot. She nearly scalped you. How can you not remember this?"

"I remember," Helen replied, her back stiffening, her lips going numb. "But I don't believe she really wanted to kill us. She . . . well, she lost her mind for a little while. I'm just saying, what did they expect Dad to do? Locking her up wasn't the answer."

"It mighta been a good start. Let her get the help she needed." Miranda's voice took on the superior tone Helen always hated. "If Dad had been at all enlightened, he'd have realized she was in a deep depression and he would have gotten her some real psychiatric help, instead of moving us all to Painter's Squat and keeping her buried at the house doing

192

'occupational therapy'. Didn't he realize that cooking and cleaning hardly made up a therapy plan? He was a total jackass and I'm not a bit surprised other people thought so, too."

"Whatever," Helen muttered. She started to curl up, shooting-pains in her left shoulder. The chiropractor would think she'd been thrown from a cliff. "It sure didn't seem to me that the hospital did Mom any good. She came out of there a zombie. At any rate, I think we're onto something here—I know it was those people we heard at the funeral, and the date tells me it all started that summer when Dad was alone. I'd gone to stay with Aunt Kathleen in Chicago, remember? Val went to summer music camp, and you'd taken off just before that."

"Ah yes." There was the sound of a smile in Miranda's voice. "San Francisco. Loved it. So, imagine, while we were all away, Dad began skulking around town, snapping incriminating photos of his enemies. And after he gave me hell for spying on Valerie and Tim. Who'da thunk?"

"You don't have to gloat over it. Maybe it was your spying that gave him the idea."

"It's ironic, that's all. I keep thinking of Dad's advice to me about not blaming other people for my own miseries. Never mind."

Helen had other worries. "So why do Boyer and Mr. Turbyfil think I'm spying on them now? They both practically accused me of picking up where Dad left off. They said someone's been shoving photos under the door, and knocking on the walls. It sounds completely creepy to me. I'd never do anything like that."

"Oh, they're just old coots. Probably a little nuts themselves."

"No, Miranda. Someone's been doing something. Someone who's got access to the photos…oh no." She could feel her hackles rising. "You didn't—you haven't….please tell me it's not *you* whose been bugging them."

"What if I have? They're old; they need some excitement in their lives."

"But they think it's *me*! They don't even know you're back in town. For gosh sakes, Miranda, you've got to stop. You've got to clear this whole thing up!" She started to shake. To realize she'd been used this way, that Miranda thought it was all a big joke. Damn it! Helen had to *live* in this town; she didn't need any false accusations or suspicion. "You've got to quit! That stuff should all be locked away again in the trunks, don't mess with it."

"Oh, all right. I was just having a little fun. Sheesh. You don't have to get your panties in a wad over it. Loosen up, girl, or you'll have a heart attack."

Helen snapped her cell phone shut and sat down suddenly on the porch step. Miranda had always had a perverse sense of humor, but for crying out loud, this was over the line. More than anything, all Helen wanted was to gather her husband and kids in their house and lock everyone else out. Why was it so damned *difficult* to hold a family together? Phil kept pulling away, the children were heading out on their own paths. Her father's final illness and death had been enough of a nightmare, and now all these secrets being uncovered made it so much worse. If she couldn't count on her family, her own *sister*, to help resolve things, then what was it all for? Why struggle so hard to keep those ties going if they were going to come back to strangle her in the end? *And Dad—why did you leave all these things behind for me to find when it was too late to ask you any questions? Was that fair? You could have just kicked me in the guts; that would have been easier to bear.*

Saturday, May 2, 2009
"More Than 400 Schools Closed by Swine Flu", (US News & World Report)

Erica and Devon sat at a table at the University Place Chick-Fil-A, waiting for Latham to get off work. Through the windows, they could see him standing out by the highway, waving at passers-by, dancing in his cow costume. "Moonwalk," Devon intoned. "Snake-arms. Scooby-Doo. Diddly Hop. Crankshaft."

"How do you know the names of all those moves?" Erica asked, watching Latham in fascination.

"I make 'em up," Devon replied. "That one looks like he's got the squirts."

Erica rolled her eyes. "Not everything in life is connected to crap. Seriously, Dev, you've gotta get over your obsession."

"I try, but then something else sets me off. Went to the lake house yesterday, looked like a whole herd of turkey buzzards musta shat on the patio. Seriously, some bird had major diarrhea. The pile was photo-worthy." He leaned over to show her the screen on his cell phone. Erica waved him away. "Enquiring minds want to know. Have you no intellectual curiosity?"

"What I have is finals coming up." She stood as Latham finished his stint and came into the restaurant, stopping to give hugs to little kids that ran up to him. After he changed clothes in the back, Latham came back out, his hair sweated up and looking more bizarre than usual. "Hey, babe," he said and gave her a hug.

No one could have been more astounded by Erica's relationship with Latham than Erica herself. He was nothing like the other boys she'd dated. He wasn't gorgeous or buff or popular, and definitely not well-dressed. Basically, he looked a lot like Shaggy on the *Scooby-Doo* cartoons—tall, skinny, with a scraggly goatee and bad haircut. He tended to wear baggy cargo pants and T-shirts emblazoned with the names of software companies, the kind of T-shirts that came free, along with a mug and a mouse pad, whenever one of their products was ordered online. He had virtually no money either, despite working two jobs, since he was putting himself through college.

Nevertheless, they were crazy about each other. Coming out of Lit class one day, he complimented her on the intelligence of the paper she wrote on *The Master Puppeteer,* and the sheer novelty of someone noticing her mind instead of her figure prompted Erica to invite him to go for coffee, during which she revealed that she hoped to teach Middle School English some day. He admitted he had signed up for the Kid Lit course thinking it would be easier than a regular literature course. "Wrongo," he added.

A few days later, she went to a party off-campus and found him sitting on the floor in a corner, nursing a beer. "What are you doing here?" she asked, gracefully dropping into a lotus position next to him. "This isn't your crowd."

"Nope," he said, gazing at the rowdy hearty-partying group. "But sadly, it's my apartment."

Later, after helping Latham's roommate Gordon clean the place up once the party had ended, she carried a load of trash out to the garbage cans and Latham reappeared, much the worse for drink. "Lemme," he mumbled, taking the overloaded bag from her. He tripped on the steps and landed full-length on the ground.

"Are you okay?" Erica gasped, and tried to help him up.

He lay there, dead weight, and stared at the sky. "I appear to have fallen for you," he said. She looked down at him, and he looked so pathetic she couldn't help kissing him. He came alive then, and there must be something said for chemical reactions, because they'd been together ever since.

197

Now, ignoring Devon's presence, they exchanged a kiss. Before they could speak, Dee came rushing in. "Thought I'd find you here," she said. "I need help." She pulled her computer memory stick from her pocket. "I think Bryan wiped my files. Everything I had for my history paper was on there."

Latham took the stick and examined it. Erica said, "What does Bryan have to do with it?"

Dee pushed her hair back, leaving it in spikes. "He's been following me around, trying to bug me. You know what a weasel he is. Anyway, I was working in the library at the writing center, left my stick in the computer for a few minutes while I went to the reference desk, and when I came back, everything was gone. He musta erased it all."

Latham handed it back to her. "Probably all still there. Unless you've downloaded anything else since the files went missing, all your data is still there, just marked to be overwritten." He pulled his laptop from his backpack and set up shop on one of the restaurant tables. "Here. Give." Inserting the memory stick, he messed around for a couple of minutes. "These your files?"

Dee leaned over to look. "Oh thank you, Jesus. Or, rather, thank you, Latham. I swear, if I could just *catch* Bryan at some of his tricks…"

"I warned you," Devon said. "What else has he done?"

"Followed me home from the library once when I stayed there too late. He didn't do anything, just followed close enough so that I could hear someone behind me, without being able to see who. Gave me the creeps." Dee put her memory stick safely into her purse. "Once I was on the U-bus and he 'accidentally' knocked me on the head with his book bag when he got off. Stuffed my mailbox with shaving foam, sent porn to my email, listed my cell phone number on Craigslist. I can't prove he's doing all this stuff, but I know it's him."

"You need to set a trap," Latham said. "Something he wouldn't be able to resist, and then let us help catch him." He hooked an arm around Erica's shoulder and stared down at her, then at Dee. "We shouldn't let him get away with this."

All the way back to the dorm, they discussed ways and means. Devon split off to go to chemistry class, but Latham walked with the girls up to their room on the seventh floor. Erica reminded him she had to leave soon to pick up Aunt Reenie for her swimming lessons. "She's planning an underwater sequence for her movie."

"Underwater?" Dee asked. "Is she crazy? She's eighty million years old!"

Erica shrugged. "I dunno. That's the plan, apparently. Aunt Val arrives in a day or two, and so does the director Aunt Reenie hired. He's got an RV or something that he's going to stay in, so there'll be loads of people at Grandpa's." She went to pull her key out of her pocket, but was stopped by the sight of an already half-open door. "Dee, did you leave the room unlocked?"

"I don't think so."

They pushed gingerly at the door and it swung open to reveal a scene of disaster. Clothes were thrown on the floor, mattresses tipped up, the TV lay on its side, and all the posters on the walls had been ripped down. "Holy crap, Batman," Dee whispered. "He got me again."

Monday, May 4, 2009
"World Bank Says Poor Need More Money", (NorthJersey.com)

Overwrought and depressed, Valerie had a hard time deciding what to pack for Painter's Creek, which ended with too much luggage, resulting in a hefty fee. There had been security issues with her cello because, accustomed to traveling with the whole orchestra and their efficient road managers, she hadn't thought about the problems involved. The cello had to be scanned before they let it on board, and she'd nearly had to pull it out of the case and play a few bars of the Elgar concerto to prove it wasn't harboring weapons or drugs. Alex wasn't exactly a boon companion; he slept most of the way. To top it off, she had a raging headache.

When they finally made it, Seth picked them up from the airport. As they passed the water treatment plant, Valerie noted a large flock of turkey buzzards perched on the metal railings. Ugly birds. Two of them were on the ground, circling each other with menacing attitudes. What would turkey buzzards fight over? Territory? A particularly juicy dead possum? That buff female turkey buzzard with the alluring gland secretions?

Drawing closer to the lake house, Val felt an increase of gloom. The House That Killed Her Mother would be a fitting resting place for her own dead career. She would end her days sitting on the swing in the gazebo, staring out over the water as her mother had, in the days when the river crept up inch by inch until it surrounded the island. Her cello would turn brittle and crack into dust, her bow arm would drop off, and her name would only be whispered as a cautionary tale: "Valerie Heron? Went berserk. Forced a cello student to eat his own sheet music after she taught *Go Tell Aunt Rhodie* too many times."

They approached the causeway and Seth glanced at her. "You'll notice a few changes," he said. "The director arrived yesterday."

He wasn't joking. A dozen cars and an '80s vintage Winnebago stood along the driveway in front of the house. All the barn doors were open, including the loft, and she could see ladders and scaffolding, men hammering and shouting to each other. Reenie and a gaggle of older ladies stood on the porch, clearly anticipating Alexander, because they all started jumping up and down, and screaming as the car pulled up. It was quite a sight. Val glanced at Alex in the back seat and saw him fingering the knot in his tie and smoothing back his hair. "Ladykiller," she muttered and he grinned. "Please don't give them heart attacks. With that group, it could be a serious threat."

"I shall endeavor to control my devastating charm. Turn the wattage down, as it were." He and Val exited the car.

"Welcome," Reenie called, extending her arms. "We're so glad you're here. Alex, let me introduce you to a few of my friends."

The bevy of belles immediately swallowed Alex up, and Val sourly lugged Baby and Hopalong inside. Someone, probably Helen, had done wonders. Flowers bloomed in the garden and in pots on the porch. Inside, the heavy drapes had been banished and sunshine flooded the main room, allowing shafts of light to penetrate the gloom. The room had been thoroughly cleaned and cleared out of all extraneous items so you could finally appreciate the hardwood floors and the eclectic mix of building materials from bricks to stone to cedar shingles. Pretty, homey touches had been added—colorful cushions, a large bowl of fruit, framed family photos. One could almost imagine a happy family lived there. Damn. She'd been looking forward to settling down into a deep, dark funk. How was she supposed to do that now?

She expected to be using the downstairs bedroom again, but the twins had loaded it up with a ton of their stuff, so she was unhappily assigned to the guest room upstairs. She just didn't like this room—it had belonged to her parents before Mom died. After that, Dad switched with Grand-dad Hec, but the memories lingered.

Alex had Dad's room next door. After unpacking, Val searched for Aunt Reenie. She found her in the barn, talking with the director, a skinny young man, with numerous tattoos and piercings, a goatee, bright yellow hair and black plaid eyeglasses. "Shane Underwood," he introduced himself, rigid with politeness. "It's a real honor to meet you." He was deferential toward Reenie, Val noticed, and nearly inarticulate when Alex walked up a moment later.

"I wish to have a word with you," Alex intoned, and Shane paled. They headed off toward the woods.

Reenie shoved a clipboard at Val. "Sign this. It's a release for the 'making of' documentary, just in case."

"In case what?"

"In case you end up in it by chance. Oh, and here are my notes on the music. I've decided against light classical." Reenie dug in her shoulder bag, plopped a thick sheaf of steno pad pages covered in deeply slanting penmanship on top of the clipboard, and took off, shouting to one of her girlfriends, "Mitzi, no! What have I told you about leaving the crew alone? Put him down!"

Val looked down at the notes. The top page said, Hospital scene, cigarette fire. Maybe something Bollywoodish?

Bollywoodish? Well, it wasn't going to be dull, Val decided. Yep. There went that nervous breakdown she'd been planning.

The afternoon quickly wore away and most of the cast and crew adjourned to Jack & Louie's Fine Dining out on Campground Road for dinner. Helen had invited the family and a few special friends over for a cookout at her place—grilled, herb-marinated flank steak, grilled okra with lemon-basil sauce, tomato-cucumber salad and, of course, sweet tea with lemon. Twenty people attended, eating at tables set out on the lawn.

Val wasn't too sure how well Alex would take to this. He was such an urban soul and not exactly a fan of family togetherness, but he seemed to be enjoying himself. Helen, Val noted, looked especially pretty that evening. Her cheeks were pink with heat and excitement, and her hair curled in little ringlets, something Helen always deplored and Val always envied.

"Your sister looks so familiar," Alex commented, dropping down next to Valerie and mopping the back of his neck with a handkerchief. "Has she ever visited you in New York? I'd swear I've met her before."

"I don't think so, but I have photos of her and the family at my apartment. Well, *had*. All packed away in storage now." Val glanced around at the backyard, dressed up for the occasion with colorful flowers stuck in glass jars, twinkle lights strung up in a few trees and across the back porch, sun beds floating on the pool surface. Helen's vegetable garden looked tidy and prolific. "God, Helen's such a domestic creature. She has all the instincts Miranda and I lack."

"Oh yes, I've met Miranda," Alex said, smiling with one eyebrow lifted. "Now she's quite a character. Offered to do a tarot reading for me."

The Trips arrived and were introduced to Alex, but the girls were obviously much more interested in meeting the young director. Alex shrugged lightly. "Not my demographic," he muttered, even though he'd starred in a blockbuster sci-fi summer film no more than three years ago. As if reading Val's thought, he added, "You have to remember, I wore heavy prosthetic makeup in *Jupiter Falling*. These kids won't know me." She suspected it bothered him nevertheless when he rose to help Helen carry out a tray of ice-filled glasses. Alex didn't like aging any more than she did.

Reenie arrived with Miranda, having left her gal pals to join the film crew's dinner. With oversized sunglasses perched atop her head and oversized reading glasses on her nose, she resembled Mr. Magoo. "What a day," she said, fanning herself with a street map printed by the Painter's Creek Downtown Development Association, known locally as PCDDA or Peak-Daddy. "Tomorrow, Shane and I have to make final decisions on a couple of locations and then Wednesday we begin filming." She stopped fanning and gave an enormous smile. "I'm so excited. Now, has everyone signed their release forms?"

Phil had just taken the steaks off the grill and announced it was time to eat when two sheriff's squad cars captured everyone's attention. An impressed silence ran over the group when Sheriff Burnette and Officer Sigmon walked up to Reenie. "We've come about your permits," the sheriff said. "Not sure they're up to snuff."

"What is all this?" Phil came over to the group. "Hey, Burnie, what's the problem?" He held out his hand to shake but the sheriff pointedly ignored it.

"I'm here in official capacity," he responded, peering over his reading glasses at a clipboard full of papers. "Your aunt has failed to file all the appropriate paperwork for that little shindig she's got going over on the island."

"Bullshit!" Reenie pushed her way forward and stood toe to toe with the sheriff, five foot zip to his six feet four. "You think I'm not a professional? I've got one of the best location managers in the business, Rita Talmadge. She and her husband worked on over twenty movies for Warner Brothers in the sixties, *and* she danced in Elvis Presley's *Girls, Girls, Girls,* and *Roustabout*, which is more than I can say for you. I've got all the paperwork on view at the barn, which is where it's supposed to be, so if you've got issues with that, you come over there tomorrow instead of breaking up a party like you're some big shot."

Sheriff Burnette blinked a couple of times, but otherwise his impassivity didn't break. "I'll be by tomorrow then." Glancing around at the three sisters, but especially Helen, he added, "Best make sure you have all your ducks in a row. We don't like lawbreakers here in Painter's Creek." With that, he and his silent deputy strode off.

"*Lawbreakers!* Who's he kidding? Glorioski, you'd think they'd be happy to have something going on around here.

Seventeen percent unemployment and rising. And I'm using local contractors," Reenie complained. "What nimnols."

"They almost seemed to have it out for us," Phil commented. "What the hell?"

No one answered. Valerie glanced at Helen and saw all the color had faded from her face. What the hell, indeed?

Chapter Eleven

Saturday, May 9, 2009
"Missouri Town Re-Elects Dead Mayor", (Duluth News Tribune)

NINE PM. BY THE TIME MIRANDA DROVE down the mountain to Painter's Creek, it would be going on midnight. Perfect time for a little look-around.

And why not? The semester was over, the store would be quiet for the next couple of weeks until the summer visitors began to arrive. Evadena was quite happy to be working overtime; she wouldn't complain a bit if Miranda didn't show up again until Monday, or even Tuesday.

The last few weeks had been rather fun, poring over all that old junk of Dad's, putting the pieces together. She now knew whom he'd spied on, what he learned, how he blackmailed them, and what they used to pay him off. It was fascinating, the secrets that a small town hid. Dwight Canfield, the county commissioner, had pocketed many a bribe when it came to zoning restrictions, building codes and minor political offices.

He had a hunger, though, for antique glass paperweights and when Dad produced proof of Dwight's goings-on, he'd paid off with dozens of the elaborate orbs. Then he turned around, pronounced them stolen, and got the insurance money. Dad was stuck with the paperweights then. Even if he wanted to sell them, he'd be unable to for fear of being arrested as a thief.

Some of the other payoffs were much more liquid than Dwight Canfield's paperweights; not only the cash, but also the stamps and jewelry. Why had Dad hung onto those? Or hide them better, if he wasn't going to use them? She'd never understand.

Well, *men*. It was hard to understand any of them. She'd floated around that Alexander Rippon all evening last Monday but he only had eyes for Helen. *Helen*, for crissake. It simply didn't make sense.

She made good time on the highway and came up the road toward the causeway by twenty minutes before midnight. It would be harder now, to find a place to hide her car. Val and Alex were staying at the lake house, and that director and his two buddies lived in the decrepit RV parked by the barn. And one never knew when the Trips might show up at the house. Along the road leading to the causeway, there were a few houses that weren't lived in full-time, but she couldn't park there; deputy sheriffs often patrolled to keep an eye on the houses, especially now that Burnie Burnette was on Helen's case. She couldn't help but laugh about that.

When Miranda had first started spying on Dad's old victims, it was just out of curiosity. Then, a malicious imp seemed to jump on her back and she found herself wanting to bug them—moving their trash cans, leaving branches and other debris on their front porches, tapping on their windows, messing with their mailboxes. Just enough to show that somebody had been there, not enough to cause any damage. She couldn't help it; she liked making people nervous. And then, to have them suspect Helen—what a bonus! Saintly little old Helen, suspected of foul deeds. It was too delicious.

She found a spot to park, backing in alongside a ramshackle shed on Mrs. Penn's property. Miranda had brought an old bed sheet, navy blue, which she tossed over the car so no stray beam of moonlight would reflect off the glass or chrome and catch anyone's eye. Mrs. Penn was another of the people Dad had watched, but apparently to no avail. Hundreds of photos, but none of them depicted anything but harmless pursuits. She was their nearest neighbor, and used to spend time with Ma, but Miranda didn't really know Mrs. Penn well. She was boring, a widow full of nothing but housewifely pursuits.

Okay, then. Across the causeway, over to the lake house under cover of darkness. Miranda made her way around to the back and climbed onto the short wall edging the patio. She could see over the deck and into the two bedrooms. Val was practicing the cello, sawing away. No, that wasn't fair. Val didn't saw away, she glided the bow across the strings. She looked beautiful, really, the cello between those long legs, her red hair swaying over one shoulder. A familiar sour pain filled Miranda's heart. How could anyone ever compete with that? Alexander was nowhere in sight, but she heard laughter coming from the RV.

She carefully made her way over to the barn. The RV doors and windows were open, plenty of light inside and out. They were playing cards, four guys, seated around a picnic table, smoking up a storm. For a moment, she considered stepping into the light and joining them, but no, she wouldn't be welcome. Alex was making comments in that resonant voice of his, cracking everyone up. Of course, they hung on his every word, the dolts. He probably loved that. The guy was a total attention junkie.

So, nothing cooking there. Miranda slunk back over the causeway, beginning to feel a little chilled. She rubbed her arms as she walked toward Mrs. Penn's house. What about Tim? Maybe she could drive over to his house, see what he was up to. She pulled the sheet off her car, and wondered whether she should phone him first or simply show up and see whether he had any overnight company.

"What are you up to?"

Shit! Miranda jumped and clutched the sheet to her bosom. A flashlight's beam caught her face, blinding her, and she screened her eyes.

"What are you doing here?"

A woman's voice. Mrs. Penn. Old bitch had to be eighty if she was a day. Maybe Miranda could brazen it out. "Hey, Mrs.

Penn. Sorry if I scared you. There were so many people over on the island earlier that I parked here. Hope you weren't inconvenienced." She casually unlocked the car door and tossed the sheet in. "I'll be getting out of your way now."

"Bullshit." The flashlight's glare didn't lower a bit. "I know a Peeping Tom when I see one. I think you'd better come over here on the porch. I've already called 911."

Miranda nearly peed herself. She jumped into the car and started the engine but crazy old Mrs. Penn positioned herself right in front of the hood. "Give it up, Miranda. For heaven's sake, I know it's you. What will you accomplish by running? Get out of the car."

Well, hell. Slowly, Miranda turned off the motor and got out. "I haven't hurt anything," she said sullenly. "Haven't touched one precious stone or brick on your place. What did you have to call the police for?"

"Give me your keys," Mrs. Penn demanded. "Toss them here."

"Go screw yourself."

"Oh, nice. Very nice. You always were an uncouth little girl." Mrs. Penn finally lowered the flashlight beam. Miranda's eyes were still half-blinded, she could only see the old woman as an outline, lit from behind by porch lights fifty feet away. "Come in the house and let's talk. I guess I owe Leland that much, anyway. He and I were good friends, you know. Long, long ago."

Miranda opened her mouth to speak and shut it again. Dad had been friends with someone? Ol' Mister Lone Wolf? Sweet mystery of life. "Okay," she said. "I'll come in. But first, you call that damn sheriff's office and tell them it was a mistake, all right?"

Sunday, May 10, 2009 Mother's Day
"The Box Office Boldly Goes Where No Star Trek Film Has Gone Before", (Entertainment Weekly Online)

Miranda spent Saturday night at Reenie's, sleeping on the narrow couch. She didn't care. It was just someplace to lay her head. She wasn't going to get any rest anyway.

Not after talking with Mrs. Penn. *Edith* Penn, she learned. Former Navy nurse, former surgical nurse at Providence Hospital, mother of two, grandmother of five, and a real pistol.

"I caught him," Mrs. Penn said, "the same as I caught you. Sniffing around my house with that damned camera of his. I was scared to death, too. I barely knew him back then. Thought he'd come to rape me." Mrs. Penn actually chuckled at this and shook her head. "Couldn't have been more wrong. Your poor father was nearly out of his mind with grief in those days, and harmless as a fly."

"Well, except for the blackmail and stuff," Miranda ceded.

"Oh, blackmail shmackmail. He wouldn't have gone through with it if any of those idiot fools would have just sat

213

down and talked with him. They blamed him for your mother's death, you know. Thought he hadn't tried to help her."

"Yeah, gee. Wonder where they got that idea?" Old resentments bubbled to the surface. Sitting there at Mrs. Penn's kitchen table, an '80s era laminate-wood top with cream-colored metal legs, chairs with well-padded seats and backs on swivel bases, Miranda couldn't help thinking what a sheltered life the woman led. Kitchen all tidy with flowered curtains and a cookie jar and even a cozy over the toaster. What did she know of strife, of mental illness and conflict and death? "As far as I could see, Dad was just plain embarrassed by Mom. He couldn't deal with the local gossip back in Raleigh after her crazy spell, so he brought her down here and virtually buried her on the island."

"No, he didn't." Mrs. Penn, leaning on one elbow, chin in hand, drew designs on the tabletop with her fingertip.

"Yes, he did! What do you know about it? Whatever bullshit sob story he gave you, he was a tyrant at home. Total disciplinarian. Rules up the ying-yang."

"All from a teenager's point of view."

" Bringing us down here away from everything we knew. Burying Mom in a landslide of household and gardening chores. It was right after the dam was built downriver. She watched the waters rise, week by week, encircling the house, creating the island, and knew she was cut off forever. You think that wouldn't make any woman nuts?"

"She was already pretty far gone. You know that. Manic-depressive, they'd call it now. Bi-polar, and severely depressed. But thirty years ago, they didn't have the same treatments."

"You didn't know her, the way she was before Gary died. She was completely different—energetic, upbeat, fully engaged with us kids." Miranda shook her head at the memory. "She wanted so badly for each of us to have a career, to carry it through life the way she couldn't. She was a dancer, you know, before she married Dad. A ballerina. Beautiful." Miranda swallowed, and her next words came out more harshly. "After we moved here, there was nothing left but a shell. That's what I hold against Dad. He didn't help her."

"He didn't know how."

Restless, Miranda surged to her feet and prowled the kitchen. She read the cents-off coupons magneted to the refrigerator door, examined the African violets on the windowsill. "So, after you caught him spying on you. What then?"

"We became lovers." Her answer, coming so composedly from this elderly lady, caught at Miranda's throat and she began to cough. "Oh, grow up," Mrs. Penn said. "Not right away, of course. He started coming over for tea and sympathy, I guess. I tried to get him to give up the idea of 'getting back' at Dwight Canfield and the others. Thought he had, actually. He stopped going on about them, anyway. We became good friends, and then, one night, we became lovers. Remained friends and lovers right up until he had his stroke. Then Helen was over there all

215

the time and I backed off." A light went out of her eyes and Miranda thought for a moment of Ian. Mrs. Penn cleared her throat and sat up straighter. "So, anyway, why are you prowling around now? What do you hope to gain?"

"I'm just curious," Miranda shrugged. "I never suspected this side of Dad before."

"And why should you? Parents have a right to have secrets from their kids."

Miranda shook her head and settled down at the kitchen table once more. "I dunno. Would have been nice to see his human side. He was such a bear with us." Feeling a bit skeptical, she added, "I suppose you *are* telling the truth."

"Suppose whatever the hell you like." Mrs. Penn got up to put a kettle on. With her back to Miranda, she said, "Too bad you never came back after you grew up. Maybe your relationship would have been better if you'd known him after you were an adult. My sons and I had terrible relationships when they were teens, arguing all the time. It's a difficult thing, releasing the bonds of parenthood. Kids always wanting freedom long before they can handle it; parents always wanting control long after they should relinquish it. I don't know how my boys and I survived. But we did, and we got close again after they were in their twenties. And let's face it, you were a real pain in the ass. And then you were gone and your dad never got a second chance."

Miranda hadn't stayed long after that. It was clear Mrs. Penn had her own opinion of things, and besides, it was a lot to take

216

in. The rest of the night, she tossed and turned on Reenie's cat-scented couch, which only made her lonesome for Nikki-stix, and the memories came zinging back.

January 1970, two weeks after Gary's funeral. She was fourteen and a half, in ninth grade at Broughton High School in Raleigh, finally getting some tits, perennially fighting zits. She had a huge crush on Paul White, but knew he was out of her league, and a small crush on Vic Jablonsky, who was a little on the stupid side but a good kisser. Not that she could truly judge; he was the *only* boy who'd kissed her, so far. A very secret crush on Kurt Russell after seeing him in *The Computer Wore Tennis Shoes*. She shared a bedroom with Helen. It had twin beds, twin dressers, green carpet, and pale lilac walls covered with posters of Creedence Clearwater Revival, The Doors, and Sly & the Family Stone.

Helen, as always, slept in a tight little fetal curl in the other bed, surrounded by stuffed animals including two huge stuffed piggies that Miranda and Val had discarded. You could barely see Helen amid all the plush. Miranda lay awake, enormous brush rollers in her hair, beloved patched and embroidered jeans draped over the foot of the bed. She imagined herself walking in the park with Paul White. Or maybe Kurt Russell. They'd go by the bridge, throw love notes into the creek, she'd have many witty and remarkable things to say, and then she'd lean back on the railing and Kurt—or Paul White or Jim Morrison—would come close and...

A screech from down the hall ran through her like lightning. She froze in her bed while hearing Dad's voice yelling and the sound of thuds. Mom shrieking, "You didn't stop him! None of you stopped him!" Miranda threw back her blankets and ran toward the door. Most of the house was dark, but a nightlight in the bathroom threw some feeble rays into the hallway where she saw her parents struggling. They grappled each other near the top of the stairs, Mom in a billowing nightgown, with the big kitchen knife in her hand and Dad in his underwear, blood running from a wound in his shoulder. Miranda stood in the doorway, her hands over her mouth in horror.

"*What's happening?*"

Helen's fearful voice came from behind and Miranda whirled back into the bedroom. "Get under the bed," she whispered. "Right now!" She could see the whites of Helen's eyes as her sister scurried to comply. New screams broke out, Mom's and Val's voices mixed, and Miranda wavered. Go to Valerie's aid or hide in the bedroom?

She peeked through a crack in the door. Dad kept trying to subdue Mom, to hold her arms down, but she broke loose. Valerie huddled in the doorway of her bedroom, holding her hands up to shield her face and Mom yelled, "You didn't care! You didn't care!" Mom's knife carved a long line from Val's wrist to her elbow and blood began pouring out. Val stared at it, the color in her face drained, and she slumped to the floor.

"No, Mom!" Miranda screamed.

"Don't come out," her dad yelled but she couldn't help herself. She ran to Valerie, whose eyes rolled back in her head, scaring the bejesus out of Miranda. Dad pinned Mom's arms but she lifted her feet and they both fell to the floor. "Go get Mr. Hamilton," he grunted, wrestling Mom down, getting on top of her. "Get help!"

Miranda turned to run for the next-door neighbor. Mom got one arm loose and clawed at Miranda, who backed up and fell halfway down the stairs, hitting her foot hard against the newel post on the landing. Mom managed to get free, kicked Dad in the face, and ran into Helen's bedroom, jerking her out from under the bed by grabbing her hair. "*No!*" Dad yelled, and slapped Mom's face with all his might. The sound rang in the air and Mom went over like a falling timber, hitting her head on the foot of Helen's bed. And then it was over.

Mom lay there, moaning, and they all sat for a moment, gasping for air, sobbing. Dad checked on Valerie. "She's losing a lot of blood," he said. "We've got to call for an ambulance."

By the time morning came, word had gone round the neighborhood. When Miranda returned to school the next day on crutches with her foot in a cast, all the kids whispered behind her back—and some right in front of her too. Val was in the hospital for a week. Mom was in the psychiatric ward for a month. And their whole family was in hell for a long time after that. Seemed like forever.

Monday, May 11, 2009
"Wind Turbine Noise Suspected of Killing 400 Goats",
(Columbia Herald)

The noise was almost unbearable. Sound bounced off the tiled walls of the YMCA pool room, magnifying what was already a cacophony of voices, hammering, splashing, beach balls bouncing against the wet floor and the constant flap of flip-flops.

Reenie sat on a bench, wrapped in a terry robe, closed her eyes and leaned her head back. They were almost done for the night. The pool scene with all her ladies was a take. They'd had to shoot it during the wee hours when the Y was closed to its regular patrons, and Reenie had been awake since 7 am. There was so much to do, so many details to cover. Bubble wrap consumption had gone up to three rolls a week and the small muscles between her thumbs and first fingers ached.

In front of her, bobbing up and down in the deep end of the pool, the new camera girl who'd been brought in to do the underwater scenes tested various fabrics for the other pool scene that came at the end of the movie. Reenie wanted something that would be gauzy and move well under the water, but they also had to figure out what color would be best. "I just imagined black," she told the girl, who went by the outrageous name of Vanity Press.

Vanity, who looked like a druggier, more anorexic version of Amy Winehouse, shook her head. "You'll end up looking like a

220

dementor from the Harry Potter films. Or one of those nazguls from Lord of the Rings."

"Red, then? I've always looked good in red."

Vanity shook her head. She was wearing an extremely tiny bikini, which had caught the attention of many, particularly the director, Shane. "Nope. It would look too much like blood. She turned to one of the college kids who'd turned up the first day of shooting, offering to help in any way they could, without pay, just for the sake of getting some experience. "Take the green one, the gold one, and the blue and go under with them." The girl promptly submerged with the swatches of fabric, and Vanity put on a snorkel mask and dropped under the water with her camera.

All around the room, people were packing up for the night. The pool scene with her ladies, which opened the movie, would only last about two minutes in the film, but had taken more than four hours to set up and shoot. Several other students helped Shane dismantle the rigging for the lights. It was great having some young, strong bodies around, and Reenie was gratified by their constant praise and admiration, but they wore her out. Questions, questions, questions. One kid asked her to mentor him. Nice kid, although those Dumbo ears of his needed to be pinned back, but she didn't have the time or energy to be anyone's mentor. It was taking all the stamina she had to survive. Thank God the kid didn't seem to be in evidence tonight. In fact, when she thought about it, he never was around when there was hard physical work to be done.

Truth was, she didn't want to be anyone's mentor, not when she had so many fears to combat. Everything was riding on this film. Oh, not the money. She had tons of money and only a few years left, no doubt, to spend it. But this was her reason for getting up in the morning; it was her last chance to make something that would last, to create a beautiful vision and a real legacy. That final pool scene alone, if it came out right, would be worthy of a serious footnote in cinematography. She could *see* it so clearly—an underwater dream, her character and Alex's in a beautiful slow-motion dance that captured all the longing and the impossibility of their love, finally together in a way they never could be throughout the rest of the movie. The viewers would really understand the agelessness of her character, the way emotions cannot be limited by a place or time. *If* she could only get it right.

A loud whistle interrupted her thoughts. She turned and saw Burnie Burnette and his squad of mouth breathers standing in the doorway. "Y'all need to clear out now," he said. "Enough for one night."

"We have the pool until five a.m.," Shane replied, disentangling himself from the lighting set-up. "We still have two hours—"

"I don't give a crap," Burnie said, frowning down at the smaller man. "Enough is enough. It's my job to make sure things are cleared away before the morning rush. Last thing's we need is a traffic jam."

"Oh yeah, a traffic jam in Painter's Creek. That'll be the day," Miranda muttered. She had shown up, unexpected and unwanted, for the late night shoot. "What's this really about?" she called across the pool.

"I'll tell you," he shouted, "it's about being fed up with people who think they should get special treatment. Now I said to get out, so *get out!*" He shot a venomous look at Helen, who immediately began clearing away the coffee and donuts, her shoulders hunched as though avoiding a blow.

Alex, standing nearby, put out a hand to stop her. "You don't have to put up with this nonsense," he said and she burst into tears. Alex put an arm around her shoulders, turned and barked at the room in general. "Right, that's quite enough." He looked at Shane. "Aren't we nearly finished anyway? Let's call it a night, in an *orderly* fashion." Shooting a frown at the sheriff, he added, "I presume that's acceptable. We will leave as soon as possible, but we're not going to tear down in a careless fashion."

Burnie blinked, apparently baffled by Alex's accent. "Just so long's you *tear down* immediately."

Alex ignored him and began talking softly in Helen's ear. She nodded and he handed her his handkerchief. Reenie joined them.

"I can't believe Burnie would act this way," Helen murmured, wiping her eyes. "We used to be friends."

Reenie huffed contemptuously. "He has to answer to a higher power."

223

"God?" Alex asked.

"No. His mama. Women like her don't like women like me."

Sheriff Idiot left and Reenie headed for the lockers to get dressed. All her ladies followed, chattering until Reenie thought she'd scream. What was Burnie really up to? And what the *hell* was Alex up to?

She'd noticed him being very attentive to Helen and had spoken to him about it just that morning. "A man's got to amuse himself," he'd replied, but under her glare, he shrugged and muttered, "I'm not doing anything terrible. Something in her just calls out this very protective attitude in me."

"Well, don't protect her right out of her marriage. She's one of the few happily married women I know."

"Believe me, the 'protecting hero' is not my usual role. And she's not my type at all, but there's just something about her..." He started to walk away, but returned. "I'd swear I knew her in a previous life. Seriously, Reenie, it's driving me mad."

She went to the locker room to change. When she came out, she saw Shane talking with Morris, his shaggy-headed second cameraman, who was doing most of the filming for the 'Making of' documentary. She hoped he'd gotten Sheriff Doofus on tape. Helen, Valerie and Miranda stood in a corner, discussing something in hushed voices. Tension radiated off Helen and Val, their arms folded tightly against their waists, and their eyes trained on the floor, but Miranda appeared to be exasperated with the conversation, hands on her hips, eyes wide, her whispers just as quiet but furious in tone. The rest of the crew were packing up, except for Alex who kept prowling the craft table, obviously waiting for Helen. He kept picking things up and putting them down, and when he saw Reenie watching him, he abruptly strode out of the room.

Upon their return to the lake house, Helen and her sisters immediately went out to the barn. Reenie waited in the car, anxious to go home to her apartment and get some rest, but having to wait for her ladies who now were quite enthusiastic about the idea of going out for breakfast. Who could think about food at this time of the morning? She watched as two crew members carried some equipment into the house. The moment the lights went on, one of them ran back out, shouting "Hey! There's been a break-in!"

Reenie groaned and climbed out of the car. She pushed her way to the front of the crowd on the porch and stood in the doorway. The living room was a disaster. Furniture had been upturned, glass smashed, curtains torn down, and some kind of foul-smelling liquid had been splashed around the room. "The door was unlocked," Morris said, as he immediately began filming the mess. "I was able to walk right in."

"Who was the last one out? Where's Helen?" Alex asked. "Stay back, everyone. Don't touch anything. Now we *need* the bloody police and, of course, where are they?"

Someone ran out to the barn to find Helen, Val and Miranda, and when they returned, white-faced, Valerie took charge. "Okay. Everyone out. Let me and Helen walk through

225

to see what other damage there might be. Miranda, call the sheriff, damn it. This is malicious damage." She wrinkled her nose at the odor. "I do believe that's someone's urine." Reenie maintained her position in the doorway and watched as Helen, obviously shaken but holding herself under control, checked the kitchen while Valerie made her way over to the bedrooms. After a thorough exam, they decided the damage had been limited to the living room.

At the sound of a siren's wail, Val muttered, "Okay, now it's gloves off." She shot a dark glance at Miranda, who jutted her chin. "Could everyone please go outside? Except Morris. You can stay. I want everything filmed for the record."

Reenie got one of her ladies to drive them all out to Waffle House for breakfast. That was a big mistake. The cackle pack, as she was beginning to think of them, were full of discussion over the break-in, and Reenie could practically see antennas going up over every head in the diner. By noon, the entire town would know about it. The community was already overly-interested in the filming anyway. Well, who wouldn't be? Especially in a burg like this where nothing ever happened. Practically half the town had shown up at one time or another, offering to help or just plain gawking. With all the unintended publicity, it wasn't surprising that the house had been broken into—somebody was bound to be nosy. To tell the truth, though, Reenie had the bad feeling she herself had left the door unlocked.

Chapter Twelve

Tuesday, May 12, 2009
"Retail Sales Drop Unexpectedly in April", (Wall Street Journal)

FIVE IN THE MORNING. ERICA HAD LOOKED forward to sleeping in. She didn't have to be at The Gap until ten, but she and everyone else in the house had been roused when Mom, Aunt Val, Aunt Miranda, and that Alex guy came home with an unbelievable tale of trouble with the sheriff and a break-in at Grandpa Lee's.

"Who could have left the front door unlocked?" Aunt Val had asked several times. "It's such a hassle to deal with that stupid lock, that we've all been absolutely brainwashed about locking it. How could anyone forget?"

"The lock could have been picked." This from that Alex guy, who slumped in his chair and plonked a tea bag up and down in a mug of hot water. His eyes kept following Mom as she moved around the kitchen like a zombie, making coffee, toasting rye bread, handing out plates. She hadn't said a word since they arrived. Dad kept staring at her too, like he wasn't sure if he should take her by the arm and lead her to bed.

According to Aunt Val, the sheriff's men had been methodical but slightly amused at the whole thing. *Well, if you don't bother to lock the door...* one of them kept saying. "Like that matters!" Aunt Val said. "It's still a case of trespass and vandalism. They ought to be more professional." She kept giving little dagger glances at Aunt Miranda for some reason, and Aunt Miranda just curled up on the couch and pretended to fall asleep. She was listening, though, to every word. Erica recognized a trick or two about that.

She wished Latham were there. He was always so calm in an emergency and knew what to do. When Aunt Val got to the part about someone having peed on the floor, Dee and Devon came alive and several glances passed between the Trips. Erica knew they all had the same thought. Bryan. He knew where Grandpa Lee's house was; he'd been there before, at their graduation party on the lake. This was just the kind of thing that snake might do. Erica stared at Dee, willing her to tell Mom. Dee shook her head, so when Mom came to the table with a platter of toast and scrambled eggs, Erica began. "Mom, we might..."

Mom didn't seem to hear. She stared at the eggs like she was in a trance, and interrupted Erica, saying, "We know who might have done this. Or, at least, we know of some people who might think they have motivation." She gave a nervous glance at Miranda, who still feigned sleep on the couch. With another look at Val, who nodded her head almost imperceptibly, she added, "There's a secret I've been keeping, but I think it's time

228

to come out." Pausing a moment, she pushed her hair back from her forehead with both hands. "Just before Dad died, I found some things he'd kept hidden from me. He'd been—"

"Oh. My. God." That Alex guy's voice broke into the room, making Erica and everyone else turn toward him. He stared at Mom. "Now I know why you looked so familiar—you're Nell Cates! I *knew* I'd seen you before. You were in *Night Blind*. You played the girl who gets killed by the rockslide. Oh my god, no *wonder* I've been—" He stopped himself and pursed his lips, looking down at the table top. He drummed his fingers on it a second and looked up again. "Why didn't you tell me? I saw that movie a dozen times."

Miranda roused herself suddenly. "Why *should* she mention it to you? It was a zillion years ago and she barely even had a speaking role." Heaving a sigh of exasperation, she pulled herself off the couch and strolled over to the table. Smearing a piece of toast with some strawberry jam, she added, "Jeez, why in the world would you watch that movie a dozen times? It was terrible. Almost as bad as *Attack of the Killer Tomatoes*."

"Mom was in a *movie*? Why did I never hear about this before?" Erica stared at her mother with new respect. "A *real movie*?"

Mom sat down abruptly and her face finally looked awake. "It was just a bit part," she mumbled. "In '76, when I went to stay with Aunt Reenie for the summer. She was shooting a movie at the same studio and I guess she wanted me out of her hair, so she arranged for me to work as an extra."

"You weren't an extra," Alex said, so loudly that Dad raised his eyebrows. "You had a speaking part. Small, but significant." Jeezy creezy, he was getting worked up. "I was in New York the following winter, absolutely dying in an off-off-Broadway play and living with a pal of mine, Jeramie Lemming. Remember him?"

Mom gave a little nod, but she looked embarrassed and kept her eyes focused on the tabletop. "He was the male lead."

"He made me watch that damned movie every day for two weeks when it came out; he was so thrilled to have a lead part."

Erica stared at him. Whoa. He was really getting het up. Leaning forward on his elbows, his face all intent, his eyes were like drilling holes in Mom. Even Dad noticed and was sitting up straight. "Wait a minute," she said. "How come we've never seen it?"

Mom gave a little smile and thawed a bit. "It was such a stinker. I don't think it's ever been put on video, and they sure don't play it on TV unless maybe three in the morning when nobody's watching."

Alex was shaking his head. "When you did that just now, smoothed your hair back, it suddenly came to me why you looked so familiar. My God." He sat back, nodding a bit and patting the table. "You were good." Mom shook her head. "You *were*. I always wondered why I never saw your name in credits on anything else."

Dee had by this time pulled out her laptop and was scanning IMDB for the movie. "Here it is. *Night Blind*, starring Jeramie

230

Lemming, Rachel duBois, and Robert Rhining Howard. Can't say I've heard of any of them. *A group of campers are picked off one-by-one by a blood-slurping mutant lizard.* Yep, here it is! 'Lisa' played by Nell Cates. Your character didn't even get a last name."

"But Mom's a terrible actress," Devon blurted out, the jerkface. Erica glared at him and he continued. "You know what I mean. She can't lie to save her life. No poker face. You always know when she's upset…" He shut up when he saw the reception he got.

Mom didn't seem to mind. She even laughed. "He's right. I'm a terrible actress. But I was playing someone who was scared, so that was easy." Finally she seemed to relax. Shaking her head at the memory, she said, "I thought it would be fun, but it didn't take long to realize that everyone there took it deadly seriously. This was what they hoped would be their big break, they really *cared* about acting, and I was terribly ashamed to be such a duffer, just doing it for fun. I was only supposed to be in a couple of crowd scenes, but the director gave me a few lines. Probably because he was a good friend of Reenie's. If he'd only known I was much happier in the crowd. But I was too shy to tell him."

"He could see you were good. You were the only bright spot in the whole film. Even Jeramie said so, and he's a conceited bastard." The Alex guy smiled and his shoulders relaxed. "So…little Nell Cates. Unbelievable."

Hot damn. Emily was wide awake now. *He totally had a crush on Mom.* This confirmed it. She turned to look at Dee and

231

Devon, and could see they'd realized the same thing. Everyone had. Dad was frowning at him, ol' Aunt Miranda looked pissed as hell, and even Aunt Val raised an eyebrow. Only one who seemed clueless was Mom herself. "Let's eat," Mom said, completely oblivious to all the tension at the table. Ya gotta love her, Erica thought, as the moment broke and everyone began passing eggs and toast around. Holy spit.

And *then* Mom dropped the bombshell about Grandpa Lee and his blackmail, which was even more unbelievable than the fact that Mom had been in a movie, and then Aunt Miranda admitted she may have stirred things up further by going out in the night, and playing weird pranks on people, which was actually totally believable, considering it was Aunt Miranda, but still unexpected as all get-out. *I can't wait to tell Latham.* Summer had just started and already things were getting exciting!

Wednesday, May 13, 2009
"Chrysler Wants to Eliminate 789 Dealerships", (Detroit Free Press)

The azalea bushes in Helen's front yard were in mortal danger. Every day for the past week, she'd been 'trimming' them with a set of loppers, two bushes a day, cutting them back until they were no more than a whimpering shadow of their former selves. They'll grow again, she thought to herself. They were getting too large anyway.

The fact that the lopping used up a lot of excess energy was not to be considered. Nor the way that slaughtering the foliage was preferable to slaughtering human beings; her sister Miranda, for example.

It was seven in the morning and the branches were still wet from an overnight rain. Phil came out of the house, dressed for work, an unhappy expression on his face. "Well," he said. "Wish me luck."

Helen set down the loppers and stripped off her gloves. She straightened the collar on his golf shirt, emblazoned with the *Mitchell Furniture Specialties* logo. "Good luck. What time are you going to do it?"

"Noon. Just before lunch. I have a meeting with the bank this morning, so when I get back from that." He sighed and glanced around the neighborhood, very quiet this early. He bent to give Helen her good-bye kiss. Shifting his computer bag to the other hand, he frowned and said, "I feel sick about the whole thing. When I think about the greed that started this whole downward spiral, and I look at what it's doing to people...well, I'd better not get started on that."

"Do you want to come home for lunch afterward? I can be here."

"No." Phil shook his head and shifted his computer bag again. "I won't be hungry."

"Well, even if you don't eat...I mean, I'll be here. If you want to talk or anything..."

"I'm all right, Helen," he sighed. "Talking just makes it worse." Off he went to the car. Helen watched him drive away, and then resumed her trimming with a vengeance.

Okay, fine. If he was going to continue to resist any sympathy, any empathy, fine. She didn't envy him. He was letting two long-term employees go, after all. Not caving in to his mom, but just doing what couldn't be avoided any longer. What else could he do? Nobody was buying furniture, not the kind Phil created—expensive, hand-made Shaker and Craftsman-style pieces or one-of-a-kind special-order chairs and tables and bookcases. Their orders had been dropping for months. Phil had cut expenses to the bone, including his own salary, but the numbers didn't lie. He *had* to let people go— there was no work for them to do anyway. And then, the final blow, three customers returned large orders they couldn't afford. He had the furniture back, sure, but he couldn't sell those pieces right now and the materials and work-hours had already come out of his pocket. It represented a huge loss. He couldn't even hire his own son to work for the summer, not when he was letting two men go who had families to support. She just wished Phil wouldn't feel like he had to bear it all alone.

At this rate, Helen thought, we might have to pull the kids out of college. Out of the dorms, for sure. And how are we going to pay for the expenses of Dad's house? The check Reenie had written to use the place for filming her movie would cover the property taxes, but there was still the ongoing cost of electricity, water, and general upkeep. Of course, there was the stash from his blackmailing efforts…

Helen took a final whack at the azalea and forced her thoughts into submission. She would *not* touch that money. Gathering up armfuls of wet branches, she stuffed them into a garbage bag to take to the compost heap at the lake house.

Dee came out to the driveway in her flannel pajama bottoms and a Sponge Bob oversized t-shirt from seventh grade. "Mom, I gotta talk to you," she said. "I think it might be someone else who trashed Grandpa Lee's house."

Helen listened as Dee told the tale of the sleety night at the bus stop and watching from Devon's window. "That was dangerous," she said, horrified, "and stupid! *Never* tease a boy about sex. Even if to get him back for being an A-hole." Dee's eyes widened. "Oh, not that I blame you. I never liked Bryan anyway. Remember when you got suspended from riding the school bus in kindergarten because you hit him over the head with your lunchbox?"

Dee laughed. "I had to. He kept insisting that Power Rangers were real crime fighters. What a dweeb."

"He was always so full of himself. Thought he knew everything. When I think of his parents, I can understand why, though. They always looked like they were about to drop on their knees in front of him, wailing *We're not worthy! We're not worthy!*" Helen set the full trash bag by the bumper of her car. "Do you really think he'd go that far, though?"

"I dunno. He's a big enough weasel to *think* of doing it, but maybe not brave enough to carry it out." Dee wrapped her arms around herself and shrugged. "But I thought you should know. Just in case. I gotta get ready for work now. They're shooting the Midol scene today." Laid off from her waitressing job, Dee was spending the summer working for Reenie—running errands, shuttling people and equipment, doing whatever needed doing. "I love the bit where her son says, *You tried to kill yourself with an overdose of Midol? How old was that stuff? The last time you had cramps, John Travolta was dancing in a white suit!*"

"Yeah. Hilarious." Helen didn't like to think about them shooting an attempted suicide scene, even if it was supposed to be funny and just a drama-queen action on the part of Reenie's character. Suicide wasn't funny to Helen.

Dee hugged her mom's waist briefly. "Okay, well, see you at dinner. By the way, the screen on my laptop is cracked. Any chance we can get a new one?"

"At the rate we're going, I'll be lucky if I can buy you each a new pencil this fall." Helen made the remark lightly, but she couldn't help thinking it was true. By September, Mitchell's Furniture Specialties might be extinct. She and Phil had always hoped the kids would take an interest some day and bring his grandfather's company into its third generation, but now those hopes seemed rather forlorn. Gazing at the ragged little azalea in front of her, Helen reached out and snapped off one more branch. The azalea would survive, no matter how ragged it looked right now. But would her family? Phil seemed so far away right now.

*

After shooting wrapped for the day, and the crew had finished off the food on the caterer's table, or crafts table as she was learning to call it, the sky was already growing dark. Helen walked out on the pier for a breath of fresh air. The big umbrella had blown over, despite its heavy stand, and she straightened it up. A breeze blew across the water and she enjoyed having a moment of peace and quiet. Then, feeling the pier shake a bit beneath her feet, she turned and saw Alex walking toward her.

"Nice night," he said, standing at the railing next to her. He turned to glance back at the yard. "You have a lot of fireflies. A conflagration." He smiled a little at his poor joke. She felt her chest rise. He was a very attractive man. Older, but still very attractive. And that voice! Deep and sexy and unique. "Little Nell Cates, at last we meet. I remember that movie so well. It was a terrible winter in New York. Cold. Absolutely peeing with rain every day. I had this cough I couldn't kick. And Jeramie dragged me to the cinema every day for two weeks until the film moved on." He propped one elbow against the railing, bringing him eye to eye with her. "I was miserable. Contracted to do a terrible play in a horrible theater. Thought

237

my career was over. And then force-fed this dreadful movie. It got so the only bright spot was you."

Helen shook her head. His intense gaze was making her feel so…so…*gushy* inside.

"You *are* like a little bright spot," he insisted, his voice dropping to just above a whisper. "Everyone depends on you, but nobody notices you. Why is that, when you shine so brightly all the time, this ardent spirit?" His hand reached out and smoothed a strand of hair from her cheek.

"That's not true." Her voice shook.

"You seemed so fragile in that film. That part on the beach, you were so … I wanted to wrap my arms around you and stop your shaking." His fingertips slid up her arm. "You could still be a fine actress. If you ever came to New York, I could help you, introduce you to people."

Helen shook her head again. "I can't act. Don't even want to. I'm no good at pretending."

He pulled away slightly. "Acting's not pretending! It's revealing truth." He frowned down at her and then relaxed again. "Seriously, why don't you plan a trip to New York soon?" Alex leaned in and his voice dropped a bit. "Even if you just want to see the sights. I could—"

Helen's breath stopped for a second when his lips touched her brow. She swallowed and said, "Um, Alex, look. You're a real nice guy."

"Very nice." He kissed her temple.

"And…and…I have to admit, you're very attractive and I even had a dream about you one night, but—"

The pier lights switched on automatically, now that it was dark, and she saw a smear of vivid orange on the edge of the boat slip. "What the heck?" Helen stepped around Alex's encircling arm and down onto the bobbing boat slip. Someone had spray-painted the pontoon boat! Bright neon-orange streaks covered the engine and seats and pontoons. A gooey slime of orange bubbled at the water line. "*Damn* it," she yelled. "Damn, damn, damn, damn, damn! I don't believe it." She bent down to see if the paint was still wet, but it had dried. Whoever had done it must have come in with a boat, probably after dark. "That's *it*," she said. "I have had just about enough!" She pointed furiously at the paint, stomped her foot, and charged up the pier past Alex. "This has got to stop." She ran toward the barn.

Alex ran after her. "Wait a minute, wait a minute! What was that you said about a dream?"

By the time he caught up with her, she'd burst into the barn and shouted to everyone assembled there that the boat had been defiled. "This makes me so *furious*," she cried. "I've spent my whole life trying to keep from upsetting anyone and now, here I am, the victim of some stupid idiots bent on revenge, revenge owed not to me but to my dad, my sister, and my… my… other people." Her voice trailed off as she glanced at Dee. "It's going to cost a fortune to clean that up. Money we don't have."

Now was not the time for her to have this tirade, she realized. Shane and his crew were still there, Reenie's gal pals, the Trips and a couple of their friends. But damn it, how much more did she have to take? She thought about Phil, trudging off to work that morning, his heart heavy. "Tomorrow we are sending everything back. The money, the paperweights, the stamps, everything! And we're—"

"Hold on." Miranda emerged from the shadows. When had she arrived? "Have you thought about the fact that the stuff doesn't belong to you? Based on Dad's will, you have to divide anything that's his among the nine of us. Personally, I want my share."

"Personally, I don't give a crap," Helen said through gritted teeth, ignoring the startled expressions on her children's faces. "It's going *back*. That's the right and honorable thing to do. Dad was wrong to start the whole thing in the first place, so now we're going to set it right."

"Miss Self-Righteous. How typical. Did you ever think these people got what they deserved? If they hadn't been doing something shady in the first place, Dad never could have gotten to them." Miranda strolled forward, hands in her pockets, a big smile on her face. "Frankly, it's the first time I've had any respect for the old fox."

Helen caught a glimpse of Morris behind his camera, filming the whole thing. "If one scrap of this gets into Shane's documentary, I will sue your ass down to the ground and out the park," she shouted, pointing at him. "*Do you hear me?*"

"Uh, yes, ma'am." Morris's voice was hoarse and his big fingers fumbled for the lens cap. "I sure do, Ma'am."

In the background, she could hear Devon's puzzled voice. "Out the park?"

Helen glared at Miranda. Trying very hard to keep her voice level, she said, "I have been the one left to deal with every ….*friggin'* issue that has come up with this family for the past thirty years. You've missed your chance to be in charge, baby. I said that stuff is going, and I mean it. And if any of this kind of nonsense continues after that, I will find the perpetrator and I will fry his biscuits. Now I am going home," she finished and turned to go. Shooting a glance at Alex, she added, "to my *husband*."

Saturday, May 16, 2009
"Miracle Mike, Headless Chicken, Feted at 12th Annual Festival", (Fruita Times)

Within a day or two of arriving at Painter's Creek with the realization that she'd be staying a while, Valerie began trying to lay down new rituals for herself. She didn't have the option of walking in Central Park or swimming at the YMCA, so she had to work out a new exercise plan for herself. Up early, shower and dress, then a brisk walk from the front door to the barn, where the caterers were always already set up with coffee and donuts. Then, with brave intentions, a casual stroll along the causeway. She always had a chance to study the clouds billowing from the steam plant a mile away—so thick and solid-looking as they emerged from the stacks, and then evaporating to nothing within seconds. Rather like her career.

Next, reminding herself to get to work, she'd head back to the house and her laptop, ostensibly to check her emails and see if anyone had sent an offer of a job but, of course, found nothing. Nada. Zip. Bupkes.

Then she played solitaire or sudoku on the computer for an hour. Or two. Or three.

Oh, she knew she couldn't go on like this. She had to get going on the music for Reenie's movie, but with the script still a bit up in the air, and no scenes truly completed yet, all she could do is work on a few themes and ideas. Truth was, she felt frozen in place, without direction, made worse by knowing that Reenie depended on her. She hardly recognized herself any more, and if she kept eating those damn donuts, no one else would either.

It was ridiculous. She'd never been so useless in her life, not even after her divorce. Of course, back then, her career had sustained her. She was able to keep doing the thing she loved most, playing in the orchestra. Now, no wonder she felt as lost as the proverbial City Mouse, out of her element.

Worse than that, she felt assailed on every side by memories. She wasn't just a City Mouse plonked down in a field—she was a City Mouse plonked down in her *home* field. Everywhere she looked, she saw familiar things that each held its place in her

242

recollection. The house itself, despite any changes, had certain spots that brought pictures to her mind. The corner of the living room, with the jigsaw puzzle cabinet wall, where she used to set up her cello for practice. The gazebo where she used to sit and swing, and dream about a career in music. The bench down by the lake, where she and Jack used to kiss. Too many memories were flooding back.

The family had already been in turmoil when they moved from Raleigh to Painter's Creek. Gary's death in Viet Nam, Mom's attack and subsequent breakdown; both had taken the family to a point of collapse, and it was no wonder that Dad wanted to go back to his roots and move in with Grand-dad Hec. It was a natural conclusion for Dad, but for everyone else, it was sheer hell. Mom hated the countryside, Miranda hated the small rural high school, and Valerie hated what she thought might be the end of all her musical aspirations. Raleigh wasn't exactly a center for the arts, but it sure beat Painter's Creek. In addition, Valerie's arm hadn't completely recovered from the wound it received on the day of her mother's knife attack. When she realized what she'd done, Mom had apologized over and over, but it still took a long time for the muscles to regain flexibility and strength.

From that point on, Valerie had made music the most important thing in her life. It was her lifeline, a strong but slender thread that pulled her out of her sorrows after Mom's death, out of Painter's Creek, out of family drama and mayhem, and into a world of harmony, order and grace. Playing the cello was her primary function, and everything else—even her marriage, if she was being honest—came second. And now, where had that single-minded concentration gotten her?

Meanwhile, she had to get to work on Reenie's movie score. The story line had some great elements; an elderly lady rebelling against the nursing-home scenario her family wanted. It was a tale of conflicting wants and needs, and overall it was a beautiful love story, between two people whom situations separated. Even more, and this was what Reenie wanted to accent, it was an adult coming-of-age tale. Young people weren't the only ones who had to figure out and decide who they were and what they wanted to be. Those kinds of questions occur to adults again and again in their lives. At least, they did if the person wanted to live fully. Valerie thought it was wonderful, and so like Reenie to still have that zest for what each day would bring. She wished she felt that same zest herself. She had all the questions but, so far, none of the answers.

Each day she would convince herself to practice, to plug in Hopalong and run through her warm-up routine. Instead of her usual scales and arpeggios, she played along to a couple of old Carpenters songs—*It's Gonna Take Some Time This Time, Close to You*, and *Flat Baroque*, the last of which really gave her a workout. However, they also took her back to high school and conservatory days and made her remember who she used to be, sometimes right down to the shoes and perfume she'd been wearing. Then she would move on to Reenie's outrageous

244

suggestion of Bollywood-style music. Valerie had downloaded *Bollywood Hits 2008* to her I-Pod and discovered the music of Akshay Kumar, Labh Janjua, Naresh, Udit Narayan and A.R. Rahman. They were a revelation and with the earphones on, she could follow along on the cello, just getting a feel for the complex rhythms and fascinating harmonics.

This morning, she forced herself to sit on the deck outside her bedroom with Baby, just messing around. She wanted to create a truly memorable piece for the opening and closing sequences of Reenie's movie, the infamous underwater scenes. Originally, Val had imagined adaptations of Handel's *Water Music*, but now that seemed too hackneyed and predictable. She needed to find some creativity, to pull something new from inside herself, but she didn't feel anything but old inside.

Alex came out of his own bedroom and dropped onto a lounge chair. "Your sister, Helen, doesn't like me," he complained. "I merely asked how she was this morning and she scuttled away like a hermit crab."

Val reluctantly laid down her bow so she could listen better. "What did you expect?"

He poked at a potted plant on the low table next to him. "A flirtation. A few kisses. A little is all I ask."

"I told you she wouldn't. Shame on you for trying."

Folding his hands across his stomach, Alex glared at her. "When are we going home?"

"Are you going to sulk?

"I was thinking about it." With a lunging movement, he was on his feet again, staring broodingly across the back lawn to the lake. "We've got that damned pool scene tomorrow."

"I thought you were looking forward to it. Really, I think it's going to be sensational. Very moving."

"It's a lot of work. Do you have any idea how difficult it is to hold your breath and not have any bubbles escape from your nose? I'm not at all sure I'm up to it. What with my heart being lacerated and all."

Val smiled. She wasn't the only one out of her depth. "Why don't you try Miranda? I bet she'd be eager to oblige."

"Where's the charm in that?" Alex muttered, but when Val picked up her bow and began playing again, he sighed and walked back into the house.

When she heard—or rather, felt—footsteps on the deck again, she expected Alex had returned, but it was Jack. A little zing ran through her. *Why?* It was just Jack. "What are you doing here?" she asked.

He grinned and raised an eyebrow. "Wow, what a welcome. Makes me feel tingly all over." Ignoring her silence, he made himself comfortable on one of the lounge chairs. "Told Seth I'd come over and look at the place. See if we can't beef up security around here."

"What do you know about it? You handle computer security, not buildings."

"A fellow picks things up here and there. I figure between me and Seth, we ought to be able to come up with something not too expensive. An alarm system, motion-activated security lights, that kind of thing." He nodded at the cello. "What were you playing? I liked it."

Valerie frowned and leaned Baby against her shoulder, laying the bow across her lap. "Nothing. I don't know. Well, an idea for Reenie's film. I'm not used to working without a more finished product in front of me. When I did the nature film, most of the footage was complete. I'm not exactly sure …well, never mind." She smiled ruefully at him. "There's nothing like being decisive. And this is nothing like it."

"Maybe you're trying too hard. Take a couple days off. Clear your brain. That's what I do when I'm blocked." He leaned forward, hands loosely clasped. "We could hop in the car and drive. Head up to Asheville or some place like that, get a new point of view."

Valerie stared at him. This was the old Jack, full of good humor and spontaneity, instead of the cool politeness they'd mastered. "I'd love to get away, but I can't run out on Reenie right now. All hands pitching in, that kind of thing."

"A couple of days couldn't hurt." He shrugged, but she could see the hint of hopefulness in his eyes.

Oh, God. It could be so easy. Jack had never wanted the divorce. He'd wanted her to quit the orchestra, which was like asking her to kill herself as far as Valerie was concerned, but he never wanted the divorce. It was Dad and Mom all over again, each one unable to understand the other. She shook off further thoughts. "No, I'd better keep at it. I'm having a hard time concentrating as it is. This place seems to get me rattled."

"I know. It's weird." He laughed and ran a hand through his hair. "Being back on the island is setting off old memories. Takes me back to the days of my youth." He smiled that one-sided, eye-crinkly smile that worked so well. *Used to* work so well. "There were some good times. And you know, Val, people do learn from their mistakes. *I've* learned. There are things I'd do differently, if I had the chance."

Before she could respond, Dee came running up. "Aunt Val, come quick. Mom's having a cow!"

Valerie and Jack hurried out to the barn, followed soon after by Seth, to find Helen up in the loft throwing a fit. She'd apparently come by to pick up all that stuff of Dad's, with a view to sending it back to his victims, but Miranda beat her to the punch and everything was gone.

"I can't believe it! I know Miranda is sneaky but this is unbelievable!" Helen gestured at the trunks, their lids thrown open and most of their contents gone. "How did she do it, with so many people around? One of you must have helped her!" She glared at the small group—Dee and Valerie, Jack and Seth, the caterers who were setting up lunch.

Valerie hauled herself up the ladder into the loft. A bit out of breath, she grabbed one of Helen's arms. "Now calm down. Where is Miranda? Is she here today?"

"Somewhere. For all her complaining about her business going downhill, she sure doesn't seem to spend much time there. Oh, I could just kill her. Just absolutely *kill* her!"

"You could *try*." Miranda strolled into the barn. "What's all the noise about?"

Helen leaned over the railing and glared down at Miranda. "You know. What did you do with all the stuff?"

"Why does everyone think of me first when there's trouble?" Miranda laughed and looked around, but shrugged when she saw Valerie's scowl. "Okay, okay, I took it. It's safe, I haven't done anything with the junk. I just wanted to slow you down before you did something foolish. I'm not the government. I don't believe in throwing money away."

Helen whipped around the end of the railing and started coming down the ladder so fast she was a blur.

"Better watch out, Miranda," Jack called, obviously enjoying himself. "I think Helen could take you!"

Helen got about halfway down the ladder when she missed her grip on the railing. Her foot shot between the open steps and, as Valerie watched in horror, Helen flew downward, her upper body arcing through the air and slamming against the ladder, leaving her dangling from one knee caught on a rung. She hung upside down for a second, then Seth lunged forward and caught her shoulders, supporting her weight. He was followed by Jack, who lost his grin in a hurry and began issuing instructions in a calm, quiet voice. Slowly and carefully, they disentangled Helen's leg.

"Be really careful of her back and neck," Jack said. "Call 911. And call Phil."

"I'm okay." Helen's voice wafted back to Valerie. "I think I'm okay." And with that, she fainted.

*

"Ow! *Ow!* Stop it!" Miranda tried to pull loose, but Valerie dragged her into the back seat of Jack's SUV and blocked her in place on one side with Dee on the other. Jack drove.

Phil rode in the ambulance with Helen. The EMT guys said they thought nothing was broken but they put Helen in a neck collar anyway and headed for the hospital.

As soon as they were rolling, Val turned on her sister. "I've always known you're self-centered, but this takes the cake."

"Oh, get over yourself. Like *you've* ever been concerned about anyone else, except maybe Seth. And you even short-changed him, whenever it conflicted with your career. But of course, you're the *talented* one, so everybody forgives you."

"Oh, jeez, give me a large break. I never described myself that way. And God knows, I'm nothing to write home about now. The problem is you always acting like somebody owes you something. Sooner or later, you're going to have to realize there are consequences to what you do. Where's Dad's stuff?"

"Not far. It's safe. And I bet you want your share. I know you're hurting for money."

"I'm not *that* desperate."

"It's not about the money!" Dee shouted, giving Miranda a sharp elbow to the ribs. "You guys are killing Mom. She loved Grandpa, don't you get it? She hated finding out this stuff about him. My God, you're as bad as the film crew. They've done nothing but gossip about all of this for days. They've even got a pool going on who will prevail, Mom or Miranda. Y'all make me sick."

"Who do they think is winning?" Miranda asked and got another elbow in the side. "Ow! Have a little respect."

"Mom better not be seriously hurt, or you'll be sorry," Dee warned.

"If you want *my* opinion…," Jack began.

"We *don't*." Three voices responded.

"All I was going to say, was…"

"*Shut up!*"

He did.

*

They were not allowed into the triage set-up and had to stay in the emergency room waiting area. Since none of the four members of their little party were speaking to each other, they mostly sat and watched a runny-nosed toddler tear up old issues of *Good Housekeeping* and *Road & Track* while his mother held a cold can of Coke to her rapidly-blackening left eye. Valerie felt too restless to sit. She leaned against a wall, waiting for Phil, who came out every so often and told them what was going on. Helen was sent for X-rays, and they awaited the results. Then she was sent for an MRI, and they awaited the results. Dee texted her brother and sister with updates. Jack paced up and down, and repeatedly offered to go to the cafeteria for some really bad food, but no one was interested. He kept looking at Valerie, but she avoided meeting his eyes.

Finally he dropped into a seat next to Miranda, one knee jouncing at a fast rate. "How's business?"

Miranda gave him a long look. "Eh. Good news, bad news."

"What do you mean?"

"Oh, you know. Good news, I'm still operating in the black. Bad news, just barely." She warmed to her subject and crossed her legs. "Good news, students always need art supplies. Bad news, art supplies alone won't pay all my bills. Good news, I worked out a deal with Charlie Messenger's photography shop. He moved into the store with me and we share the rent. Bad news, now we're both a little tight for space and I had to move my office and storage upstairs. Good news, my kitchen makes a pretty good office. Bad news, now I have to keep my kitchen clean."

Jack laughed. "You always land on your feet."

"Yeah, but I'll never be able to wear high heels."

Val observed this little exchange. Miranda and Jack had always gotten along well. "Why don't you put some of that wisdom to work for the family?" she asked Miranda. "Figure out a way to salvage the lake house. Can't sell it, can't afford to keep it. What's the good news there?"

Finally, Phil came out, said there were no broken bones, but probably some pulled ligaments. "She'll be pretty sore for a while," he said. "They're icing her now and they've given her some pain pills. I'll be taking her home in a little bit but you can see her for a moment." He gave Miranda a stern look. "Except you. She doesn't want to see you."

"Phil, I didn't make her fall."

"You know what? Don't talk to me. That'd be best."

Jack, Valerie and Dee went into the treatment room. Helen lay on her stomach with ice packs on her back. She looked sleepy.

"Gosh, Helen, if you wanted company, you shoulda thrown a party," Jack quipped. "I'd have come."

Dee crouched down near the head of the bed so her mother wouldn't have to twist to look up at her. "Don't worry," Dee said. "I'll take some time off from helping Reenie to stay with you. You won't have to lift a finger."

"Don't be silly," Helen murmured. "I'll go see the chiropractor and I'll be fine in a day or so."

"I *hate* Aunt Miranda."

"No you don't. But thanks, Deedle, that's sweet of you." Her words slurred. "Is Val here?"

Dee left to text the other Trips and Valerie took her place, perched on a rolling stool and holding Helen's hand. "Shall I kill Miranda for you?"

"She'd just come back to haunt us." Helen started to shake her head, but gasped and stopped. "I can't believe I said that, about killing her. No matter how angry I am. If this," she said, waving a hand to indicate the hospital setting, "isn't a wake-up call from God, I don't know what is." She lay quiet a moment, eyes squeezed shut, and then relaxed and continued. "I've tried with Miranda. Really tried to keep her close to the family. I invite her to everything; she rarely comes. What's her problem? Why does she hate me?"

Valerie shrugged. "She doesn't. She just hates letting someone else call the shots."

"She used to be nice. Remember after we moved here and I didn't know anyone at school yet and it was my birthday? She set up that haunted house in the basement and invited all the girls in my class over and scared the bejesus out of them. They loved it and I had a million friends from that day on."

"Yes, but first she had the pleasure of scaring the bejesus out of them. That's Miranda."

Helen was silent a moment. Her eyes kept drifting shut. She opened them with obvious effort and said, "Why does she always push people away?"

"I don't know." Valerie sighed and stretched her arms in front of her, rotating her wrists. "Why do any of us do what we do? Here I am, knowing I can't keep up with the orchestra any more, but wanting to run back to it just because it's familiar. It's like we get gucked up early in life and then we just keep banging our heads against the wall until we pass out. We're doomed."

"Well, I'm not. Not any more. If after twenty times you don't succeed, regard it as an omen." Helen shifted her weight, winced, and settled down again. "Look, please take care of Dad's stuff. I know you'd rather not get involved, but I'm asking you. Give it back to the original owners or throw it out, or split it up between you and Miranda and Reenie. Whatever. Just leave me and my kids out of it. Okay? And don't even tell me what you did with it. I never want to hear about it again."

Val looked up at Jack and he shook his head. To Helen, she said, "But, honey, I don't know what to do with it."

"What do I have to do next?" Helen's voice rose. "Throw myself off the roof? It's *your* problem now, I've had enough. You're part of this family, damn it. You can't get out of everything. Once in a while, you've got to get your hands a little dirty."

She struggled to sit up and Jack pressed her down. "Helen, we'll figure out something. Valerie and Seth will put their heads together and come up with a solution. Don't worry. Something that suits everyone." Valerie mouthed *We will?* at him and he shook his head again. "So just rest and don't worry yourself about it, okay?" He excused himself, leaving Valerie and Helen alone.

Helen murmured, "He's so nice. Remind me again why you guys split up? Oh yeah, you can't remind me *again*, you never told me why in the first place. One of these days, you've got to do that."

"One of these days," Valerie said. When Helen raised her eyebrows and waited, Val added, "But this is not that day." She kissed Helen's cheek and left the room. Jack was waiting just outside the door. "So, Mr. Genius, what am I going to do, now that you've left me holding the bag?"

"*I* don't know. I said you and Seth would figure it out." He grinned and took her arm. "But first things first, we've got to get hold of that loot and keep Miranda from absconding with it. God knows, she's capable of almost anything." They headed down the hall and he continued, "Boy, this takes me back. Life with your family is never dull, is it?"

"No," Val said. "And no thanks to you. Somehow, I'm going to have to deal with Miranda. Guck, I hate drama! Guckety guckety guck."

Chapter Thirteen

Still Saturday, May 16, 2009
"Senate Passes Credit Card Overhaul Bill", (Nashville Post)

MIRANDA GLANCED AROUND THE WAITING room. Phil had buried his face behind a year-old copy of Auto Week. "I didn't make her fall," she repeated. "It's not my fault."

Phil lowered his magazine and shot her the angriest look she'd ever seen from him. "Nothing ever is. Your problem, Miranda, is you just don't give a shit about anyone but yourself. When are you going to grow up?" He gave his salt-and-pepper hair a brisk, hard rub, threw the magazine down and leaned forward, putting his head in his hands. "Well, listen to me shooting my mouth. I'm at fault, too. Helen's been an uptight mess for months. We both have. So much for trying to protect each other from bad news. We're idiots. Well-meaning, but idiots." He sat up again and glared at her. "But that doesn't excuse *you*. You set out deliberately to make trouble. Nothing new there. You know, she'd really like it if the three of you could be close. She loves you, for some damn reason. You ever think about loving her back?"

What the hell, Miranda thought. Helen already had a million people who loved her. Why was she still so needy? Miranda had never been anyone's favorite and she never would be. She glanced around the waiting room again. Valerie and Jack would be coming out of Helen's room in a moment, no doubt. She didn't relish the idea of driving back to the lake house with them, but there she was—no purse, no car, no money, no cell phone. How did that song go? *Clowns to the left of me, jokers to the right. Here I am, stuck in the middle with you.* Except she was stuck all alone. And here came Valerie with a look of determination on her face.

Miranda patted her pockets. Ah, at least one break—a battered pack of cigarettes with two smokes left. "I'm going out for smoke," she hastily told Phil. "Be back later."

Phil had also seen Valerie's approach. He just smiled and said, "Wimp."

Miranda scurried down the sloping path that led to the parking lot. Once she got to the road, she pulled out a cigarette, straightened the kinks in it, and lit up.

Who needed Valerie and the rest with their self-righteous attitudes? She had enough to worry about, with the store doing poorly. For twenty cents, she'd sell the whole thing and just take off. Actually, that wasn't a bad idea. Hit the road with a duffle bag of clothes and a sketchpad and wing it. She'd done it several times before and the experience could be liberating, unleashing loads of creativity.

Miranda walked along the path toward the highway, puffing furiously. Jeez—who needed all these headaches? She didn't have much in the bank, but she had a decent car, and could work out some arrangement for moving her stuff out of the store. Charlie Messenger might even be willing to take over if she cut him a great deal. She could eke out a living. Hell, she could waitress at a Waffle House, if nothing else. She'd survive.

Her lips grew warm and she felt the telltale rise of heat as a hot flash began. Sometimes the rising flush seemed like it would choke her. Suddenly, her cigarette tasted foul and she ground it out. Tears came to her eyes and she spun on her heel, wheeling about, trying to get fresh air. She could survive. But it was a lonely kind of survival, now more than ever. At fifty-three, she didn't want to start all over again. God, wasn't she ever going to find herself a home? Someone to love?

A car horn startled her. She looked up to see Hayley behind the wheel of a very familiar-looking banana-yellow SUV. *Her* SUV, her Jeep. Hayley grinned and lowered the side window. "Need a ride?"

"What the hell are you doing?" Miranda jerked open the driver's door. "Move over." She slid behind the steering wheel as Hayley clambered over the stick shift into the passenger seat. "Did you steal my keys?"

"Your whole purse. You left it behind." Hayley grinned even wider and held up the patchwork leather hobo bag. "I thought you might welcome some wheels."

"How'd you know where I was? And what do you know about this whole thing?"

"Oh, I know all, I see all." Hayley dug in her jeans pocket and held up her cell phone. "Dee tweets."

*

By the time they got back to the lake house, Hayley had explained everything. "Dee's been posting like mad, including photos, to everyone at the shoot. They're all over at the steam plant, you know, setting up the highway scene, except for Reenie and Alex, who are in the house rehearsing. Dee's been keeping everyone updated about Helen."

"So the whole crew knows? Holy smoke, how much information did Dee put on her posts?"

"Just about Mom and the hospital. Why?"

"Well, does she want the whole world knowing?"

"Nah. Just people on her Twitter list."

"That could be throngs!"

"Oh for pete's sake, will you listen? It doesn't matter. The crew knows almost all of it anyway. They're the biggest set of gossips I ever met, especially Reenie's girlfriends. People say teenagers are bad, but we don't have anything on those folks.

Shane has a super-hot crush on that weird girl, Vanity Press. He says he can't resist a girl with a strong inner bitch. But she likes Seth." Hayley frowned. "And I don't know who Seth likes." After a moment, she added, "I was supposed to help him clean the boat today, but then he said he and his dad were working on security for the house instead. I brought my swimsuit and everything but, of course, now that's all ruined anyway, with Aunt Helen getting hurt."

Aha, Miranda thought. Another hopeless case. Poor stupid girl.

Hayley brightened up. "But anyway, when I read Dee's tweets, I decided you'd probably want your car so I brought it. I have my license, it's okay. And I want to help." She turned in her seat to face Miranda. "I looked in the back end, I know you stashed everything under that sheet. What should we do with it?"

They crossed the causeway and Miranda pulled up in front of the barn. Shane's Winnebago was parked alongside; he'd moved it from its previous spot on the lawn in order to shoot a scene under the river birch near the water's edge. Miranda turned off the engine and leaned back to get a good look at Hayley. "What do you mean?"

"I want to help! Quickly, before everyone gets back from the hospital." Her eyes lit up with excitement. "We could hide the stuff somewhere else and have some fun with it. Don't you want to? I mean, even if they make you return it, why not stir things up? Dad says that's what you're good at. I thought, that

Dwight Canfield guy who got the insurance for his paperweights might be a good target. We could return the paperweights one by one, real slowly, so he has them hanging over his head. He can't display them openly or sell them because he'd have to pay the insurance company back—which he won't want to, I know that loser—but he won't be able to resist keeping them. It'll be pure mental torture. Don't you love it?"

"No." Miranda felt yet another hot flash beginning, another warm flush crawling up her cheeks. She suddenly felt sick, but not from the hot flash. Hayley's idea was too close to what Miranda had envisioned. Keeping the cash, splitting it up among the family, but leaving a few of the victims twisting in the wind. She'd even considered using some of the photos for a terrific collage on small town life. Blurring out the faces, yes, but enjoying the burning frustration of the subjects. Damn. Was this what it was like to be a parent? Unable to indulge in your own vices because of the responsibility to the next generation? Good thing she'd never had children. And Tim. His throwaway comment to Hayley about Miranda being good at stirring things up. Strange, how that stung.

"No," she repeated. "I'm sick of the whole mess. I don't even want that crap any more. Val and Helen can deal with it. I'll probably just go back to Boone. I have work to do there and nobody wants me here." She cut off any further self-pitying remarks. Nobody liked a whiner. "You need to stay out of this. You'll only get yourself in trouble."

Hayley folded her arms and slumped back. "I'm just trying to have a little adventure. *You've* had plenty of adventures, why can't I?"

Miranda turned to face Hayley and drew a deep breath. "Adventures are great. I'm all for having an adventurous life, a full active interesting life. But watch what you wish for, Kid. Sometimes adventures aren't all they're cracked up to be. There are consequences." She paused, thinking *if my sisters could hear me now! They'd slap my face!*

"Oh yeah, consequences. You think I don't know that? You think my dad hasn't preached it at me a million times a day?" Hayley slammed her hand against the dashboard. "What do you think my life is like, with Mom in jail? Kids laugh at me. They talk shit to me, or even worse, they act all sympathetic and *sorry* for me. God, I just want to get out of this crummy town. Or at least have some *fun*, if I'm stuck here. I thought you'd understand." She turned away, arms folded across her chest.

Holy shit.

For maybe the first time in her life, Miranda found herself without a snappy comeback. She reached out in sympathy, but Hayley jerked away. Hell, what was there to say or do anyway? The kid had been dealt a lousy hand, and the last thing Miranda wanted to do was spout any platitudes, but she also didn't want to take a chance at screwing up Tim's kid. Tim might be a hopeless fool for clinging to his teen dreams of Valerie, but he was still a nice guy, damn it. He tried to be a good father, at least. He probably just didn't know exactly what to do.

Any more than Dad did.

"Well, crap," she said finally. "This is where I should be telling you that life will get better if you just behave yourself and be nice to kittens, or something. It doesn't work like that. Life doesn't get better unless you make it better. Look, I gotta take care of something right now. Promise me you won't do anything crazy, and after I'm done, we'll figure something out. Okay? You say Reenie and Alex are inside?" Hayley kept her back turned to Miranda, but she nodded. Miranda pocketed her keys, got out of the car and headed for the house.

She found Reenie and Alex out on the sun deck, theoretically running lines but in reality engaged in competitive name-dropping. "Van Johnson was a great guy, a lot of fun," Reenie said, "but when it came to dates, my favorite actor was Brian Keith. Oh, what a good-looking guy he was. What *shoulders!*"

"Shoulders are very well and good," Alex replied, lazily leaning against the railing, "but Jackie Bisset had other valuable attributes." He straightened up when he saw Miranda approach. "How's Helen?"

"She'll live." If Alexander Rippon preferred white bread to something far more exotic, so be it. No skin off her nose. "Nothing's broken. She'll be sore for a few days. It was an accident. Not my fault." Somehow, those words were beginning to ring hollow, even to herself. Maybe one or two things were her fault. Possibly. "I have a major headache," she added, just then realizing it.

The doorbell rang. They all turned toward the sound and Miranda went to the door. It was Burnie Burnette once again, alone this time. "Oh jeez, Burnie, what now?"

He looked uncomfortable. "I have reason to believe there is contraband on the premises."

"Say what?"

He shifted from foot to foot. "I have reason to believe there's contraband on the premises. He hooked his thumbs in his belt and finally met her gaze. "I want to examine the place."

She could see his Adam's apple bob up and down. Somehow he seemed almost tentative. "Where'd you hear this?" she asked.

"I got an anonymous tip."

Damn those tweets! "You have a warrant?"

He held up a folded paper. "Barn, house, and car." His left shoulder inched up toward his ear and he gave a half-glance back toward his squad car. "We can do this the nice way, or I can radio for some help. It's your call, 'Randa."

For a moment, she felt rage building inside. 'Randy Randa'—that was what some of the guys called her in high school, even though she hadn't been all that loose—not with *those* jerkfaces, anyway. Burnie, she remembered, had been on the football team, a big beefy horndog with mush for brains even then. "Fine," she said. "You want to see what's in the barn? Fine. Let's go. Although I don't think you'll exactly want it hitting the five o'clock news when you do. Nor will your *Mama*."

265

Burnie turned a whiter shade of pale, but stuck to his guns. Literally. He put one hand on his holster as if for courage and shoved the warrant into his back pocket. "Let's go."

She threw a glance of dismay back toward Reenie, who nodded almost imperceptibly. "Okay," she said to Burnie. "Don't say I didn't warn ya."

Still Saturday, May 16, 2009

"BankUnited FSB Collapses in Year's Biggest Failure", (Financial Times)

Reenie was able to figure out just enough to know that Miranda was in trouble. If Burnie found those letters in the back of her car, it would be enough to incriminate Leland as a blackmailer. And even though Lee was dead, Reenie didn't want her brother's transgressions to be front page news. Not to mention Dwight Canfield's stupid paperweights, which he'd reported stolen, the old fool. Miranda could possibly get charged with dealing in stolen merchandise or something. Reenie wasn't sure exactly what could happen, but she did know one thing. All of this would result in delays to her shooting schedule, damn it. She couldn't afford that.

She wheeled around and stared at Alex. "What can we do?"

Before he could answer, they were startled by some taps on the glass door that opened from the back deck. Reenie turned to see Hayley out there. "What are you doing?" she asked, as she let her in.

"What did the sheriff want?" Hayley asked, her eyes bright with excitement. "The stuff? The loot? The ill-gotten gains?"

"What, precisely, do you know?" Alex sounded exactly like Inspector Crawford, the character he played in *Parlor Games*.

"It's okay, I moved everything to Shane's RV."

Reenie jumped in. "Why? When? How could you move it so quickly?"

"I was…well, I was kind of already moving it before he arrived." She had the grace to look embarrassed. "I had some plans. Anyway, the RV was handy and unlocked."

"Okay, here's what we need to do." Reenie conferred with the other two for a moment. Despite Hayley's protests ("At least I have a driver's license! He doesn't even know how to drive on the right side of the road and you can barely see."), Reenie decided Hayley should stay behind and text-message the rest of the gang out at the steam plant that they were on their way. "If anything goes wrong, I don't want you to be named an accessory." Alex would drive the RV to the steam plant, which was only a little more than a mile away. "What can go wrong in that distance?"

Quite a bit, as it turned out. They checked to make sure Burnie and Miranda were still out in the barn, but by the time Alex had manhandled the stupid RV out of the driveway, he had run over several azalea bushes and knocked the cannon off its cement foundation. "Bugger, bugger, bugger," he muttered, steering carefully between the stone gateposts. They crossed the causeway and were headed down the road when old Mr. Finger, who lived past Mrs. Penn, pulled out of his driveway in his pickup truck, and Alex nearly caused an accident, swerving instinctively to the left. Old Mr. Finger went into a ditch, his dog Rocko barking hysterically. "Bugger *all*." Alex pulled over to the side of the road and turned off the engine. "I'm going to kill someone if I do this."

Reenie pushed Alex out of the driver's seat and took over herself. She could barely see over the steering wheel and had to sit on the edge of the seat in order to reach the pedals, but by God or by Golly, she would get this thing going. As they careened down the road, Jack's car shot past them, going the other way. In her rear-view mirror, Reenie could see him hit the brakes, turn around, and follow them, laughing his fool head off. They passed Helen's street just as Phil's car turned onto it and before she knew it, Reenie had a convoy going, including Old Mr. Finger's truck, honking hysterically at her to stop. Good thing the steam plant wasn't far ahead.

Possibly a little too far, though, because she could also faintly hear the sound of a police siren.

The film crew location was a stretch of abandoned roadway that had been diverted when work was being done on the steam plant last year. It curved to the right while the new road curved to the left and ended at a traffic light opposite the plant entrance. In between was an empty lot, knee-high in weeds, where some of the crew had parked their vehicles. A temporary track had been cobbled together by Shane's crew to allow a camera to run alongside the abandoned part of the road so that a scene could be shot inside a moving car. Reenie's character was supposed to argue with Alex's while he drove and then the car would 'crash' into another car. It was the most difficult scene to shoot, after the underwater scene, and Reenie's budget didn't allow for too many takes.

Reenie hurtled at forty miles per hour toward the lot, closing in on the scattered vehicles like a bowling ball gone berserk. Her little fleet followed right behind her.

"Curve to the right!" Alex yelled in a rising crescendo. "Hit the brakes! *Hit the bloody brakes*!"

Reenie curved to the right and pressed the brakes hard, one foot on top of the other, but the RV hurtled through the weeds, crashed through a number of saplings and didn't stop until the front wheels plunged into a ditch. The back of the RV flew up in the air and thudded back down, and they finally came to a stop four feet from the highway. She knew they were only four feet from the highway because cars flashed by practically right under her nose. She and Alex had been pelted with loose items from the back of the RV, and after pulling a damp towel, a saucepan lid, several dirty paper plates, some Cheez Doodles and a sock monkey from her lap, she switched off the engine and sat there a moment, panting. When the roaring in her ears lessened, she looked at Alex and said, "You scream like a girl."

Then all hell broke loose.

First, there was a lot of shouting and people running toward them, then her door was jerked open and she nearly fell out. Jack pushed her back in and shouted, "Don't move yet. Are you all right? Did you hurt yourself anywhere?"

Shane jumped down into the ditch to look at his RV, holding his head and screaming "Oh my god! Oh my god! Somebody tell me they caught this on film!" and Alex produced a flask out of heaven knew where, took a long swig, and spewed forth a string of profanity, beginning with the words 'bloody hell' and ending with 'shite'. Other car doors slammed and Old Mr. Finger came around the corner, ranting about how he'd nearly been killed, with Rocko on a leash barking spastically at everyone.

Her right foot hurt where she'd mashed down on the brake and she felt a strange buzzing in her ears. Then Jack lifted her down from the car seat and carried her over to his car where he sat her on the warm hood. "Are you okay?" he asked again, peering into her eyes.

Burnie Burnette's siren nearly deafened her as he pulled onto the lot, barely squeezing into the remaining empty space. The siren stopped and he heaved himself out of the car, slamming the door, his face almost purple with rage. One final car arrived, pulling onto the shoulder, Miranda's Jeep with Miranda and Hayley inside.

"Hail, hail, the gang's all here," Reenie murmured. "Quick, Jack, lock up the RV. He doesn't have a warrant to search that." She shook her head, hoping her vision would clear up. "Ohhh. Everything horrible happens to me."

*

It took several minutes to sort things out. Burnie ordered everyone not immediately involved to retreat to neutral territory. Since nearly every person there insisted that they *were* involved, this was easier said than done, but eventually he narrowed in on the three sisters—Valerie, Miranda and Helen. "And you, too, Reenie," he shouted, pointing a fat finger at her. Not even Phil was allowed to remain.

"My wife's just sustained an injury," he kept insisting. "I'm not going to let you browbeat her."

"You and all the rest of them folks are going over there by that whatever it is," Burnie insisted, "that track thing, and you're gonna stay there until I'm ready for you. Unless you'd rather I start writing people up." He glared at Reenie. "Especially you. I know you ain't got no license. Or if you do, it's about a million years out of date. I could throw the book at you—*and I will*—if the rest of this bunch don't shut up and keep out of my way. Got it?"

"Go with the others," Helen said to Phil. She adjusted the neck brace and looked surprisingly calm. "I'll deal with it." When he showed reluctance to leave, she added, "You have *your* family emergencies, I have mine. Now go." He wasn't pleased, but finally allowed himself to be led off by Dee and Erica, grumbling all the way.

"All right now," Burnie said, hoisting up his britches. "Miz Reenie, can you walk?"

"I certainly can," she snapped, although her ears still rang. There was no way she was going to miss whatever came next. "If the girls will help me…"

Valerie and Amanda took her arms and Burnie herded them all around the far side of the RV, out of view of their family and friends. He took a deep breath and put both hands on his hips. "Now," he said, "we can do this the easy way or we can do this the hard way. I want that contraband."

"You've never adequately identified exactly what you're talking about. Could you please elucidate?" Miranda asked, going all hoity-toity. He frowned and his face began to turn dark red again.

"Burnie," Helen said, putting on hand on her arm. He looked down, seemingly discomposed by her neck brace. "Burnie, we've been friends for a long, long time. Your kids went to school with mine, we've sat through PTO meetings, and T-Ball and school plays and football games. Why all this ugliness between us now? We haven't done anything wrong."

He shifted his weight but held his stubborn frown. "Let me in that RV, Helen. I want to see what's in it."

Reenie could have told Helen that a little honey wasn't going to work with this guy. Before she could say anything, Valerie spoke up.

"Do you have a warrant?"

"I do." He patted his back pocket.

"I'd like to see it, please." Valerie could do hoity-toity pretty well, herself. In fact, even better than Miranda. It was impressive. "Just to make sure it's in order."

Burnie blinked and squared his big shoulders. "Okay, if you're gonna get technical about it, then no, I don't. What I do have is an old lady driving a vehicle without a license, driving a vehicle that requires a special license, and driving said vehicle in a reckless manner resulting in property damage, and if I'm pressed, I'd bet I could think up a few more charges. Plus that English fellow, who I'm guessing doesn't have a license either, putting another driver in danger. And his dog. Old Man Finger would probably be quite happy to press charges."

"Old Man Finger is a danger on the road himself!" Reenie snapped, and was immediately hushed. "Well, he is. And his dog stinks to high heaven."

"*Enough!*" Burnie roared. "Now open up this RV!"

Valerie looked at Miranda who looked at Helen, who turned, wincing at the effort, to look at Reenie. "Well, fudge," she said. She handed the keys to Burnie.

He waved the women out of the way and was about to unlock the door when Miranda said, "Wait a minute! I have an idea!"

What's she up to now, Reenie wondered.

"Let's strike a deal, okay?" Miranda took a deep breath and glanced from person to person, looking unbelievably sincere. "I

273

mean, we each have a vested interest in the outcome, so let's try to make everyone happy. Look, Burnie, we all know what we're talking about here. You want to protect your Mama. She made a mistake once—more than once, actually, but we don't have to go into that now. After all, what do I care that she liked visiting Cunningham's department store and coming home with little 'gifties' back in the 1970's? You clearly don't want it to haunt her. We understand." She turned to Helen. "And our dad went a little nuts and did some stupid things, too. So, we all want to protect our family's honor, right?" Helen nodded, a trifle unwillingly. "And Aunt Reenie and Val, they just want to put all this behind them and get back to work on their movie. So, how about this idea? You and me, Burnie, we go inside and I'll give you everything that pertains to your Mama." Miranda's voice took on a confiding tone and she even slipped her arm through his as she urged him toward the side entrance of the RV.

"What's she going to do?" Helen whispered. "Seduce him?"

"Or stomp his ass," Reenie muttered. "She could probably kick the shit out of him. Come on." Herding Valerie and Helen in front of her, Reenie followed Miranda and Burnie into the RV. "I want to see this."

Miranda's eyes rolled in exasperation when she saw everyone crowding in, but she continued talking to Burnie in a soothing voice. "All the photos, the letters, the money she paid him, everything will go to you. But that's *all*. The rest of it, you leave alone. We'll make sure nobody is bothered any further. You leave us alone, too, and stop badgering the movie set.

You're happy, we're happy, your Mama's happy. It's a Happy Happy Town." She kept nodding at him and gradually, he began to nod back. Being Miranda, of course, she added a kicker. "And we'll make sure none of this gets into Reenie's movie or documentary." Burnie's eyes widened and he threw a quick glance out the window of the RV where, Reenie noted, Shane's main camera guy was hard at work, filming them. "I promise, no repercussions of any kind. Let's agree to do this, out of respect for our parents."

"You, showing respect? That'd be something new," he grunted, but finally agreed. It didn't take long to find where Hayley had stashed the cartons in the shower. Helen used the opportunity to apologize again and again to Burnie for any problems they'd caused. Reenie thought she overdid it, but at least the big fart seemed pacified. Once he got the large envelope filled with the photos, letters and cash relating to his Mama's little shoplifting hobby, he fixed Miranda with a final glare and said, "Remember, I'll be keeping an eye on you," and stomped off.

As soon as he was gone, Valerie turned to look at her sister, giving a one-sided grin. "Out of respect for our parents? I never thought I'd hear that from you."

Miranda mirrored Val's grin. "I know. That's twice today I was due to get slapped. Don't read too much into it. I still think Dad was a stubborn old cuss. But, lord, I'm tired. Too much excitement here in Painter's Creek. Who woulda thunk?"

Phil and the twins climbed up into the bus, followed closely by Jack and Alex. They were full of questions about what happened, and under cover of the hubbub, Reenie leaned close to Miranda and asked, "Okay, so 'fess up. What do *you* get out of this little game?"

"Why, Reenie," Miranda responded, eyes wide. "Whatever are you talking about? I'm cut to the quick that you would question my motives."

"Oh, bull hockey. You have something up your sleeve."

Helen came up to them. "Thanks, Miranda. You saved the day." She made a move as if to hug her sister, but the neck collar and maybe something else held her back. Instead she turned it into a tentative elbow-bump. "Now, we're still going to sort out the rest of the mess and deliver things to their rightful owners, right?"

"But we don't have to, now! I mean, we could split up the cash, at least, ..." Suddenly, Miranda threw up her hands. "Okay, okay, okay! I get it. You're going to take all the splendid spoils and give them back, just toss all those assets away. This pains me, you know, deep down in my soul. It's sad to discover your youngest sister is completely mental. I hope it hasn't rubbed off on the kids."

"Well, *I* hope you can put your heads together and help me figure out how to create a scene using the RV-in-a-ditch," Reenie said, feeling rightly that all control of the situation had slipped away from her. "Because we're not moving it or going ahead with anything else, or getting any supper until we've exhausted every possibility of filming something here. You don't get a golden chance like this every day." She rubbed her hands together, feeling incredibly energized. There was nothing like a lot of family angst or a little vehicular terror to get the old creative juices flowing, and both at once was like manna from heaven. Just as she thought things were coming to an end, they started up again. Jimmy Stewart had it right. It *was* a wonderful life!

Still Saturday, May 16, 2009
"California Faces Bankruptcy; Some Suggest Splitting the State into Four", (The Charlotte Observer)

The day seemed to last forever. Helen sat in the car, listening to Reenie and Alex and Shane argue about how, or if, to include the footage of the RV shooting into the ditch in the movie. "It's not every day you get an opportunity like this," Reenie kept insisting.

"It. Does. Not. Matter." Alex said, his words practically dripping icicles. "My character's motivation has been set by this point. You can't inject something now that's not organic. Do you want to completely ruin the dénouement?"

"Look, it's not a problem." Shane put an arm around Reenie's shoulders. "We can use it in the documentary. It'll be fabulous. The angularity of the RV, with its ass up in the air like that, will be a great metaphor for the whole endeavor. Great visuals. I've got big plans for the footage." The three of them finally pried themselves away from the rushes and Shane called it a wrap for the day, so that the crew finally could break things down.

Personally, Helen had had enough. Her back hurt and the neck brace itched. All she wanted was to go home and go to bed. The crisis was over, Burnie was off their case, life could return to normal—or what passed for it around there.

Phil asked Dee to bring them some carry-out food for dinner and got behind the wheel. As they headed home, he said, "Jack and I moved the boxes of your Dad's, um, *valuables* to Jack's car. He said you wanted him to dispose of it. I'm not sure all the paperweights made it intact. That was quite a jolt they took." He glanced over at her. "It's a lot of stuff, Babe. A lot of cash. I didn't realize how much until I saw it. You're completely sure about what you want?"

"Completely."

"Nobody's cared about it for over thirty years."

"I'm not passing the sins of the father—or grandfather—onto our kids. Don't cross me on this."

Phil reached over and patted her knee. "Okay. Just checking." He grinned. "Once again, it's all about you."

"All about us, buddy. All about us."

It really was all about them. And about *all* of them, she realized. Not just her 'gang', her little circle of Phil and the Trips. The decision affected her sisters and Reenie and Seth, too. They all needed money—well, maybe not Reenie—and

278

even divided by nine, the sum that could have been realized from selling the paperweights, stamps, and jewelry might have been significant. Enough, maybe, to help with the kids' tuition, or put some into Mitchell Furniture Specialties, or keep the lake house going for the short term.

"The house!" she said suddenly, smacking Phil on the arm.

"What's the matter?" he asked, startled.

"I forgot all about it. We're not out of the woods yet. We've got to decide about the lake house."

"*Now?*"

"Yes. While we're all in a good mood. While Miranda's all softened up. She might never be this mushy ever again. Turn the car around; we've got to go to Dad's."

Phil groaned. "Aren't you tired? Haven't you been beaten up enough for one day?"

"No, this will work. Can you reach my purse? It's on the floor."

"What do you want?"

"A pen and paper. I've got some ideas and I'm going to make a little list."

"A list. Well, why didn't you say so?" He shook his head with resignation and handed her the leather handbag. "I mean, if you've got a *list*, then why should I worry? Although, I think you should consider this—didn't your Dad's nefarious schemes start out with a list?" Helen batted his arm, and he laughed and held up his hands. "I'm just saying."

"Okay, I hear you. Now, let's get over to Dad's."

When they got to the lake house, the only people there were Hayley and Miranda, comfortably established with several large cushions on the floor of the living room with a bunch of family photo albums spread around them. Hayley lay on her stomach, flipping through pages while Miranda explained who was who. As Phil helped Helen get settled in the recliner, Hayley said, "We've been looking at old pictures when your dad and Great Granddad Hec built this house. I just think it's so cool. I never knew there used to be an iron archway over the gateposts. What happened to it?"

"Oh, I can explain that." Miranda folded herself into a yoga position and twisted her spine left, then right, with audible cracking sounds. How did she do that, Helen wondered. How did she stay so loose and flexible? "The original farm was called LynnCrest, right? For our great-great-grandpa, Lynn Cates. He passed it on to his son, Virgil Cates, who passed it on to Grand-dad Hec, who passed it to Dad. When Hec built the place, he made the archway saying LynnCrest, but he and Great-Grand-dad Cates argued about something so after the old man died, he tore it down. It's a family trait, you see? We build things up and tear 'em down. It seems to be all we're good at." She winked at Hayley, glanced significantly at Helen, folded herself into a lotus pose and closed her eyes. "*As we see, so we become.*"

"Who said that?" Hayley asked.

"I did. Didn't you just hear me?" Miranda opened her eyes again and grinned. "I'm a strong believer in family traditions."

Before Helen could respond, Dee came through the door with Erica and Latham, carrying several Chick-fil-A bags and a couple of six-packs of Coke. "Food," Dee said, unceremoniously dumping her bags on the dining room table. "Let's eat, I'm starved." Erica found some paper plates and began setting the table and Dee went over to her mother. "How are you feeling?"

"Like I've been beaten and dragged," Helen said.

"You pretty much were." Dee glared at Miranda.

"Hey, don't give me those daggers!" Miranda responded. "You contributed to the problems today too, with your Twittering."

"*Tweeting*. And I did not!"

"Did, too!"

"Did not!"

"SHUT UP!" Erica shouted. "What a pair of children!"

Dee whirled away and marched into the kitchen.

"I'm not feeling the love," Miranda muttered and, for a while, silence reigned.

So much for family unity, Helen thought. Phil offered her another pain pill but she waved it off. Now was not the time for fuzzy thinking. If the usual family traditions continued, Miranda would head back to Boone tonight, now that there was no reason to stick around, and they wouldn't see her again for six months or a year. Of course, if they didn't, would it really matter? If everything went back to status quo….no, that wasn't possible. Going back to how things were before meant Dad would still be around, and he wasn't. Would never be. And all the problems of the lake house would still be there, waiting for someone to solve them.

The rest of the family arrived—Reenie, Val, Jack, Seth. "Shane's waiting for the wrecker to pull his RV out of the ditch," Reenie said, "and Alex has gone off with Mitzi and Rita and the other ladies to The Landing for a drink. Thank God. Actors can be so self-absorbed."

Everyone gathered around the table and before they fell on the food like a pack of hyenas, Helen said, "Look, since we're all here together, except Devon, isn't this a good time for y'all put your thinking caps on and try to come up with a plan for what we're going to do with the house? I mean, we pulled together and got the ninety-day inventory done. We've handled the whole Burnie Burnette thing. Certainly we should be able to reach some kind of decision on how to deal with the estate. Miranda, you've come up with ideas on how to keep your store going in hard times. Can't you think of anything that would help with our situation?"

"Sure. I think we should sell everything and split the cash." Nobody responded, so she shrugged and said, "Hey, you asked."

Seth pointed out that it was a bad time to sell real estate. "If you could hang on for a couple of years, maybe three or four, prices for lake property might come back up where they belong. Although I still don't really want to sell."

"It's a bad time to sell the antique furniture, too," Valerie said. "Everyone who's got anything they don't need is selling it, and cheap. If none of us are in completely dire straits, we should wait."

Erica knocked on the table to get attention. "We should vote, right now, on selling or not. I vote no."

"Oh yeah, sure, vote. Like your family doesn't already have a majority just by itself." Miranda shot french fries into her mouth with machine-gun-like rapidity. "Why do I feel like this is Thanksgiving all over again, and I'm about to get railroaded?"

"We have other problems, too, don't forget," Dee said. "Like who's messing up the house and boat. I'm totally betting it's Bryan, that s.o.b. What do we do about him?"

Hayley leaned on one elbow and said, "I kept hoping we'd find buried treasure. Something nobody knew about or cared about, that you could sell to make a fortune, so you could keep the house."

"We do have a fortune." Helen looked around the table, making eye contact with each person there. "Dad left us something important, okay? Only it's not buried treasure. It's this house and the island and all the things we've always done here and all the things we could do if only everyone would pull together and just figure a few things out. I mean, maybe that was his whole point! He left it to *each* of us. He gave us this opportunity and it's up to us to run with it. We each have a stake in making it work. And we all have each other, or we would if only we'd stop fighting and bickering all the time."

283

"Then do something about it," Hayley suggested. "Get along. Work things it out."

"Easy for you to say," Dee pointed out.

"Oh really? Wait until you have a mother in jail, and then tell me how easy things are." Hayley's eyes flashed and her voice shook a little. "Y'all stop feeling so damned sorry for yourselves and start working on a plan. Jesus Christmas! You've got a family that basically likes each other, right? Okay, so maybe Miranda's kind of a bitch, but heck, she just keeps things lively. Figure out some way to make the house pay for itself. Just stop all your whining, you make me gag."

"Hey, okay, let's calm down a bit." Phil reached out and grabbed each girl's wrist. "Let's try to think of this like a business decision, something based on logic and not emotion. How can we make the house pay for itself?"

"I've been thinking," Valerie said slowly. She glanced around the table and looked down at her fingers, curling a paper napkin around them. "Maybe I'll stick around for a while. Through the summer, at least. If I paid for the insurance and utilities and the regular maintenance, would that count enough as rent? I could afford that, and it would buy time. Give us a chance to think about other options." She flushed a little as Jack leaned forward to look at her. "It would give *me* time, too, to think about my options."

"That would be great," Helen said. "This is what I'm talking about, coming up with ideas together. I've been thinking, too, about some of the stuff that we could sell now. I've learned enough about consignment shops to know what kind of things go quickly—usually, it's the worst junk, you'd be surprised—and they're things we could do without, but might bring in enough money to help with some of the repairs we need." She turned to Miranda. "Really, sis, don't you want to get in on this? You're probably the most creative thinker here."

Miranda made a face and squirmed a little. "Oh, man. This is getting all lovey-dovey. You know I don't do that shit. It makes me throw up in my mouth." Helen waited, and after a moment, Miranda said, "Okay. Well, if you're going to look at it as a business operation, then you have to look at your assets and your liabilities. The biggest asset, really, is the property itself, the lakefront footage. If you're not going to sell, then use it some other way. Turn the place into a bed-and-breakfast, although that would take a lot of renovation. Rent it out during the big race weekends when people come from twenty states to watch NASCAR. If Val stays on here, then just use the exterior space. Hold weddings here. I always thought, with the gazebo and the lake view, that an outdoor wedding would be real pretty. The big gothic door downstairs is a perfect place for wedding photos, use it in the advertisements. Hold corporate picnics. Fix up the barn, put in a couple of bathrooms and you'd have a place for receptions. The only reception hall around here is the VFW hall and it's ugly as dog shit. Rent the barn out to dance groups—shaggers, line dancing, Zumba. Or a summer theater group. This could be the Flat Rock Playhouse of Painter's Creek. Or—"

"Jiminy cricket," Reenie said. "When you get going, Miranda, you get going."

Miranda looked down and smiled. "I'm just norbal."

Helen had been scribbling all the ideas down on her list. "Zumba," she murmured, "summer theater. You're a genius! We could get all our ideas organized this summer while Val's here and start a campaign in the fall. I love you! This will save everything." She looked up and saw her sister's eyes looking unusually shiny. "This will save everything," she repeated, softly. "Thank you."

"Oh god, we're not going to start blubbering now, are we?" Miranda pulled at the neck of her shirt and actually blushed. "Damn, another hot flash." She gestured helplessly at the rest of the group. "Oh, jeez, I can't take all this quivering mass of love goop. Somebody, please, cut a fart!"

"Sorry," Dee said. "Devon's not here."

Chapter Fourteen

Friday, May 22, 2009
"In Tough Times, Even Amoebas Turn to Family", (Science Digest)

Devon glanced around at the crowd filling the streets in downtown Painter's Creek. The "Alive After Five" party was in full swing, with beer for sale right on the square and an oldies band on top of a flat-bed truck, slaughtering the B-52's *Love Shack*. The local Harley Davidson shop was sponsoring the event, which meant the place surged with aging bikers, bandannas tied over their balding heads and long gray ponytails proclaiming their so-called rebel status. Some rebels, he thought, oh yeah. Most of them were familiar as the town's handymen, auto-shop owners, physical therapists, and dealers in hardware.

He'd missed all the excitement, of course. The big fight between Mom and Aunt Miranda, the trip to the hospital, the slo-mo car chase down Cates' Island Road, the crash of the RV, and most of all, the showdown with Sheriff Burnette. Dee had filled him in, going on and on about everything until Erica pointed out that it was Dee's love of all things Twitter that was responsible for Sheriff Burnette showing up at all. "We still don't know who yocked to him," Erica said, raising her eyebrows significantly, "but we can guess." Then, she'd curved herself under Latham's arm in a way that was really starting to get on Devon's nerves. Latham was always underfoot these days; it was like he and Erica had become Siamese twins, and now Devon and Dee were orphans. Orphans who didn't get along very well, to boot.

The whole past week had sucked. His job at the car wash paid good tips but he hated coming home sweaty and tired. The worst part was that Hayley had a job there, too, looking cute as all get-out. She seemed to love her job and worked hard, flirting with all the male customers, and pocketing the biggest tips of anyone there. No wonder she loved it. She was driving him nuts.

The band began to murder Wild Cherry's *Play That Funky Music, White Boy*, and the girl singer took a break. Not exactly a girl, though. The singer in the low-cut sequined top was Mrs. Duffy, Devon's fourth grade teacher, although back when he was in love with her, she'd been a holy vision, not shaking her jugs and tapping a tambourine. That wasn't right.

His mom walked up, finally free of the neck brace. She had her camera and was taking photos of everyone and everything like some kind of kamikaze papparazi. She'd been amazingly upbeat all week, even when she and Dad had sat the Trips down to tell them they wouldn't be able to stay in the dorms

288

next school year, and they'd have to live at home and commute every day. "Things are tight, I won't lie," she'd said, smiling in what she probably thought was an encouraging way, while giving the death knell to his social life, "but we're confident we can handle your tuition and books. You'll have to help out with your other expenses, but that's a good preparation for when you're on your own anyway. Your dad and I each held multiple part-time jobs while we were going to college, and we know it can be done. And we're going to start organizing the lake house—I mean, LynnCrest—as a business property." And she'd given Dad a goofy, lovey smile.

Erica, the traitor, had actually been enthusiastic. What did she care, after all, since she had Latham? But he felt his own heart sink. He'd just begun to enjoy some freedom, and now the jail door was clanking shut. Damn.

"Dad's gone to get us some drinks," Mom said. The band began to destroy ZZ Tops' *Sharp Dressed Man*. The sound vanished for a few seconds while a freight train rumbled through the center of town. Small mercies. Glancing around the crowd, Devon saw Dee and Murph approaching. Not hand-in-hand, but darn near. He might have to spew.

Dee was excited about something, practically hopping up and down. "Mom! Aunt Reenie and Shane and I have been talking and we're going to try to feature the lake house as much as possible in Reenie's 'making of' documentary and we think it can be a starting point for publicity for the house. Plus they're going to go to Uncle Jack's place in Wilmington in June to work on editing the film, and Reenie says I could be a big help with running errands and stuff. Can I go?"

Mom started to respond but her attention was caught by someone else standing nearby. Bryan. Devon hadn't seen him since that night outside the dormitory, when Dee had left him standing in the cold rain. Bryan sauntered closer, hands in his pockets. He'd cut his hair super-short and now his ears stood out wider than ever. Jerk.

"Whassup, Dee?" he smirked, his gaze taking in Murph, who moved slightly closer to Dee.

"Don't talk to me," Dee snapped. "After what you did to my Grandpa's house and our boat? Don't even come near."

Bryan rocked back on his heels and smiled. Just like a snake. "What are you talking about? What would I want with your Grandpa's broken-down old house? Looks like a crazy man built it. You must be just as insane. You crazy bitch."

His smirk suddenly disappeared as a fist smashed him right in the nose. *Mom's* fist.

"Oh my god," she said, obviously shocked. "Did I do that? I'm so sorry, Bryan!" He put one hand up to his nose and swore at her and she socked him again with her other fist. "Oh no. I don't know what to say. Are you all right? I've never done anything like that before."

Murph started laughing and Devon insinuated himself between Mom and Bryan, whose nose spurted big time. "Time to go, Bryan," he warned, trying to keep from laughing himself. "You never know what she'll do when she gets riled up. It's a form of Tourette's. We've lived in terror for years." As Bryan's eyes filled with tears and blood dripped through his fingers, Devon pushed his mom behind him.

She kept trying to move forward, pulling a pack of tissues from her purse. "Oh, somebody give him these. Bryan, I'm so sorry. I can't believe I did that. Does anyone have some ice?"

Bryan gave them one last furious, agonized look before he pushed his way out of the crowd. Devon turned around to see Dee and Murph laughing their asses off, while Mom stuffed the tissues back in her purse and looped the purse over her arm. "Unbelievable," she muttered, starting to grin. "I guess that Wii just paid for itself." Dad came up then, holding a couple of beers, his eyes round with astonishment.

Devon gave up. "I'm out of here, Killer. Y'all are too much for me." He walked away, shaking his head. His family was crazy, *crazy*, he thought, with an obscure sense of pride. The band began mutilating The Dixie Chicks' *Good-bye Earl*. With the memory of Bryan's rapidly expanding nose in mind, Devon whistled along. Maybe this summer wouldn't suck so bad after all. And he had Camp Meeting to look forward to in July. They spent two weeks every summer with his dad's family, and those people were even crazier than his mom's. All you can do in this stupid life was laugh, he decided. Just laugh. Which he did, all the way across the square.

Saturday, September 12, 2009
"Grand Opening, Lynncrest Island, the Perfect Setting for Your Special Event", (Painter's Creek Chronicle)

Monday, November 16, 2009
"UNC-Charlotte Music Department Adds 'World Class' Composer and Cellist to Faculty", (The Charlotte Observer)

Wednesday, December 2, 2009
"New Film starring Reenie Cates and Alexander Rippon to Compete at Sundance Film Festival" (Los Angeles Times)

Thursday, January 6, 2010
"Stolen Paperweights Resurface Thirty Years Later; It's a Miracle, Happy Owner Proclaims", (Painter's Creek Chronicle)

Acknowledgements

***

A big *thank you* to:

My children – Joanna, Katie, Becky, and Danny, and my two sons-in-law, David and Brandon, who are so supportive and who also inspire me by the stories they tell about their own lives. Thanks also to my sisters – Lori, Deb, Kim, Jacki and Linda. We've never had to overcome the kind of estrangement that the Cates sisters had, but the love we share certainly gave me the longing to write about sister relationships. We share a history with our siblings that is matched by nothing else. I give thanks to my late parents, Lynn and Evelyn Steele, who never left me any mysteries to solve, but lots of antique paperweights and cameras, and a love of laughter. I hope they'd be proud of this story if they knew.

I also offer thanks to my critiquer and friend, Michael Mendershausen, who helped me get this manuscript into final shape, and to Barbara Kidd Lawing, whose Monday afternoon writing classes helped me stay focused and enthusiastic.

And most of all, I thank my husband, Matt, who has always offered me love and support. He's my biggest promoter, not only with my books, but in my life, and I'm glad to have him.

293

Carolyn Steele Agosta is the author of "The Pleasure of Your Company", "Every Little Step She Takes", and over 35 internationally-published short stories. She graduated from the University of North Carolina at Charlotte and lives with her husband in North Carolina. Her website is www.carolynagosta.com.

Look for more books from Carolyn Steele Agosta soon, including two anthologies of her short stories.